REVIEWS

"Richard Alan Hall's latest novel, *They Call Me Machete,* is a fun and inventive ride that will keep fans of the thriller genre, or anybody who enjoys a lively story, turning pages. In this tale—Hall's fifth novel in the series—the author takes us into the world of his darkest character, Machete. We learn of his childhood roots in a Mexican ghetto, witness the deadly forces that shaped his boyhood and the deadly forces he, too, harnessed to survive, turning him into a brutal and remorseless killer.

Machete's story, though, is anything but predictable, as Hall's love of plot twist and startling storyline shines through, taking us from small-town America to the world of international crime. Also shining through is Hall's innate sense of the timeless struggle between good and evil both among our tribes and within each of us as individuals. We watch as Machete's dark world closes in on him and wonder if he'll be able to, or even want to, find a way out."

> Jeff Smith, Author
> Editor, *Traverse* Magazine and MyNorth.com
> Traverse City, Michigan

"Part prequel, part tale of justice and retribution, this fifth installment in the Big Bay series is as sharp and as savage as its namesake, Machete. The taut, no-nonsense dialogue rips like a California forest fire through the pages. Another stunning tour de force by Richard Alan Hall."

> Jim Rink
> Editor of *American Wine Society Journal*
> Lake Leelanau, Michigan

"Thrilling, heart pounding, gut wrenching, all mixed together with love. Richard possesses a raw and pure talent for writing. His characters are vivid and alive, sharing their hearts and souls. While reading, I hear their voices and see his words come to life. The battle against deep-seeded evil, their love and trust; the vulnerability and bonds are gripping. Be prepared not to put this book down. Thank you, Richard Alan Hall for another incredible journey and sharing the significance of the color blue."

Barbara A Ely, Reviewer
Rockford, Michigan

"If there ever were masterful playbooks for confronting the relentless pursuits of evil, Richard Alan Hall certainly writes his share of them! Novel after novel, Richard draws you in, opens your heart to full-faith capacity, and makes you never look back. *They Call Me Machete* takes all who are courageously willing to the 5th level in the Big Bay series of adventures on the never-ending course of what unconditional love can do."

Brenda DeNoyer Girolamo, Artist and Author
Chandler, Arizona

"Richard Alan Hall has done it again but with more thrills than ever before. I could not put *They Call Me Machete* down and finished it in three days. It is very definitely a page-turner. It is one of those books that you swear you'll stop after the next chapter and then just keep going until you finally can't hold your eyes open one more second. Who is the enigmatic character Machete? Where did he come from? How did he come to be part of the Usual Suspects and in many ways part of the True Believers? You are about to find out and Machete's story will absolutely surprise you. It did me. What's next Mr. Hall?"

Patrick Mazor, Author and Reviewer
Slaton, Texas

"Where to begin! I absolutely loved *They Call Me Machete*. Machete is one of my favorite characters in the Big Bay series. It was tough to put the book down. I felt many emotions and embraced each page as I read. I was captivated by the characters and could not wait to read what would happen next. Bravo, Richard Alan Hall, for being an amazing story teller."

Marciana Williams, Reviewer
Grand Rapids, Michigan

"In this new Big Bay adventure, we get the complete picture of the man Machete. We learn about a young, vulnerable boy named Marco, whose survival skills and instinct drove him to become the fearsome man with the name Machete. We see innocents lost and watch as a villain is transformed by the love for his little sister. We cheer as Machete goes from a feared foe to a beloved friend and adversary of evil. *They Call Me Machete* is an adventure of heroic proportions."

Wendy Murton-Helmka, Reviewer
Graysville, Tennessee

"Love is when we show unselfish, loyal and benevolent concern for one another. Richard Alan Hall shows us this love in his fifth novel, *They Call Me Machete.*"

Adell Maksimowicz, Reviewer
Traverse City, Michigan

Other novels by Richard Alan Hall

Big Bay Novels

Remarkable

Seldom As They Seem

No Gray Twilights

For Better or Worse

For Bernard Carl Rink, my friend.

ACKNOWLEDGEMENTS

Thank you, Lisa Mottola Hudon.
You make me a better writer.

Thank you, Angela Saxon of Saxon Design
for designing this book and cover.

Thank you, Jim Rink, for your help and insights.

Thank you, Jill Johnson Tewsley.
You are an amazing publicist and friend.

Thank you, Debra Jean Hall.
Once again, this is your fault.

And, thank you always to our Eternal Daddy.

TABLE OF CONTENTS

PROLOGUE

We do not blame the alley cat for doing what is
necessary to survive in that hostile world.
In fact, we secretly admire the alley cat.

RICHARD ALAN HALL

CHAPTER 1

THE COLOR OF PAIN

Stanley McMillen missed the second step in the darkness, stumbling on Dora's Place's dirty concrete steps.

"Damn!"

He touched a ragged gash below his right knee with sticky fingers.

"What a klutz!" Stanley pulled open the restaurant's blue screen door, and watched Moses yank the little brass chain, turning off the Avenida Street neon *ABIERTO* sign.

Moses pushed the fingers of her left hand against her lips and came quickly toward Stanley. She wiped at the little streams of blood moving down his shin with a green bar towel, and then pressed the towel against the jagged wound.

"You need dat stitched er someding."

"I'll have Danielle dress it when I get home. Tell me more… what's going on with your husband?"

Moses nodded in the direction of Machete at his table in the dim corner. They watched the little man, sitting in the dim light, patting Little Miss on the top of her golden head, over and over.

"He says dat he sees da color of de pain."

"Anything else?"

"He be sick to da stomach. Wen de headaches be bad, he throws up. Please help him, Stanley."

"Just spoke with Doctor Gonzalez; we have a plan."

"My man trusts you…God bless." Moses put her arms around Stanley's waist, and she squeezed with all her might.

Machete Juarez leaned back in the wooden chair and turned his blind face toward Stanley when the wooden floor creaked.

"You been cheating at cards, again?" Stanley said. He pulled a chair over to Machete's table.

Machete attempted a grin.

"That's never been a proven fact, amigo."

"It's a documented fact that poker cheaters have more headaches. Moses is worried."

Machete shrugged and caressed his dog.

"If it were Moses, you'd be worried."

"I would be sick."

"Exactly. Let's see if we can find your problem and fix it."

"Probably the bullet," Machete said, rubbing his forehead. "Maybe it moved or something. I have never felt such pain, even when I was shot, not like this. I can see the color of pain."

"I spoke with Doctor Gonzalez this morning. He has a friend at Havana's Institute of Neurosurgery; moved from London last year…one of the top neurosurgeons in the world. They spoke and Doctor Gonzalez called right before I walked over. Have you scheduled for a cerebral angiogram Tuesday at 10 a.m. in Havana."

"Seems like you would have asked me first. You driving?"

"Sorry. Got involved pulling strings and calling in favors. Angiograms are booked out six weeks. Not knowing won't make things better, Machete."

"Thank you."

"Unless you want to drive," Stanley chuckled.

"I loved driving," Machete retorted. He closed his blind eyes and gently rubbed them both.

"What color is pain?"

"White. You are a hard man to win an argument against."

"Because I care."

"I know."

Stanley watched from the Diagnostic Cath Lab control room while Doctors Gonzalez and Congdon performed a cerebral angiogram.

Doctor Congdon turned toward Stanley and pointed at a small caliber bullet lodged in the chiasma of the optic nerve. Doctor Gonzalez injected contrast dye, and both men pointed.

"See the aneurysm in the Circle of Willis?" Doctor Congdon asked through his mask.

"Nope," Stanley replied.

"Watch this next injection...the right ophthalmic artery, next to the bullet."

From a new position, the protruding aneurysm became obvious.

"We need to go to O.R. today," Doctor Congdon said.

●●●

"They're taking Machete to O.R.," Stanley said on his cell phone to his wife, Danielle.

"When?"

"Going to bump the schedule, as soon as a room opens up."

"Why, what'd they find?"

"Pulsating aneurysm in the Circle of Willis."

"I'll find someone to take my shift. How's Moses?"

Stanley watched Moses rocking back and forth on the waiting room couch.

"Not good. She needs you."

"I'll be there soon...rush hour."

"O'Malley's helicopter is headed to the helipad."

"You called Quinn."

"It'll be a quick trip, honey."

"I love you. How's your knee?"

"Haven't taken your dressing off. Love you, too."

"Please Jesus, save my man…da man you send dat be wid me… please…please…please…." Danielle heard on her husband's phone.

"Chloe's calling, see you soon," Stanley said, glancing at the call waiting message.

"Hi Honey, what's up?"

"Daddy, something's wrong. I have a terrible ache inside."

Stanley's skin prickled in waves. The man who had kidnapped little Chloe from their home in Big Bay, insisting that their little girl was his sister, reincarnated; the little Mexican who never doubted this for an instant over the years, and somehow now Chloe felt the doom.

"Machete is in the hospital, honey."

Moses looked up from the couch.

"What's wrong?" Chloe asked.

"Brain aneurysm. He's going to the operating room soon."

"Which hospital? I'm coming."

"Institute of Neurosurgery, two-hundred Maximo Gomez."

"I'll be there soon, Daddy. Tell Moses I'll be there. Does Mom know?"

"I just talked with her. She's flying in Quinn's helicopter. Moses called Dora; she's on her way here, too. Quinn is in France with Richard.

"See you in a little bit. I'll call Uncle Fidel on the way."

● ● ●

"I will never forget the phone call," Danielle said.

Machete's friends huddled close around a little square table in the surgical waiting room.

"When the babysitter called me in E.R., screaming," Danielle continued, "I CAN'T FIND CHLOE! Or, the ride up the hill to our condo with you, Stanley."

"God bless Doug. He and his dog Malcolm tracked Machete

to a vacant house, and there you were, rocking in the dayroom with Machete," Stanley mused.

"I was little, but I remember rocking with Machete and then Doug telling him to put me on the floor and Malcolm pulling on my pajama arm. He dragged me to the other side of the room and then licked my face," Chloe said. "I remember Malcolm going back to Machete and sitting next to him, resting his chin on Machete's knee."

"You never told me that part," Danielle said.

"It was like he felt sorry for Machete."

"Dat night wen de bad ones come an' all de men went wid you, Stanley, to get you an' da family out to da airport, den Machete an' me guarded Poor Joe's all alone, an' I know'd he be da one."

Three hours into the operation the waiting room door opened, and Fidel Castro entered. He simply hugged Moses, silently, and then sat next to Chloe and hugged her.

Together, the six sat in the waiting room, mostly silent, often with their heads bowed.

● ● ●

Hours later the waiting room door opened again.

CHAPTER 2

TWO BROWN GLASS BOTTLES

Marco Juarez's mother, Lilliana, worked the streets of Mexico City as a prostitute. They lived in a one-room, tar paper and lath shack deep in the Iztapalapa ghetto. When it rained, the brown water running in the streets smelled of animal leavings and urine.

Uncertain who fathered her son, Lilliana named him Marco. She had a hunch, but it didn't matter. The ghetto prostitute knew very well the father of her blue-eyed daughter, Maria. She knew him as Mark and that Mark worked for the United States government. And she knew his job to be dangerous. Mark visited her often and treated her and her son with a kindness she worshiped.

Marco had just turned seven when it happened, after a birthday party with his very first birthday cake and candles, too. He made a big wish before he blew as hard as he could.

Mark hugged Marco and rubbed the top of his curly black-haired head "for luck" before slipping out the back door into the narrow alley and the dark night. Lilliana found Mark in the morning. His throat had been severed, and he lay on his side, his head twisted strangely backwards.

Eight months later Lilliana gave birth on the ragged green couch in her one-room shack, with the help of two ladies from down the street, to a blue-eyed baby girl. She named her Maria.

Marco watched from the corner, next to the cook stove. The ladies tied off the umbilical cord, twice, using a shoe string and cut the fleshy pink cord in the middle between the ties, using a butcher knife the younger lady found on the table next to the cooking stove. The old lady with gray hair wrapped the baby in a pillow case. She handed Maria to Marco, and when he took her in his arms, the baby girl abruptly stopped her shrill cry and looked up with wide open blue eyes.

They were never separated after that moment except early most mornings when Marco left the shack to steal food from the outdoor market. He fed her, changed her diapers and rocked her to sleep every night in the white wicker rocking chair he had found on the doctor's front porch just west of the market.

When Maria became sick with dysentery, Marco carried her to the doctor's office, three miles from their shack.

"My sister is sick," he said to the nurse sitting at the desk just inside the doctor's small office.

"How are you going to pay?" the nurse asked.

"I will find money someplace," Marco replied. "Please give me medicine to fix Maria."

The doctor with a black mustache and goatee opened the door from the patient room and stopped walking, looking at Marco and the baby. He shook his head no at his nurse before turning his back.

"Boy, you must leave now," the nurse said, standing. "Come back when you have money."

Marco gently placed his shivering sister on the gray tile floor and walked close to the nurse. Looking up, he stared at the lady dressed in white. She glared at the besmudged boy while the fingers of her right hand tapped the desk top.

"Do you know what is wrong with my sister?"

"Probably dysentery," she retorted. "It is going around in the ghetto."

"Give me medicine."

"You must pay."

Marco learned closer to the nurse, his right hand pointing up at her face.

"If you do not give me medicine for my sister right now, I will find your house and burn it down in the night and then the doctor's house the next night."

The nurse turned without replying. She walked to a tall white cupboard and opened the doors. Leaning back, she handed Marco two brown glass bottles.

He stared at the labels marked Ciprofloxacin.

"One teaspoon every twelve hours. Do you know what a teaspoon is?"

"Yes."

"Do you have a teaspoon at home?"

"Yes."

"And you must give your sister lots of water. One bottle of water every four hours."

"I will."

"Now go, and never come back here."

Marco did not sleep for three days. He bathed her hot little body and worried when she developed little red spots all over. He gave Maria one teaspoon of the medicine from the brown bottle every twelve hours and fed her water flavored by crushed mangos he had stolen from Fausto's Market.

Two weeks later Marco carried his sister back to the doctor's office. The office nurse looked up from her desk when he opened the door.

Alarm glistened in her eyes.

"Thank you," Marco said.

He waved at the nurse and pulled the door closed.

CHAPTER 3

WITH EACH HEARTBEAT

When he was five years old, Marco would cover his head with the ragged yellow blanket he had slept with since he could remember and try to muffle the sounds of gun shots coming from the street in front of where he lived—and sometimes from the alley behind, too—almost every night. Now that he had turned nine, he no longer cowered. Instead, he felt anger and hoped the sounds would not wake his little sister.

Tonight, the sounds of a battle between two drug lords grew closer and louder and more intense. Marco listened from his bed on the floor next to the cast-iron, two burner cook stove. The green couch, although now more brown than green, sat in the middle of the room between the stove and Maria's crib. His sister's rickety white crib leaned tight against the wall, next to the front door.

BOOM......BOOM...bang...bang...rat-ta-tat...rat-ta-tat... BOOM!

Marble-sized beams of yellow light from the lone street lamp at the intersection outside instantly violated the complete darkness of their shack.

BOOM......BOOM...more holes through the tar paper wall. Several bullets struck the cook stove chimney-pipe, and the middle section of the chimney fell on Marco. The hot metal burned his right cheek. Coal smoke filled the room, creating bizarre beacons of yellow streaming through the holes.

Marco rolled away from the hot stove pipe and watched his drunken mother leap from the couch towards Maria's crib then stagger backwards several steps before lurching forward.

I have no pain, Lilliana thought in amazement, looking down at her chest in the smoky yellow light, watching blood gush from the buckshot hole above her left breast with each heartbeat. She tried to breathe and could not.

Gurgling, her mouth opening and closing without breath, Maria's mother crawled to her baby's crib.

Looking up, Lilliana watched the dark drops coming down through the blankets and thin mattress. She watched the dripping through the yellow beams of light before she closed her eyes.

Marco crawled around the couch on his hands and knees away from his bed which had now burst into flames, crawling toward his slender mother lying next to Maria's crib. From the floor, he watched the blood drip...drip...dripping, then stood in the smoke and lifted the blanket.

Marco's nine-year-old body trembled.

●●●

"Do not be afraid of fear," Mark from the United States had told him. "It will make you brave." Marco admired Mark. His mother had told him, after Mark's death, that he had been a C.I.A. spy for the United States and Marco admired that, too. Marco wondered, though, if Mark had been afraid the night the cartel enforcers had killed him.

*I will not be afraid...I will not...I will not be afraid...*Marco repeated over and over in his mind, crawling to the front door. With the top of his head, he pushed the door open. Marco ran from the burning shack, away from the street light. He stopped in the darkness and watched the black smoke from the burning tar paper swirling through the light of the street lamp.

Nine-year-old Marco stayed long enough to watch the corrugated metal roof collapse into the inferno. Touching his right cheek with his fingertips, he walked three miles to the doctor's office and waited for the nurse to arrive and unlock the front door.

CHAPTER 4

SHINY BLUE BARREL

Fausto's Market is located at the intersection of San Lucas and Victoria streets. Canned goods, dry goods, fresh meats, and alcoholic beverages are available inside. A large outdoor market, protected under a flat, corrugated metal roof, is attached to the main store on its west side. Lettuce, cabbage, sweet corn, plantains, green beans, bananas, avocados, and other produce are presented on long wooden tables. The market has been at this location for nearly 100 years and is currently operated by Miguel Fausto, the great-grandson of the founder. In order to supplement the store's cash flow, Miguel also rents office space to Raul Veracruz, his son Diego, and grandson, Cesar.

Black Mercedes-Benzes with tinted windows are often seen parked in the back of the market, outside the Veracruz office.

● ● ●

The nurse unlocked the office door. She came close to Marco and pushed his hand away from the burn.

"That hurts," she said. "Wait here."

Marco shrugged.

She walked up the three steps and into the office then turned and motioned for Marco to follow.

Gently, she washed his burn with iodine while watching the expression on the young boy's face.

"You don't cry, do you?" she asked while applying a thick coat of brown salve to the burn.

Marco unclenched his jaw and smiled a faint smile.

"Thank you, nurse. You are very kind."

"Where is your little sister?"

"In heaven with Mother."

For a brief instant, the nurse saw Marco's eyes glisten and his lips tremble before he clenched his jaw again. She patted him on his back before saying, "Put this salve on your cheek every morning and every night until the jar is empty. If it is not healed by then, come back…early like today."

"Thank you."

Marco walked to Fausto's Market. He sat on the green metal bench next to the front door and waited. He knew Miguel Fausto's routine.

Miguel exited the driver's door of his Ford produce Van and walked toward the front door, looking at the boy with the burnt cheek.

"I am here for work, Mister Fausto."

"Why would I hire a thief? I have watched you steal from my store, boy, for many years."

"It is only stealing if you do not get money. I am here to work."

Miguel studied Marco's face.

"How old are you?"

"Nine."

"You do not think like a nine-year-old."

Marco shrugged.

"What about your classes?"

Marco shrugged again.

"It would be easier just to have my friends feed you to the wild pigs that live down at the dump."

Marco smiled and then winced. He touched the burn with the fingers of his right hand and glanced at the brown salve on his fingertips.

"Then I would be dead and you would still have people stealing avocados and plantains and some asparagus."

"Good point, boy. What is your name?"

"Marco Juarez."

"Where do you live?"

"In the shipping crates behind your store."

"I've not seen you there."

"Just starting today. I think I will love it here."

"Well, young Marco Juarez, come into my office, and sign your name on a piece of paper, and you will have a job. I expect the best from my workers."

They entered the store. Miguel flipped a large black switch which made a hissing sound before all of the store's lights flickered alive. Marco followed the store owner to the rear of the store and into his office.

"Sign here." Miguel pushed a blank sheet of typewriter paper across the big desk.

Marco stood next to the desk and carefully wrote, moving his tongue with each letter.

MARCO JUAREZ

"How did you learn to write?"

"Mark taught me."

"Where is this Mark?"

"Heaven, with my sister and mother."

Miguel stood and extended his hand down toward his youngest employee.

"You are hired, young man. You are my produce security officer." He smiled a distant smile.

"Do I get a shiny badge?"

"I have something even better."

Miguel Fausto reached behind the desk and retrieved a single shot .22 caliber rifle which had been leaning against the corner wall.

"This was given to me by my grandfather when I was your age. Be careful."

Marco touched the shiny blue barrel.

"Shoot someone only if they are going to hurt you."

"Yes, sir."

"And, if that should happen, knock on the door next to this office, and tell them what has happened."

"Yes, sir."

"Do you know about the men in the office next to us?"

"Yes, sir. That is the office of Raul Veracruz, the drug lord."

"Exactly right. Tell me, young Marco, were you burnt in that house fire last night, down in the ghetto?"

"My mother and little sister, Maria, died there last night."

"I am sorry, boy, that this has happened to you."

"Someday I will find the men who did this, and I will kill them."

Miguel Fausto studied Marco's brown eyes for several seconds before replying, "I have no doubt of that."

He pulled the top drawer of his desk open, reached in, and handed Marco a box of .22 caliber, long bullets.

CHAPTER 5
ONLY A MONGREL DOG

Marco constructed a large lean-to against the outer wall of the Ve-racruz office, using the wood from shipping crates and several long boards covered on one side with green moss he found down by the creek. He had nearly finished when a tall man with a thin mustache opened the door from the drug lord's office and walked around the corner. He stopped and watched Marco and then looked at the rifle leaning against Fausto's cement block wall.

"It is going to leak when it rains," the man said.

"Yes, sir. I hope not much."

"Would you like a canvas to cover it?"

"Yes, sir, very much."

Marco looked up at the man who extended his hand.

"I am Diego Veracruz. This is my father's office."

"Yes, I know that."

"I will have a canvas delivered today."

"I do not have money to pay."

"I did not ask for any."

Diego walked toward his black Mercedes Benz then stopped briefly, turned, and said, "Someday we may have need of your help, young man." And then he drove away in the direction of downtown.

• • •

Marco hid the rifle under one of the green military blankets that arrived with the brown canvas. During the day, he patrolled the outdoor produce market. When he spotted shoplifters, he would approach the offender and simply state, "Put that back or I will follow you home and burn your house down."

On a Tuesday, a wrinkled man smoking a cigarette pulled a knife and laughed when Marco ran.

Marco returned, pointing his .22 rifle at the man who stuffed another cabbage into his full canvas bag.

"Right boy, you would shoot me for cabbages, three avocados, some green peppers, and sweet corn?"

He put the bag down and pulled the large knife from his belt, waving it. Puffing his cigarette through puckered lips, he walked toward Marco.

The trigger pulled easier than Marco had anticipated, and the stunned look on the man's face surprised Marco before the bright blood spurted from the man's forehead, and he collapsed.

The customers in the produce area watched briefly then turned away, shopping as if nothing had happened. The door to the Veracruz office opened. Two young men surveyed the situation before backing a blue Ford pickup close to the shoplifter's body.

One young man grabbed the man by his wrists while the other took his ankles, and they tossed the wrinkled man into the truck bed. The shorter man turned, as he got into the driver's seat, and wagged his finger several times in Marco's direction before starting the pickup and driving towards the city dump where the wild pigs live.

● ● ●

After that, Marco watched the produce area without incident. Sometimes he noticed people point in his direction and shake their heads. During the afternoons, Marco would watch from outside his lean-to while the boys and girls walked back from the Garza Garcia Grade School and San Pedro High School. He watched the boys form gangs and the bigger boys pick on the smaller boys. It made him feel uneasy and restless when some of the boys harassed the pretty girls, especially the girls who walked alone.

On a particularly hot and humid September afternoon, he watched while two of the bigger boys pushed and pulled at a young girl with long black hair, walking by herself, reading. She dropped her book, and when she bent over to pick it up, Marco saw her crying. Then the curly haired boy pulled at her white blouse, ripping it off. He tossed it to his partner who waved the blouse in the air like a flag.

"Give it back."

The boys turned to see Marco standing ten feet away; his right arm behind his back.

"What did you say, runt?" the one waving the white blouse shouted.

"Give it back, and never touch her again."

The boys looked at each other and grinned.

"You stay right here, sweet thing," the curly haired boy said to the crying girl, now holding her book up to cover her budding breasts.

They walked quickly toward Marco. Marco stepped back two steps while bringing his rifle out from behind his back. He pointed it at the curly head.

They stopped.

"You have only one shot," the boy holding the girl's white blouse chided.

"I know; it's for him," Marco replied, nodding at the curly head in his sights.

"It's the crazy boy from the market," the curly headed boy stammered. "Don't push him. He is the one who shot that man."

The boys turned and ran, taking the blouse. Marco walked to his lean-to and returned with a green military blanket. He draped the blanket over the girl's shoulders.

"Tell your friends," Marco said, looking at the girl's face, "that I will help them if they like."

"Thank you, I will."

"My name is Marco. What is yours?"

"Rosa."

"I am nine, almost ten," Marco said.

"I am ten," Rosa replied. She looked at the ground and then her eyes came up and she stared at Marco for an instant before she turned and walked away.

• • •

Diego Veracruz watched from the open door of his father's office. When Marco draped the green blanket over the girl's shoulders, he turned to his father, sitting at his desk, and said, "Marco Juarez is an old soul, Father." And, he closed the door.

"I admire that young man," Raul Veracruz replied.

"What is it, about him, Father?" Diego asked. "Why him…a strange little boy who appears from the ghetto. We have watched him steal from the market for years…and I cheered for him!"

Raul Veracruz removed some papers from the chair seat and motioned for his son to sit.

He removed his glasses and cleaned the lenses with a soft cloth. Then he spoke.

"I often visited Marco's mother, Lilliana."

He placed his glasses back on his face and looked at his son.

Diego stared at the old man who continued as if in a confessional.

"I visited Lilliana often. Your mother never discovered. Even though she worked the streets, I loved her. She did that to feed her family and purchase that shack."

He paused.

Diego simply stared.

"I always felt she loved me as well. I gave her extra money often and even more when she became pregnant with Marco. I did not go to her any longer when she told me she was about to marry a North

American by the name of Mark. I never stopped sending money…
I have never stopped loving her."

"Stand up, Father."

The old man, the head of the Mexican drug cartel, stood.

Diego hugged his father tightly.

"I'll be right back, Father." Diego opened the door and watched
Marco feed carrots to a stray dog.

"Throw me a carrot," Diego yelled to Marco. He caught a carrot and threw it high, watching the black and white dog catch it in
the air.

They sat on a bench next to the lean-to, in the shade, and
watched the dog chew the long carrot.

Marco said, "I like this dog."

"It is a nice dog. Have you named him?"

"No."

"Why not?"

"I am afraid I will lose him some day; perhaps he has an owner
that will claim him, and if I named him, I would be sadder."

"Good point, but he is only a mongrel dog."

"Yes, but now he is my mongrel dog."

They sat side by side on the bench, small Marco with a burn
scar on his right cheek and tall, handsome Diego.

"I always wondered why you never turned me in, all the years
I took produce from this market," Marco said, throwing another
carrot. "I knew you watched me. I would see you from the corner
of my eyes when I put produce in my bag. One time, I saw Mister Fausto running out to chase me, and you handed something to
him."

Diego smiled.

"Father paid for the produce you took. Every week he paid; that
is the reason the police never came."

Marco threw another carrot.

"Why?"

"My father knew your mother."

Marco looked up at Diego's face.

● ● ●

That evening Marco crawled into his lean-to, and the mongrel crawled in beside him. In the darkness, he dipped his finger into the jar of brown salve and rubbed it on his right cheek. He took a deep breath and then another, smelling the sweet melons piled in a long row on the table closest to his lean-to, and he wondered if the girl with long black hair thought he was ugly. And, he thought about his conversation with Diego.

CHAPTER 6
ZORRO

A red clay pot, with a cover shaped like a rose, sat on the dust next to his head the following morning. Marco opened his eyes and stared at the red and green paint decorating the clay and then up at the red rose handle.

Marco sat up and pulled the pot inside the lean-to and lifted the cover. He found a note and studied the inscription, shrugged, and walked to Miguel Fausto's back door.

"I am not able to read all the words. I do not know what this paper says," Marco said, handing the note to Miguel.

Miguel read it silently and smiled before reading aloud.

"Thank you. I was very frightened, and you saved me. I will tell my friends. Keep this pot where I placed it. We will leave you notes. Rosa."

Miguel rubbed Marco's head.

"You are a regular Zorro."

"What is a Zorro?"

"Ask Rosa."

• • •

The notes came at night while Marco slept. Sometimes he would try to stay awake, but those nights no one came. Even when he pretended to sleep; no notes. The pieces of paper were pleas for help—sometimes protection from bullies, sometimes for food, sometimes for prayers. Each time he received a note, Marco would take it to Miguel. Miguel would read it and insist that Marco read it with him.

"This is a family on South Victoria Street in the brick house next door to the laundry. The father was murdered last year."

"What does the mother do?" Marco asked, looking at the gray floor, recalling his mother.

"She operates the steam iron at the laundry. That job pays little. There are five children. The oldest daughter is Rosa's friend."

"What do you wish for me to do?" Marco asked, folding and unfolding the note.

"What do you think you should do?"

"I think we take a bushel of produce and place it on their door-step each week," Marco replied.

"And how do we account for our losses?"

Marco grinned. "Take it from my pay."

Miguel laughed.

"You save me several bushels every day."

● ● ●

Within six months, Marco could read all of the notes which came more frequently. His fame in the ghettos grew over the next seven years; first with the youthful problems of grade and high school, and then with more adult situations.

● ● ●

Rosa approached the lean-to at dusk. At her side walked a swollen-faced teenage girl.

Marco looked up from his chair at the young ladies. He did not recognize the young lady with shoulder length red hair.

"This is my best friend, Mary," Rosa said. She leaned down and patted the mongrel dog.

"Why is your face black and blue?" Marco asked Rosa's friend. He stood and walked closer.

Mary trembled. She looked at Rosa.

"Her stepfather beats her. He wanted sex, and she said no, so he beat her. He beats her mother, too, on Friday nights after he is paid. He goes to the cantina with his money and comes home drunk and beats her mother."

Marco scuffed the dry dirt with the toe of his right shoe. They watched the dust form a little tornado around his ankles.

"Mary's mother married the man just five months ago," Rosa continued. "He started beating her last month."

"Where do you live, Mary?"

"On Victoria Street, in the brick house next to the laundry."

Marco and Rosa's eyes met. The kindness faded from Marco's brown eyes, replaced by cold anger.

The skin on Rosa's arms formed little bumps and her tiny arm hairs stood straight up.

"What is this man's name, and where does he work?"

"Sergio. He works at the scrap metal foundry down by the city dump."

Marco gathered the girls closer with his right arm on Rosa and left on Mary.

He looked up and for the first time realized both young ladies were taller. He smiled and nodded, "It will be OK."

Twenty minutes after the young ladies left, Marco knocked on the Veracruz office door, and went in.

"I need your help," he said to Diego.

CHAPTER 7

THE PAYBACK

The boys in the gang had grown. Five had quit San Pedro High School and either drove taxis or worked as pimps at the Mexico City hotels. The curly haired boy now ran a brothel in the Iztapalapa district and was the envy of his friends. Three were still in school, all seniors. Still, they all gathered most nights at the cantina called Amigo's to drink tequila and act like grown men.

Amigo's is kitty-corner from Fausto's Market, on the south side, facing the back of the store. From the wooden benches outside Amigo's, they gathered to sit and drink and whistle at the ladies... and to watch Marco.

"Even the runt has grown," the curly haired young man said, biting off the end of a Nicaraguan cigar before lighting it. He spoke with the authority of a leader.

"I hear he is very strong," said the fellow at the end of the bench. "I hear he can pick up a full crate of bananas with each hand and put them on the table at the same time."

Now age sixteen, Marco had grown to his mature height of five foot, seven inches. His muscular body weighed 178 pounds. Pure muscle.

"We still owe him a payback," the young man sitting next to the curly haired leader said. "Crazy Marco needs to be taught respect; the runt embarrassed us, and all the girls and even the kids in grade school laughed at us until Christmas that year."

Marco had finished his midnight patrol. The young men watched while he crawled into his lean-to feet first, with his head pointing out so he could look up at the sky.

The gang of eight finished the seventh round of 80 proof El Toro Tequila when their leader pointed toward the lean-to with his cigar.

"I say this is the night we even the score with the runt," he slurred.

"I'm not getting anywhere near him," the high school senior at the end of the bench replied. "I heard three drunk guys tried to rob him one night with a knife. He woke up and bit the man holding the knife on the wrist. And then he broke all the bones in their arms with his bare hands. That is what my Uncle Raul said."

"I do not believe that story," the leader retorted. "I think perhaps the runt made that fake story to scare people."

"Well, it is working," the senior replied while kicking the dusty dirt in the darkness.

"Besides," the curly haired leader continued, "there are eight of us."

The young men drank two more shots of El Toro and felt braver.

"When he is soundly sleeping," the slender young man with a straggly mustache said, "When he is sleeping, we all grab the blanket and pull him out."

"You two," the fellow next to the leader said, pointing to the end of the bench, "wrap that damn dog of his in a blanket."

"And we kick the shit out of him," the leader commanded, "but we do not kill him. No knives, I want him to wake up and know that we have beaten him."

Marco fell asleep with his right hand on his rifle. He dreamed…

Through the smoke, he watched his mother and sister float in the air above him and embrace. He reached for them when an angel with long blond hair joined them and held Maria's hand before all three disappeared.

The first blow caused Marco to see bright lights spinning in both eyes. The second blow to his ribs forced all the air from his lungs. He rolled to his side and opened his eyes in time to see a boot descending on his head.

All black.

He awakened vaguely, enough to feel the pain of a savage beating—being kicked and stomped over his entire body.

All black, again.

The sun had risen, and he listened to the dog whining, licking his bloody arm over and over. The sensation of flies crawling on his face and lips gave him the shivers. His left eye would open but not the right one. He rolled to his back and looked up through his left eye at the school children gathered around him. He watched Rosa lean down and gently push a green military blanket under his head.

Her long hair tickled his face and scared away the flies for a few seconds.

She whispered, "I am sorry. I will get help."

Marco turned his head and watched Rosa walk to the back of Fausto's Market.

She has a beautiful shape.

She repeatedly knocked on the back door until it opened and then Rosa left for school.

Miguel Fausto and Diego Veracruz carried Marco to Miguel's office and laid him on the large desk. Ten minutes later a doctor and his nurse arrived. The nurse touched his broken face gently and turned his head just enough to look at the burn scar on his right cheek.

"He is badly injured and should be in the hospital," the doctor said after a brief evaluation. "This is what happens to these street urchins...sad waste of our resources," he continued, stroking his goatee.

The nurse grasped Marco's right hand and gave it a gentle squeeze.

Miguel and Diego sandwiched the startled physician between their bodies. Almost simultaneously they uttered, "Marco is my employee. I will pay."

"No amigos...please no...." Marco muttered through swollen lips. "I stay here. I am fine."

It was then Marco felt with his tongue all the broken teeth.

"I will be fine in a short while; if I can have a few days off, I will be fine."

Miguel and Diego smiled.

"Leave me some pain pills for the boy, and I will call if there are problems," Diego said.

The doctor glanced at Diego Veracruz with a sardonic look. He fumbled around in his medical bag before handing Diego a plastic bottle filled with white pills.

"Codeine tablets. One every six hours if he is hurting. Call me if he vomits blood."

For three weeks Marco lived in Miguel Fausto's office, sleeping on a cot behind the desk.

"They didn't get your twenty-two," Miguel said one morning while Marco sat on his cot, sucking thin corn soup through a straw.

"I love that gift," Marco said, looking up at the rifle.

"I do, too. It was my grandfather's first gun."

"Your debt is paid in full, Marco Juarez. From now on, I pay you a salary."

"Thank you. Tomorrow I move back to my lean-to."

"That place is not safe for you."

"They need to know I am not afraid."

"I would be, if I were you."

Marco turned his head and looked directly at Miguel before he continued, "I was dreaming of my mother and sister when they attacked me It is a sign. I am not afraid."

KNOCK...KNOCK...KNOCK.

Miguel looked at the TV monitor then unlocked the door.

Diego entered.

"I have something for you," Diego said, handing Marco a large machete with a shiny stainless steel blade.

"When you sleep at night, have this leather strap tied to your wrist," Diego said.

"Thank you. It is beautiful," Marco said, looking at the cane knife. His eyes glistened with defiance.

CHAPTER 8
RECKONING FOR ROSA

The intense Saturday afternoon sun reflected perfectly from the machete's polished steel blade. Marco sat in his chair at the end of the melon and pineapple table. Carefully, he reflected a beam of light across the street, flashing light from face to face and then on the curly haired leader.

"They are not worth it."

Marco looked up to his left.

"They are idiots," Rosa continued, looking down at him.

"I will not allow their evil to hold me prisoner. I refuse to let the memory of what they did ruin my life. Those worthless boys are not worth the price, Marco."

She bent closer.

Marco stood. His face looked up, just a little, into her face.

She smiled.

"My uncle Miguel told us at Sunday dinner Diego Veracruz has a nickname for you."

"I have not heard. What is it?"

"Uncle did not say, only that it is fitting."

Marco reflected light into the gang of eight faces, causing several to shield their eyes by pulling the bills of their caps low.

"My uncle is very proud of you."

"I am grateful to your uncle for many things."

One of the gang picked up a golf ball-sized stone and threw it in Marco's direction. It fell short.

"They must be punished for their evil," Marco continued. "I'm surprised your uncle has not had them all fed to the pigs."

"Uncle said the time will come. He doesn't want to offend the Veracruz family. Those guys do work for the Veracruz family, sometimes."

"Oh."

"That is why I never told uncle about the boy who tore away my blouse that day when I was ten..." Rosa paused a long pause.

"He hurt me again, thirteen days ago, in the girl's locker room."

"What!"

"Our team had just finished soccer practice, and I had dried off from the shower."

Rosa reached and took Marco's hand. It felt hot and electric.

They sat next to each other in the sunshine.

Rosa gazed at the clouds.

"Tell me, please," Marco said. He glared across the street. "Please tell me."

"I had stayed late to talk with Coach and every one had left when I took my shower. I had a towel around my waist when he walked in. He said, 'I see they have grown,' and he touched my breasts."

Marco reached up and gently turned Rosa's face toward his. He shuttered and bent over slightly, leaning toward the ground.

"My heart is aching," Marco whispered. A tingling hot current flowed from Rosa's hand. He looked up from his bent over position at Rosa's face. Dark makeup streaks now lined both cheeks.

"What did he do?"

"It hurt."

"Did he rape you?"

Rosa shook her head, *yes*.

Marco sat up and ran his left hand through his hair. He stared at the wicked, curly haired person sitting on Amigo's bench, laughing and blowing smoke rings with cigar smoke.

"Why didn't you tell me."

"I feel ashamed. I did not know how you will think of me, now."

Their hands now felt fused.

"Yes, you do."

"I am sorry, Marco."

"Why?"

"That I did not tell you—that I did not fight harder. I should have bitten his face or screamed more. I felt dirty—that maybe you would look at me with disgust."

"You know that is not true."

"I hoped."

"Does anyone else know?"

"I have told no one, not even Uncle Miguel. I bet that scum has bragged to his buddies." Rosa nodded toward the Amigo's bench. "I bet he thinks I am afraid to tell."

"And," Rosa continued, "I kept it a secret to prevent war between the Fausto and the Veracruz families."

Marco watched Rosa's eyes. Hatred glistened while she spoke, looking across at the young men sitting on Amigo's bench.

"Which one?"

"He is the bigger one on the bench next to the front door."

"Curly hair?"

"Yes."

"He is a pimp and a drug dealer. Everyone is afraid of him. The sight of him makes me nauseated."

"I am sorry, Rosa," Marco said, looking down at the machete, feeling the sharp edge with his fingers.

"I graduate next week. Then I go to work at this store for my uncle. I wish those guys would go away."

"Come here," Marco said, laying the machete on the table and extending both arms.

Rosa and Marco embraced. The gang of eight watched.

"I wish they would disappear, too," he whispered.

Rosa kissed Marco on the cheek. Then she turned his face with her hand and kissed the scar on his right cheek.

"Thank you," she whispered. "You are my good friend."

• • •

Monday morning, Marco knocked on the Veracruz office door. Diego unlocked the door.

"Come in, Marco."

"There are two that sit on the Amigo's bench that must disappear."

"Be careful, they do work for father."

"They beat me up. That I can live with; someday they will all be sorry. Two days ago, I learned the leader raped Rosa Fausto. That I cannot live with."

"Why?"

"I think of my little sister. I think about Maria and all the girls like her who must be quiet."

Diego sighed a deep sigh.

"You must not get caught. No one can know you did this thing."

• • •

Marco liked the invisibility of the nighttime. For several weeks he trailed the curly haired leader and his mustached lieutenant after they departed Amigo's well after midnight. Each of the young men would take the same drunken routes to their residences. Marco memorized the times they would arrive at various locations along their routes. He memorized the times and locations and the phases of the moon.

No moon on Tuesday, Marco thought, looking at his calendar covered with scribbled notes.

Marco waited behind a green dumpster with a puddle of reeking brown fluid underneath. He could hear the young man coming closer, singing a drinking song. He peeked around the rusty edge in the dim light of the street lamp and could see a pistol in the singer's right hand.

"HEY!" Marco shouted just as the man passed the dumpster.

The young man spit out his cigarette and twisted to his right, his arm extended, pointing the gun into the darkness behind the dumpster.

WHOOSH!

Marco brought the machete down from over his head.

Then a crushing metallic *clink…clink,* severing through the bones.

The young man grabbed his right forearm with his left hand.

His severed hand dropped to the ground. He looked and looked again, first at the bright red blood spurting far into the darkness and then at the hand in the wet grass holding his prized pistol.

Marco scooped the hand and gun from the grass next to the dumpster, tossing the hand and pointing the gun. He said nothing.

With contempt and fear, his thin mustache twitching, the young man sneered, "You will always be a runt," looking down and squeezing his right arm, watching the blood squirting between his fingers.

Marco pointed the gun at the gang lieutenant's face and squeezed the trigger repeatedly, until the gun stopped firing. The gun made a dull clank when he threw it against the full dumpster. He started to walk away, returning just long enough to thrust the thumb of the severed hand in the dead lieutenant's open mouth.

Marco ran five blocks and waited in the shadow of a large Christmas Palm at an intersection with only one street lamp. He could hear the gang leader talking to himself and laughing, coming closer and closer.

He stepped out from behind the tree and blocked the sidewalk.

"José, you should not have touched Rosa."

The curly haired man sneered, "She liked it. Did she tell you that, that she likes the big ones?" His pudgy fingers played with the wooden revolver grip protruding from his belt.

The machete hissed, moving through the air, its razor-sharp blade slashing the gang leader's throat without hesitation.

"Ahh……ohhshissss…." the curly haired young man gurgled through the frothy blood filling his mouth.

With both hands grasping at the wound, Jose´ looked to see blood streaming down his chest and covering the sidewalk before his knees became weak. The curly headed gang leader collapsed on the dirty cement, his cheek bouncing twice on the concrete. Jose's eyes opened and closed slowly, facing the large palm tree. From his face resting on the bloody Christmas palm seeds, he looked at a golden butterfly perched on a milkweed plant, growing at the base of the tree.

With each slow blink, the butterfly flexed its wings and then Jose' watched it fly away into the darkness.

Marco leaned close and whispered, "Rosa."

José's arms and legs stiffened and relaxed in rhythm three times and then he lay still.

● ● ●

Marco told no one.

Diego Veracruz knew, when he heard the news, and said nothing.

Rosa Fausto suspected and said nothing.

The remaining members of the gang choose another cantina for their nightly gatherings.

● ● ●

Marco tossed carrots high in the hot afternoon air and laughed when the mongrel dog jumped in the air and caught the treats. He had just tossed another carrot, extra high, when Rosa sat next to him.

"The guys are no longer at Amigo's," she said.

"I noticed that as well," Marco replied, tossing some peapods in the air.

"Thank you."

Rosa leaned closer and kissed Marco on the lips before walking toward her uncle's office.

"Mary said to tell you 'thank you,' too," she continued while walking away.

CHAPTER 9

A GOOD STRONG NAME

Five young men approached. Marco watched from his new padded cane chair with a sun umbrella, next to his lean-to. They walked slowly with empty hands, showing Marco, making it obvious they came without malice in the heat of the summer afternoon. Finally, the young man with a straggly mustache spoke.

The black and white mongrel dog growled a deep rumbling growl.

"We have voted; we would like for you to be our leader, Marco."

Marco looked from face to face, squinting at the eyes averting his stare.

"How many voted for someone else?"

"We all voted for you."

"You are the ones who attacked me as I slept. Why would I want to lead a pack of cowards?"

"It was José's idea. He commanded we do it," the short fellow on the right replied. He wore a frayed white T-shirt with a picture of Elvis on the front.

"Where is José?" Marco questioned. "I have not seen him for quite a while."

"His throat got slashed. He is dead," a young man with acne replied.

"What a shame, losing a brave man like José," Marco said. "How did such a thing happen?"

"He was attacked on a Tuesday night on his way home from Amigo's," the young man with the mustache answered.

"And he lost the fight?" Macro retorted.

"Yes. His good friend, Carlos, was murdered that same night."

"Why exactly are you here before me now? When José lived, you were all kicking me while I slept, like cowards, not brave enough to face me. I think if Carlos still lived, you would be laughing at me from your cowards bench."

Marco fingered the blade of his machete and polished the wide blade with a rag. He spit on the blade and polished even harder, waiting for a reply. He glanced up and looked from face to face.

"Everyone in the ghetto and in Iztapalapa district call you Machete," the fellow with the Elvis shirt said.

Marco fingered the sharp edge of the blade. He placed the machete on the pineapple table and stroked the mongrel dog sitting next to him. He fed a carrot to the dog before replying.

"I think Machete is a good name for my dog. What do you think?"

Five heads nodded yes with enthusiasm.

"I will not be the leader of cowards who have no spine." He fed the dog a handful of green peas.

"If there is trouble in the ghettos—when you see people treated poorly—you come here and tell me, is that understood?"

"Yes," they replied in unison.

The five walked away.

Marco yelled, "If I should hear that any of you commit a rape or hurt any of the children, guess what I will cut off."

They turned just long enough to see Marco pointing his machete at their anatomy and whispering to his dog.

"I like the name, Machete," he told his mongrel dog.

"And please come back to Amigo's. The owner is sad."

The gang of five walked to Amigo's and opened the rusty screen door.

Miguel Fausto listened to the entire exchange from his open office door. He had watched as the gang of five approached Marco and then left. He walked to Marco when they entered Amigo's.

"Would you like a more formal education?" Miguel asked.

"They wanted me to be their leader," Marco said.

"Of course, they did; they are weak and need guidance."

"I said no."

Miguel smiled. "Now they respect you even more."

"They are calling me Machete in Iztapalapa district and in the cantinas."

"I know. Diego gave you that name after José and his lieutenant died. It is a good strong name."

"I just named my dog Machete."

Miguel laughed.

"You did not answer my question; would you like some formal education?"

"Yes. Mark showed me how to make letters, and you have taught me to read. I would like that."

"You know that Rosa works for me now?"

"She told me."

"Rosa came to me after our family dinner following Mass and asked if she could tutor you. She is a very bright young lady—top of her class."

"I would like that."

"Good. Class in my office every evening, except for Sundays, for one hour…seven p.m."

"Thank you."

"You are welcome, Machete."

Miguel Fausto grinned as they shook hands.

CHAPTER 10

GOING AWAY

Marco's photographic memory surprised and thrilled Rosa.

"He learns with the first lesson, Uncle. Marco memorizes so easily I am jealous," Rosa said during Sunday dinner six weeks later.

"What is his favorite subject?"

"History. He loves history. He would study only history, if I let him."

Uncle Miquel smiled.

"Does he know that you are engaged to Roberto Aguilera?"

"I showed him my ring on Friday."

Miguel waited.

"He hugged me, Uncle. He hugged me very tight and told me it is a beautiful ring."

•••

Sunday morning.

Marco looked up with surprise from his chair, watching Diego's black Mercedes Benz drive up to the back of the store and park in front of the lean-to.

"I thought you would be at Sunday Mass," Marco said to the approaching Diego.

Diego sat next to him.

"I am going away for a while."

"Why?"

"Father has a job for me in a city named St. Paul, in the States."

"That is in Minnesota," Marco replied. "What job?"

Diego took several deep breaths and lit a cigar before answering.

"Father has a central distribution center in St. Paul. It has accounting problems and new problems with the Italians. He is sending me north to fix things."

"How long?"

"No idea. Until the operation is again running smoothly."

Marco smiled and then shrugged.

"You are a big brother to me, Diego. I will miss you like I miss my sister. I have always known, since you gave me the canvas for the lean-to, that you are my best friend, that you are secretly guarding me and that, especially after the gang beat me, that you put the word out no one was to hurt me again or they would face you. I heard that from Rosa. My heart will have an empty spot until you come home."

Marco paused.

"I would like to go with you."

Diego said, "I would like that, too. Perhaps in the future. This time I need to be alone."

"Be careful up north. I have heard it can be dangerous."

"Living is dangerous, my amigo."

Marco nodded yes.

"I leave Monday morning. I want you to know I am very proud of you, Machete."

Marco's eyes widened and shifted to Diego's face.

Diego's face beamed. "I think it is a splendid and powerful name and my gift to you. Use it when the time is right!"

He paused. "And, by the way, Father is moving to his new office on the top floor of the Hotel Ciudad. I have suggested to Miguel that our old office would be a perfect office for his security officer."

Marco shrugged. He looked at the ground and then again at Diego's face. "I am going to miss you."

Diego bent down and hugged Marco.

"Until we meet again, brother."

CHAPTER 11

VICTOR BONIFACIO

Timothy Fife had been conceived in a French field hospital on a wooden gurney. He was born to a single mother, a major in the United States Army Nursing Corps, on February 2, 1945. Timothy was adopted by First Lieutenant Sabrina Fife and her husband, Sergeant Major Dwight Fife.

Following high school, Timothy attended The Citadel Military College where he graduated at the top of his class and as a star quarterback.

Timothy spent four years in Vietnam following graduation. He returned home on a moonless night, with shrapnel in his body, a slight limp, and pain which he mostly ignored. At age twenty-seven, Timothy joined the Minneapolis Police Force. Four years later he was promoted to detective.

• • •

The first Monday following promotion, Timothy drove to the shipping docks at midnight, on patrol for drug trafficking. He had just turned left into the shipping yard, when a black Corvette whooshed out at a high rate of speed.

Their cars side-swiped, knocking the side mirror and door handle to the pavement from Timothy's undercover car.

Damn, he's doing a hundred, Timothy thought. He made a U-turn in the yard and activated the flashing red and blue lights hidden in his Dodge Charger's grill.

Rain splattered on the windshield.

The Corvette pulled steadily away from the Charger. Timothy glanced at the speedometer.

"There will be another day," Timothy muttered. "This is nuts." He lifted his foot from the accelerator pedal and watched the speedometer needle drift down from 125.

It seemed in slow motion; Detective Fife watched the black Corvette hit a bump and go airborne. The Corvette's front lifted for several seconds before the car crashed, head-on, into a bridge support.

The Corvette erupted in flames.

Timothy did not hesitate. Stopping twenty yards from the wreck, he ran and then crawled into the inferno through a river of burning fluids coming from under the car and disappearing in the storm drain.

Napalm…smells like napalm.

He pulled the unconscious young man, feet-first, away from the flames. In the rain, Timothy checked for a pulse and found a fast one.

The Corvette exploded, again.

Bad night…Delta night.

Timothy carried the young man with smoldering, wet pants to his car. It did not occur to him that protocol required an ambulance with EMTs be summoned. He simply drove down 10th Street at 80 mph toward St. Joseph's Hospital.

Two young night shift nurses and a trauma resident looked up from the nurse's station to see a tall man with a golden detective's badge in his left hand, carrying a smaller man with smoking clothing against his chest.

Timothy walked through the open entrance door into the

emergency room atrium, supporting the bloody head with his right hand.

"P.I.A....first and second-degree burns, head and chest trauma...unconscious," Timothy said in the direction of the E.R. staff. He placed the man on a stretcher. "He was going in excess of one-hundred when he hit a bridge support."

Timothy walked alongside while the staff rolled the stretcher into Trauma Room One.

"If you don't mind, I'll just stand over here and watch," Timothy said to the trauma resident.

"Sure, use the sink to wash-up, if you like," he replied, looking at the oil and blood on Timothy's hands.

They had taken the Corvette driver away for a CT scan when an older man who looked very similar to the Corvette driver approached Timothy.

"I hear you saved my son."

Timothy looked up and then stood.

"I'm Detective Timothy Fife."

The men shook hands.

"I'm Victor Bonifacio. The resident tells me you crawled into my son's car; you crawled into the fire and saved my son."

"Yes."

Victor Bonifacio stared up at Timothy Fife.

"He would now be dead if not for you. Someday I will find a way to repay you. I want you to know that, Detective. I am grateful."

Victor Bonifacio extended his hand again, "Thank you," and he left the room.

An older nurse with gray hair came into Trauma One and began to bag the burnt clothing and restock supplies.

"Who is Victor Bonifacio?" Timothy asked him.

The fellow stopped for a moment. "You must be new here."

"Yup," Timothy replied, "first week as a detective."

"Well, sir, Victor Bonifacio is the Midwest olive oil distributer." And he winked.

"Olive oil, huh."

"He's a very influential man."

"Good man to know?"

The nurse turned so he could look directly at Timothy before saying, "Depends."

●●●

Raul Veracruz purchased a large brick building in St. Paul at the intersection of 10th Street and Robert for the purpose of receiving traffic coming from Mexico up U.S. Highway 35. The official looking green cards and letters of introduction listed the travelers to be working as *domestic service, restaurant server, housekeeper, cook, construction worker, and security guard.* The building's location also made it an ideal distribution center for a variety of drugs.

The Italians resented the intrusion of the Mexicans into the Midwest drug and prostitution business. After several "peace summits" failed to persuade the Veracruz family to take their business elsewhere, Victor Bonifacio declared a subtle war.

At first profitable, the Veracruz business venture steadily lost market share and finally, after six years, began to lose money. An angry Raul Veracruz sent his youngest son, Diego, to St. Paul to oversee the North American operations.

●●●

"Detective Fife, this is Victor Bonifacio," the answering machine on Timothy's desk spoke. "I promised the day you saved my son I would somehow repay you. I have information I think will help you. Please call me at 800-587-2147."

Timothy dialed the old black phone on his desk.

"Sicilian Fine Foods and Olive Oil, Victor speaking."

"Detective Fife. You left me a message."

"Not over the phone. I'll discuss over lunch at The Sicilian. When's a good time for you?"

Timothy flipped through his day planner.

"This Friday at eleven thirty."

He arrived ten minutes late, intentionally. Timothy had watched Victor arrive alone, relieved that no one followed or lingered or window shopped outside the nearby stores.

Victor looked up from the table, sipping a scotch and soda when Timothy entered. The Sicilian was otherwise empty except for a waiter.

"I made a reservation," Victor said with a wry smile.

"Thank you. I hate waiting."

The waiter approached.

"Club soda with lime and one cherry," Timothy said.

"I'll have another scotch and soda," Victor ordered, "and a big plate of calamari, and oil and a loaf of bread. You like calamari?"

"Very much," Timothy answered, looking around and in the reflection from the bar mirror.

"You aware of the Mexican mob infiltrating our city?" Victor asked.

"Yes."

"You know they are running prostitutes and drugs up highway thirty-five through Nuevo Laredo?"

"I do now."

The calamari and bread arrived with extra marinara, parmesan cheese and extra virgin olive oil. Timothy tore a large piece of bread from the loaf and dipped it in the oil.

"I'm curious, Victor, how a man in the olive oil business knows all this stuff."

"I have a pizza business. I hear things from my employees at Bonifacio's Pizza Pie Company."

Timothy smiled. "Pizza and olive oil. How is business?"

"Best year ever. I tell you these things as a concerned citizen. I love our city and the United States."

"As do I."

"And, by the way, thank you for your service. I hear you were awarded the Purple Heart."

"Thank you."

"Here's a new development, something I doubt you have heard; the Mexican Cartel's Godfather, Raul Veracruz, has just sent his youngest son to St. Paul to take over the operations. His office is in the tall brick building at 10th and Robert."

"Thanks for sharing," Timothy replied.

"You are welcome. Anything I can do to be of assistance and keep our city safe."

The men finished eating in silence. Timothy motioned to the waiter and handed him a credit card.

"Your money is not welcome in my bistro, detective."

"I always pay for my meals."

"What meal?' Victor retorted. The waiter walked away.

"Diego Veracruz will be at his office tonight," Victor said, standing and swiping a cloth napkin over his lips. Then he walked to the rear door, leaving Timothy alone, except for the waiter, who stood at attention near the front door.

Timothy's hand touched the brass door knob. The waiter cleared his throat. Timothy paused.

"You will find heroin and cocaine in Diego's car under the spare tire."

"What kind of car?"

"Mercedes 500, black. It will be parked in the lot west of 10th and Robert."

Timothy handed the waiter a one hundred-dollar bill.

"Thank you, Arturo."

● ● ●

RICHARD ALAN HALL

Arturo Rossi arrived in the United States when he was seventeen years old from Sicily, for sanctuary.

Prior to his arrival in St. Paul, Arturo worked as a currier for Don Bonifacio in Palermo. The young man's future looked bright in the family business until the police arrested him with four kilos of cocaine on his way to make a delivery to a client who had turned state's evidence.

A Palermo Chief Judge refused bail after the Chief of Police informed the judge the Bonifacio family had refused to "share the bounty," over the previous year.

Don Bonifacio paid the appropriate authorities for safe passage and sent Arturo to the United States for the protection of his oldest son, Victor.

Timothy had joined the St. Paul Police department seven weeks prior to having met him. A rookie night patrolman and scared Italian boy, pulled over for a burned-out taillight.

"Driver's license and registration, please," Patrolman Fife said, shining a long, 6-cell flashlight on the boy's face.

"It is Italian license," Arturo replied, handing the green and white plastic card through the open window. Timothy watched the boy tremble.

"You need to have a Minnesota driver's license."

"I have time, still."

"Are you a citizen of the United States?"

"No. Italy."

"Do you have a green card?"

"No, only this license. I work for Mister Bonifacio."

"How long you been in this country?"

"Nearly one year."

"And, you work for Victor Bonifacio?"

"I work in his restaurant, The Sicilian. I do waiter work."

Timothy studied the young man's face in the bright light. *Poor kid.*

"Why are you here?"

The young man looked away, staring at the Camaro's dashboard.

"A big problem in Sicily, and Mister Bonifacio's father sent me here to work for his son."

"Drugs?"

Arturo stared at the dashboard.

"Were you sent here to avoid the authorities in Sicily?"

"Yes."

"What happens if you go back?"

Arturo made a cutting motion with his right forefinger across his throat.

"Tell you what," Timothy said, looking at the Italian driver's license, "I will meet you Monday morning at the police station and take you to the Secretary of State's office. I'll sign that you passed your driver's test. Now drive directly back to where you are staying and no driving until Monday."

"Yes, sir."

"The time may come," Timothy glanced at the driver's license again, "the time may come, Arturo Rossi, when you will be able to help me."

"Thank you."

"Do you understand what I just said?"

"Yes." Arturo smiled. "That is how things work in Sicily."

CHAPTER 12
NO FAVOR

In March, Sergeant Roy Dumbrille celebrated his 25th anniversary with the St. Paul Police Department. He held the politics and "butt-kissing" associated with working the day shift in disdain and refused every opportunity for promotion if it meant leaving the night shift. Plus, he enjoyed being the senior figure on a shift chronically staffed with rookies.

Fred Glen had no choice. He graduated from the police academy in April and took a position as a night patrolman in May.

● ● ●

"Who's on tonight for the warehouse district?" Timothy asked the desk sergeant.

"Sergeant Dumbrille and Patrolman Glen."

"Glen a rookie?"

"He is," the desk sergeant replied.

"I need to meet with them tonight."

"What time?"

"2300 hours."

The Sergeant typed a message on his computer. "They'll be in the conference room…2300 hours."

The night sergeant and the rookie looked up from their coffee cups when Timothy entered the small conference room with green tiled walls.

"Hi, Roy. Nice to meet you, Fred," Timothy said, shaking the hand with faint age spots and then the firm young grip.

The rookie looks kinda pale.

Timothy poured a cup of coffee and smelled it before dousing it with powdered coffee creamer.

"This stuff tastes like floor sweepings," he said, taking a sip.

"Well, at least it's consistent," the sergeant retorted.

"I need your help tonight," Timothy said, "at the intersection of 10th and Robert. A Mexican by the name of Diego Veracruz, son of the Mexican Godfather, Raul Veracruz, has arrived in our town to take over his father's operation."

Timothy handed a black and white glossy picture to the men sitting across the table.

"He has an office on the top floor of the Roosevelt building; drives a black Mercedes 500. I received intel from an informant that there will be heroin and cocaine hidden under the Mercedes spare tire."

"Any idea who put it there?" the sergeant said with a smile while blowing on his coffee.

"Don't know the answer to that, Sergeant; we'll ask him. I talked to Judge Walters and here's a search warrant for the car and office."

Timothy watched the rookie wipe at the perspiration on his forehead with a paper napkin.

"First raid, Fred?"

"Yes, sir."

"It'll be fine, young man. Your sergeant knows more about these operations than anyone on the force, just follow his lead. You a married man, Fred?"

"No, sir. Just got engaged."

"You'll have an exciting story to tell your honey tomorrow."

"Yes, sir."

Timothy unfolded a street map and walked around the table.

"I'll be in an unmarked car across the street. You wait down here; there is a big maple tree right at this intersection. When you see me get out, drive up and block the Mercedes.

"Got it. What time?" Sergeant Dumbrille ask.

Timothy looked at his watch.

"Let's go now."

• • •

Diego Veracruz rubbed both tired eyes. The books had been altered by his predecessors, and the men had been sent back to Mexico City for "rehabilitation."

Enough for tonight.

He closed the ledger, took a long sip of black Bustelo, and retrieved the car keys from the desk's top drawer.

One thirty…damn…it is foggy.

He looked down from the top step at the parking lot below, hardly able to make out his black car in the dim light and fog.

His right hand slid easily down the wet metal handrail. It felt cold.

"YOU STOP RIGHT THERE! Let me see your hands. NOW!"

"WHO THE HELL ARE YOU?" Diego yelled into the foggy dark.

"Let me see both hands!"

Diego could now see a figure walking closer to the bottom step. The man wore civilian clothing and held his empty hands open.

Shit.

His eyes now accommodated the darkness. Diego made out two uniformed police officers standing next to his Mercedes. He froze.

"I have no weapon," Diego said calmly. "Here are my papers."

He reached for the wallet inside his jacket.

"POLICE! DROP THE GUN!" screamed a shaky voice, almost falsetto.

BANG!

For a flashing instant, Diego's mind remembered the time in middle school when the foul ball off José's bat hit him in the Adam's apple, and he could not breathe.

Timothy snapped his head toward the gunshot then turned back when the sound echoed from the tall building.

Where the hell…what the hell…the rookie…damnit.

Diego's eyes opened wide with surprise. His mouth formed the word why. Both empty hands grasped at the wound in the middle of his throat above his Adam's apple.

Cold…cold…cold…bless me…Father…bless me.

In disbelief, the former Green Beret watched the bright blood gush from Diego's nose and mouth before the Mexican's knees crumpled.

Diego took both bloody hands from his throat, extending his arms up from the cold concrete, seeing Timothy's face coming closer while fading…fading…fading into the darkness with each blink.

The last thing either of the two uniformed policemen saw on this earth was the flashing from the barrel of a Thompson machine gun.

A large man launched through the brick building's front door and down the wet steps, running with a machine gun, firing without hesitation, ignoring two bullets striking his chest. He stopped and dropped the empty clip next to Diego's body and with a new clip, continued to walk toward the two downed policemen, with absolute hatred, firing bullets into the lifeless heads.

Timothy felt no fear, at all, only anger.

Another cluster…another embassy cluster…shit.

The smoke from the hot Thompson barrel drifted up into the face of the big man, now standing ten feet away.

"You did not pull your gun, amigo," the big man said in broken English.

"There has been enough death here tonight, sir," Timothy replied, raising his arms away from his body, both hands open and empty.

The big Mexican studied Timothy.

"You are a strange one, amigo."

Six men ran down the steps and formed a circle around Timothy. The tallest man with high cheek bones came close and stared. He pulled a large Bowie knife from his belt and pressed it against Timothy's throat.

"I think tonight we cut your throat," the unshaven Incan said. "That is how we slaughter pigs in our country. We cut their throats and let them run."

Timothy continued to stare at the big man holding the Thompson. They stood three feet apart.

Today is good day to die scrolled through his Green Beret mind.

The big man pushed the man holding the knife back into the circle and put his bloody chest against Timothy.

"You go now, and tell your police that Diego is innocent—that an innocent man is murdered here this night. You tell them this. Go now. We take him and we leave."

He pointed his machine gun toward Diego's body. The high cheeked man advanced with his knife. and the big man pushed him back again.

"You take great care, amigo. I have done you no favor this night." He paused and stared at Diego then reached down and closed his friend's open eyes.

"Raul Veracruz and his grandson will have questions for you, I am sure. There is a debt to be paid."

CHAPTER 13
THE ROOKIE'S FIANCEE

First Lieutenant Wendell Jackson and Lieutenant Colonel Timothy Fife met in the darkness of a hellish night.

Timothy's Special Forces unit had been ordered into Saigon to protect the United States embassy during the evacuation. During the dark confusion of that final night, Timothy grasped Wendell's arm, and together they ran toward a heavy 50-caliber machine gun, moved two dead South Vietnamese soldiers, and began firing the big gun at a large hole in the compound wall on Thong Nhat Boulevard.

Like a seasoned center fielder, Wendell leapt from his crouched position next to the hot machine gun into the dark, smoky air. He grabbed a hand grenade that had been tossed over the wall, and in a single motion, threw the grenade just as it exploded. Both men were hit. Wendell lost most of his right hand, except the thumb and forefinger, and multiple abdominal wounds.

"Godspeed. Please help him, Lord," Timothy whispered into the racket of war, watching the medivac helicopter with the wounded marine lift from the embassy roof and with the nose pointed slightly down, head east, just above the treetops.

Six months after he started working for the St. Paul Police Department, Timothy received a phone call from Wendell who now lived in a city called Big Bay. After that conversation, the two veterans spoke on the phone nearly every day. Their friendship grew, forming a bond few know.

"I'm not cut out for this shit," he said to Wendell on the phone, the morning after the Diego debacle. "It's giving me flashbacks to the delta…and the embassy."

"Well, leave."

"And do what?'

"There's an old bar for sale here in Big Bay. You'd make a great bartender."

"What's the bar called?"

"Poor Joe's."

•••

"Morning Chief."

The St. Paul Chief of Police looked at his daily planner and then up at Timothy.

"You here about the shooting investigation, Detective?"

"I'm here to resign."

"Never thought of you Green Berets as quitters."

"Chief, I'm resigning; there's a difference. Thinking about buying a bar in a peaceful little place called Big Bay."

"Really?" the Chief said sarcastically.

"Sick of watching death." He tossed his badge and service revolver on the chief's desk. "I'll finish my report and have it on your desk this afternoon. One sergeant dead. One scared rookie patrolman…dead. One dead innocent civilian…killed by our rookie."

"I'm not so sure about that innocent part, there, detective."

Timothy shrugged. "Well, unarmed civilian, then."

"You sure about that? The man you claimed was killed has never been found—no blood on the cement, not even a trace. I don't know if he didn't have a gun—not even sure he's dead. What I do know is I have two dead St. Paul policemen, mutilated beyond recognition, and a close friend at that. I've known Roy Dumbrille for nearly twenty years. Did you know young Fred? Had a hell of a future in law enforcement; graduated second in his academy class, second only to some kid with a photographic memory."

"You don't believe me?"

"What Detective O'Brian did find is one hundred and thirty-two bullet marks in the pavement, no empty casings, just bullet marks. He says looks like an ambush to him, that you walked into an ambush…thinks perhaps you froze."

Timothy smirked down at the chief.

"That's right, Chief," the former Green Beret retorted, fingering the Purple Heart always in his right pocket, "I froze and I'm a quitter."

Timothy swiveled a military turn, 180 degrees, and walked away from the chief of police, looking straight ahead with his crystal blue eyes spewing distain. He walked down the hallway past the next office then turned around and looked at the desk sergeant.

"What is Fred Glen's fiancée's name?"

The sergeant looked at Timothy while answering the phone.

"Yes, sir. Yes, sir. I'll take care of that ASAP."

He looked up at Timothy from his desk.

"Chief says you're no longer on the force and I'm to deactivate your computer and NCIC access."

"Just resigned. What's her name?"

"Erin Gray."

"Help me, here, John, I need an address."

The sergeant typed on his computer and hit the enter button.

"She lives in the dorms at Macalester College."

"Thanks."

"Here's her room number."

● ● ●

Erin Gray's eyes sucked Timothy's mind empty. The words he rehearsed driving to the dorm and practiced while climbing the stairs…gone.

Sweet diesel and thatch…liquid fire…burning Vietnamese children…good God almighty…kids on fire…mother and grandmother staring…angry despair…hollow eyes turned inward…absolute sorrow…

He opened his mouth, sucking air, desperately choking back a surging urge to weep. No words came out. Erin stood and left her friends sitting on the couch.

The complete strangers embraced. He felt her body quivering and then convulse with sobs.

For the first time since he was twelve years old and Shep, his German Shepherd, had died, Timothy felt warm tears on his face.

He squeezed Erin.

"I am very sorry, Erin, that this has happened in your life."

Erin cried.

"He was a very brave man," Timothy said, wiping his nose with the back of his hand.

CHAPTER 14

SELDOM AS THEY SEEM

KNOCK...KNOCK...KNOCK...

Twelve thirty...what the hell...

Timothy opened the apartment door.

"Didn't think you'd be sleeping," Victor Bonifacio said, "I need to talk before you leave for that Big Bay." He walked to the little red kitchenette table and pulled out a chair.

"Have a seat, Victor."

"Thank you. Just so you know, there will be a guard outside your door at all times. I think you know Arturo."

Timothy sat on the couch and stared at Victor.

"I'm not even going to ask how you know I resigned yesterday or how you know I'm moving to Big Bay."

"Good."

"Don't need a guard."

"Oh, trust me, you need a guard."

Timothy stared.

"You, my young friend, have a target on your back. The Mexican Godfather will grieve for a period before he comes for you. If you had a son, he would come for your son, so you could suffer the agony."

Timothy shrugged. "Maybe I should take a trip to Mexico."

"Bad idea...really bad."

Timothy smiled.

"That was a joke, Victor."

Victor pulled two cigars from his jacket pocket and tossed one to Timothy.

"Don't smoke anymore...since 'Nam."

"These are wonderful cigars—Fuentes," Victor replied, biting the cigar end and lighting it.

"This is a no-smoking condo."

"That's your Puritan's fault."

"What?"

"Your founders that started this country, abolishing all of life's pleasures. Did you know they placed a board between men and women in their beds? What kind of people do things like that? Pleasure is a sin. Even sent missionaries to civilize the Indians and natives in Hawaii; outlawed their dances and made them cover up. What a bucket of crap."

Timothy grinned. "So, this no-smoking law is the Puritan's fault."

"Damn right; they planted the ideas." He puffed twice on his Fuentes. "They enjoyed misery, I can only guess the reasons."

"Still, this is a no-smoking building, and I'll get fined by the landlord."

Victor puffed five smoke rings and grinned. "I own the building."

Timothy scratched the back of his head and reached for the cigar lighter.

"Things are seldom as they seem," Victor continued. "And I can tell you this with all honesty, the truth is seldom accurate."

"Please enlighten me," Timothy replied, lighting the cigar and then looking at it closely.

"These cigars are a gift from Fidel Castro, a thank you for helping. Gives me a box every year at Christmas."

"I'm not even going to ask."

"Here's the truth. The police and citizens believe me to be an Italian Mafia Godfather. And, to them, I am. The other truth is that I am part of something much greater, a group of men who are called upon, from time to time, to rectify wrongs in this world, to administer justice."

Timothy puffed on his cigar and listened.

Victor continued, "Someone close to you is also part of this organization. He appears to be a hospital custodian with a disfigured hand and a limp. At a moment's notice, that brave marine will drop everything and go anywhere needed."

"Wendell?"

Victor removed a strange looking phone, triangular in shape and yellow. "We communicate by satellite links on these phones."

"That's one strange looking device." Timothy took the phone from Victor and turned it over several times.

"Just wait until you see our helicopters," Victor replied. Then he smiled. "They are invisible to radar."

"Olive oil and pizza man, huh Victor."

"Yes, sir, and that is the truth. Our helicopters go four hundred miles per hour, and that is the truth, too. I'll let Quinn O'Malley tell you how fast the flying wing travels. He calls it the Ghost Wing."

"You gonna tell me who Quinn O'Malley is?"

"A charter boat captain in Key West. No fishing, just charters around the keys. He went to college with Fidel Castro."

"I can hardly wait for the rest of that truth."

Timothy and Victor stood in the little non-smoking apartment.

Without hesitation, surrounded by cigar smoke, Timothy shook Victor's hand.

"Welcome to the True Believers, Timothy. I am eager to see your Poor Joe's Bar."

CHAPTER 15

WORTHLESS TRASH

The lessons had concluded for Tuesday evening. Rosa extended her left arm across the desk and touched Marco.

"Mary is grateful."

Marco smiled when Rosa touched him.

"That man should not have touched her. I wish that had never happened to her...very evil."

"I think Mary likes you."

Marco shrugged before replying, "Look at me...Mary is quite beautiful, not as beautiful as you, but beautiful. She can do better."

"That is selfish of you, Marco."

"What?"

"You should not take it upon yourself to choose for her."

"Sorry. I do not look at life as you do, I guess."

"You are afraid of being rejected, Marco. We all fear that, and you came from the ghetto and think you are less because of it."

Marco studied Rosa's lips moving with the words.

"You are not a lesser person. Some of the great people you have studied came from ghettos; some were poor, even born in a barn. Jesus of Nazareth was born in a barn."

Marco tilted his head and listened.

"Dream, Marco, dream of who you want to be and never stop reaching, you are very smart."

Marco sucked in a deep breath.

"Thank you, Rosa. I will ask Mary for a date."

Rosa smiled.

"She will like that."

"Will you ask her for me?"

"No, silly boy," Rosa answered, twisting her engagement ring around and around.

●●●

"Marco asked me to marry him last night after dinner. We went for a walk during sunset and he asked me," Mary said to Rosa.

Rosa looked across the booth table at her best friend.

"It has taken him nearly seven months to work up the courage. What did you say?"

"I said I would," Mary replied, and she poured more sugar into her coffee.

"When Roberto proposed, I tingled all over," Rosa said.

Mary stirred the coffee.

"You don't seem very excited. I thought you would be happier."

"I did too," Mary replied, sipping the black, sweet coffee and then blowing on it. "Just something I need to do, and Marco is a good man. He will protect me."

"PROTECT YOU?"

"You know what I mean."

●●●

Miguel Fausto and Raul Veracruz paid for the wedding.

Initially, the priest objected.

"That young man is a heathen. They call him by the nickname Machete in the neighborhoods, and I think you both know very well how he earned that name," said Father Nieto, disdain oozing with each word. He glared at Raul and Miguel.

"What happened to, 'Let him cast the first stone who has never sinned,'" Miguel shot back.

"So now you are a theologian," Father Nieto retorted.

"No, Father," Raul said, "we are the financers that help keep this Basilica of Our Lady of Guadalupe open."

Father Nieto scratched his chin and nodded. "So, you want to play that card...I see. It is time for me to hear confessions now. Let me know when."

"I want to pack the Basilica with people from the neighborhoods," Miguel said, watching the priest flap away in his white robes.

"I will put the word on the street," Raul said. "I will have Cesar print an invitation with pictures of a great feast."

Miguel grinned. "Good. Father Nieto will burn incense for a week to rid the Basilica from the odor of the poor."

• • •

Mary came to Marco on their wedding night after the long night of festivities, in the dark, joining him on the bed, fully dressed.

Marco felt the dress and fumbled in the darkness to unbutton it. Mary recoiled.

"Please do not touch me tonight," Mary said

"It is our wedding night."

Mary rolled and faced the wall.

"Good night, Marco. We do not have to have sex to be married."

Marco stared at the dark ceiling and did not sleep, hating the stepfather who had touched his wife.

I hope his soul is burning in hell.

• • •

"Mary tells me you guys do not have sex."

Marco turned from the parsnip and carrot table.

"Hi Gabriela," Marco replied, looking at his sister-in-law. "Why would she tell you that?"

"Girl talk."

Marco shrugged.

"I like to have sex," Gabriela said. "I like it plenty. Maybe we can get close sometimes."

Marco reached for his sister-in-law's hand and nodded to his office at the rear of Fausto's Market.

● ● ●

"HOW COULD YOU EMBARRASS ME LIKE THIS!" Mary screamed at Marco.

Marco sat at the red kitchen table and said nothing.

"She's pregnant! Did the little whore tell you that? That she's having your baby; did she tell you? You didn't know my brother lost his manhood in the factory explosion, you didn't know that did you? You and Gabriela deserve each other…the whore. I hear your mother was a whore. I should have known. How many times have you been with your little whore?"

Marco walked away from his screaming wife. He closed the bedroom door and laid on the bed. The black and white dog jumped up and joined him, resting his mongrel head on Marco's heavy chest.

Rosa is wrong…I am worthless trash from the ghetto.

CHAPTER 16
THE TIME IS NOW

"How much longer, Grandfather?" Cesar asked.

Raul Veracruz looked over his half glasses from his big desk then stood, walking to an open liquor cabinet while staring at his grandson.

"Join me," the Godfather said, extending an amber glass. Then he poured a tall glass for himself to the rim.

"No ice?"

"Not today."

Raul took his glass and the half empty bourbon bottle with a little race horse on the cork and walked through the open door to the office balcony high above Mexico City.

Cesar followed.

Leaning against the black, wrought iron railing, they drank warm amber from their glasses, refilling the glasses until they finished the potbelly bottle. Silently, they stared west at the distant smoke from the city dump.

Raul looked at the empty bottle and said, "It has been long enough. The pain only grows larger in my soul. It is time now."

"I cannot believe you have waited this long, nearly five years."

Raul turned to look directly at Diego's son.

"If I teach you nothing else, I hope you learn patience from me. Those who are about to pay for your father's murder have now no idea when we are coming, perhaps even believe, after all these years, that we are not coming at all."

Cesar smiled. "I am trying. You make is seem too easy. So did father."

Raul continued, "I spoke with Miguel Fausto after Mass yesterday. I inquired about Marco. Miguel told me life is going badly for Marco and that he has moved back to the lean-to and that nearly every week he inquires as to any news about Diego."

The old man paused.

Cesar said, "I heard that after he married that friend of Rosa Fausto's, Mary, they moved into the family house on Victoria Street."

"That is true," Raul replied. "When I mentioned the marriage, Fausto shook his head and simply said, 'Life happens.' It makes me sad. It was a beautiful wedding."

"When do I go north?" Cesar asked.

"I am not going to lose my only grandson. I want you to bring Marco here to me. Go to Fausto's tomorrow and get him."

Tuesday morning and there he stood in Raul Veracruz's office on the top floor of the Gran Hotel Ciudad in Mexico City. The room reeked of a wet dog that had rolled on something dead. The old man stared for nearly a minute before speaking.

"You look like shit…and smell like it," Raul said.

Marco said nothing.

"Wouldn't your mother and sister be proud of you," the old man muttered.

Marco looked up from his gaze toward the floor, lifting his head and staring at the old man with dark, unblinking eyes, and Raul suddenly felt cold fear fill the room.

"I am sorry. That was wrong of me. I am sorry, Marco, to mention your mother and sister like this. Lilliana and Maria. I am sorry."

"Do you have news from Diego?" Marco finally spoke.

"First, tell us, what has happened in your life that you look like this? I hear you and your wife are no longer living together."

Marco continued to stare at Raul through the strands of dirty, black hair, only rarely blinking. "I was not a good husband for

Mary." He paused and rubbed his smudged face before continuing. "I wanted to have sex and she did not. Mary does not like me."

"That's rough," Cesar interjected.

"I had sex with my sister-in-law. Gabriela likes me. We love each other, and Mary discovered this when Gabriela grew large with the baby. I did not know the husband had no penis after the accident at the factory."

Raul almost smiled. "Did not go well, I take it."

"First, my wife poisoned my dog; she put rat poison in some chicken and gave it to Machete."

"I know you loved that mongrel," said Cesar.

"The next night while I slept, she poured hot water over me. Then I moved back to my lean-to. Now, tell me about Diego."

Raul Veracruz removed his reading glasses and stared into eternity.

"Diego is dead."

The old man felt the vapor of cold fear again, and tiny goosebump mountains emerged on his wrinkled arms, making the little, gray hairs stand erect. He studied the dirty face showing no emotion—absolutely no change in Macro's blank stare. Then Raul's eyes moved down, watching Marco's powerful hands open and close slowly, over and over.

Marco stood silently on the white tile floor.

Raul and Cesar looked at each other. Cesar raised his right eyebrow.

"Was he murdered?" Marco asked.

"Yes. The police ambushed him. They murdered my son," the old man said softly.

"The police in that city…St. Paul?"

"Yes," Cesar answered, "in Minnesota."

Marco stepped back and turned toward Cesar before saying, "I will go there this week and kill many of them."

"All of the murderers have been dealt with except for their leader that night, and he has moved," Raul said.

"Tell me where," said Marco.

"A city named Big Bay," Raul replied, touching a map opened on his desk. "He lives here," pointing with his forefinger, "and is no longer a policeman. He owns a bar."

"What is his name?"

"Timothy Fife. The bar is named Poor Joe's."

"You get me to the States and that Big Bay, you get me there, and I will kill Timothy Fife."

"He has friends that must be dealt with," said Cesar.

"You get me to that city and the names," Marco said, pausing and looking down at his hands, "and I will cut the pigs' throats."

"We will get you up highway thirty-five to the States and money for a bus to Big Bay. Remember these names: Timothy Fife, Stanley McMillen, and three men who live upstairs in the bar. They must all be dealt with or they will seek revenge. Here are the names."

He held out a small piece of paper.

"How much am I paid for this?"

"Five hundred thousand U.S. dollars," Cesar answered.

"I will burn that Poor Joe's down for fun." Marco paused.

"I want that money put in a bank to care for my son and his mother. I want you to do that for me."

The Godfather nodded. "What did you name your son?"

"Gabriela and I named him Diego. His name is Diego Gomez, Diego Mark Gomez."

Raul Veracruz stood from his desk and walked to Marco. He hugged the powerful, dirty, short man.

"First, we get you cleaned up and some new clothing. I will set up a bank account, I promise," Raul said, nodding toward his grandson.

Marco's large hands formed tight fists.

Soon Diego…soon brother.

CHAPTER 17
LESSONS

Poor Joe's Bar is located at the intersection of Union and Basswood, with Grant Street on the west side, in the city of Big Bay. The Big Bay River runs behind the building and is connected by a brick tunnel in the basement which exits through a heavy oak door to a steep clay bank just below the dam.

Built in 1898 by Irish immigrants, the building served as a whiskey depot and distribution center. Joe McCain purchased the building in 1929 and declared it to be a "dance hall." During Prohibition, Irish whiskey and Cuban rum arrived under the cover of darkness in small boats, to be hidden in Poor Joe's basement, behind a false wall.

The second story has six nice apartments with wallpaper, each with a bed, night stand, small closet, and a toilet enclosed in a tiny room only big enough to turn around in. During the dance hall years, these apartments became known as the *consolation rooms.* The Irish Catholic Ladies Society lodged a formal complaint with the city council, claiming illicit and immoral activities. The charges were dropped after Joe contributed $1000 dollars to the Ladies Society and another $1000 dollars the city's general fund which left Joe broke and almost out of business for several months.

When Prohibition ended in 1933, Joe painted *POOR JOE'S BAR* with green paint on a white metal sign and suspended it over the front door. It has not been touched since, and now the lettering is hardly visible through the brown rust, especially at night, even though it is illuminated by spotlights shining on it from both sides.

Timothy Fife purchased Poor Joe's, after his conversation with Wendell, from money he saved and a V.A. loan.

The *consolation rooms* upstairs are now apartments and occupied by a group of characters collectively named the Usual Suspects by the residents of Big Bay.

There is Pete, who like Timothy, is a Mekong Delta survivor. Wayne is left over from the Korean conflict and still hates the cold. Then there is Morris, who lost more than his right eye in Vietnam.

Another, Jonathon, was assigned to the Army Mechanical and Ordinance Battalion. On June 8th, 1972, his battalion moved to the outskirts of Trang Bang, watching the Air Force drop napalm on a village. The hot humid wind blew odors of petroleum, rubber, and burnt flesh from the village into the young soldiers' faces. Soon, villagers ran toward the soldiers. Women helping old men, two water buffalo running from the inferno, and children running, several mostly naked with their clothing burnt away.

The realization that human beings could treat each other in such a horrendous fashion caused Jonathon's coping mechanisms to completely implode. Two months later the United States Army discharged Jonathon with a section 8 mental disability.

The roster for the Usual Suspects is completed by Ralph, who showed up on a Sunday morning, barefoot, carrying a brown suitcase and a trumpet in a canvas bag, and Doug, who lives with his dog named Malcolm in the room at the top of the stairs.

Poor Joe's is the soul of Big Bay. It is the gathering center for occasions of glorious celebrations and times of great grief and consoling. Imbibers, Christians, Jews, Muslims, Hindus, Buddhists, Teetotalers, Christian Scientists, and even occasional Jehovah's Witness, have been known to gather as one. Every Friday evening, Chang Lee and his wife, along with their six children, come for the *All You Can Eat Fish Fry*. The lone Chinese family in Big Bay provides special sauces made by Mrs. Lee for all to share. Every Christmas Mr. and Mrs. Lee take over Poor Joe's kitchen and prepare Peking duck and pot-stickers for anyone who needs a special meal.

Even the conscientious objectors who refuse to enter what they believe to be a den of iniquity, in an honest moment, admit Poor Joe's is a collective soul.

● ● ●

The old whore house is in fact a cathedral, just another of life's lessons.

CHAPTER 18

A RIDE WITH ANGEL

Cesar Veracruz drove Marco back to his lean-to. "The canvas has holes, Marco, it is rotten now," he said, looking through the Mercedes' windshield at the sagging structure surrounded by tall thistles in bloom. "I will send you a new one."

"That is the canvas Diego gave me," Marco replied.

"How about we protect Diego's canvas with a new one on top?"

Marco nodded.

"Here is my number. Call me when you are ready to go north."

"Just tell me; I will remember," Marco said, opening the door.

My brother...my dear brother...I felt the night they took your life away from me...all these years I have known from the night it happened...I should have been at your side that night...if I had been guarding you perhaps you would still live...or I would have died at your side...either way I would be better...my heart is empty.

Marco lay in his lean-to awake and did not sleep for the entire night. When the little red and white rooster which owns the Fausto's block crowed three times, giving the sun permission to rise, Marco crawled out and sat on his bench, waiting for Miguel Fausto to open the market.

Miguel Fausto watched Marco through the Ford van windshield.

Poor fellow is surrounded by much sadness.

"I need to use your telephone," Marco said as Miguel opened the van door.

"You have a key," Miguel said.

Marco shrugged. "It is your market. I wait."

They entered the building and walked to the office.

"Want me to leave while you talk?"

"No, you listen."

Marco closed his eyes then dialed the phone.

"I am ready," Marco spoke into the phone.

"Good to hear," Cesar Veracruz replied. "I will have your papers and cards prepared and pick you up Saturday at noon."

"I want my name to be Machete on those papers," Marco said. "I will use the name Diego gave to me. Machete Juarez will go to that Big Bay and revenge his brother's death."

•••

Machete Juarez's green card listed truck driver as his occupation. The letters of introduction and reference also included security guard. Machete read the card and papers and flashed a quick smile, exposing his broken and rotting teeth.

"Do your teeth hurt you."

"Not anymore."

They drove the rest of the way to Nuevo Laredo in silence and just south of the city limits stopped at a Citco gas station and parked next to a large, green Dodge stake truck filled with musk melons.

"The driver's name is Angel. He talks very little but is an excellent driver and very convincing with the border guards. You are his relief driver."

Machete nodded.

"Do not call me while in the States; they will trace the call. Grandfather and I await your return with good news."

Machete said nothing and left the black Mercedes.

The trip up highway 35 from Mexico, through San Antonio, Austin, Oklahoma City, Kansas City, and Des Moines took three days with stops at several IGA stores and one Kroger's, unloading melons. In Iowa, the State Police stopped the truck.

"Yes, officer, I was going below the speed limit," Angel said through the open window, looking down at the trooper while watching, in the side mirror, a second trooper walk toward the passenger side with his hand on his pistol grip.

"Your passenger side taillight is out. License and registration and proof of insurance please, and your travel log."

Angel complied.

"Wait here…better yet, wait outside your truck, and your passenger, too."

"He is my relief driver."

"I'm sure he is."

The trooper walked to his car and spoke on the radio for a bit before returning and tossing the papers through the open truck door to the driver's seat.

"We need to inspect your cargo."

Machete made a soft growling sound. Angel noticed Machete's hands opening and closing slowly and stepped in front of Machete, blocking the trooper's view.

"Unload the melons behind the cab."

"Why? We have done nothing wrong."

"Unload the melons for inspection or we impound the truck for inspection."

Gently, Angel handed Machete one melon at a time for 45 minutes. When the bed behind the cab was empty, the trooper shined his flashlight on the wet wooden bed and then at the pile of melons on the side of the highway. He walked to the melon pile, selected a big one and smashed it on the pavement. He sniffed the smashed melon before saying, "You are free to go. Get these melons off the road."

"That will be three dollars," Machete said.

The trooper turned.

"What?"

"You owe us three dollars for the melon."

"Is he kidding?" the trooper said to Angel.

Angel nodded in Machete's direction. "Feel free to ask him."

The six-foot two-inch trooper walked closer and looked down at Machete, into dark eyes looking up with no hint of emotion, and the same old feelings returned, those he experienced as a twenty-year-old Marine recruit during his first live ammunition obstacle course…the urge to evacuate his bowels. He reached into his pocket and retrieved a five-dollar bill.

"Keep the change," he said to Machete and walked to the police cruiser.

"What was that all about?" the younger trooper said to the driver after they drove away from the truck.

The senior trooper said nothing for several minutes.

"You had to be there," he finally responded. "You had to look into those shark eyes and know this was about to turn very bad real fast."

From a St. Paul parking lot, next to the Greyhound Bus Depot, Machete watched the empty, green truck turn south and disappear in the darkness then he climbed the silver steps of the bus and took a seat at the very rear.

The bus's diesel engine sometimes lulled Machete to sleep. It took three days and changing buses four times before Machete arrived in Big Bay.

The illuminated neon clock arms across the dark, wet street from the bus station pointed to 9:10. The sign under the clock said *JEN's Cuban Diner*. Machete walked there.

A lone waitress stood behind the counter. The young lady looked up from cleaning the coffee maker, watching the short man walk past her and sit in the end booth.

She handed him a menu and smiled a tentative smile.

"Would you like coffee…maybe café con leche?

"Speak Spanish?" Machete inquired while looking at the menu.

"Sí!"

Machete continued in Spanish, "Good, my English is poor."

"Are you hungry?"

"Very."

"Try the special, puerco asado, everyone likes it."

Machete smiled at her. "I like the way Cubans make roast pork. Thank you, I would like that."

She is very pretty.

"Where is the toilet?"

The slim waitress pointed to the other end of the diner. "Men's room on the right."

He walked back to the booth at the same time the waitress approached with a large plate heaped with marinated pork, black beans, yellow rice, sweet plantains, and a piece of Cuban bread.

"I hope you like it," she said quietly, bending over enough to expose most of both breasts.

Beautiful.

"Thank you. Are you allowed to join me? I have questions."

The waitress looked around the empty diner, walked to the counter for a cup of coffee, and slid her bottom on the shiny blue booth seat across from Machete.

"What is your name? My name is Machete."

The young lady giggled. "I've never heard of that name."

"It is a nickname my brother gave me."

"Oh. My name is Nancy."

"Do you know this city well?"

"Pretty good," Nancy replied. "I've been here for three years. I came from Miami with my boyfriend. He left, I stayed. Why do you ask?"

"I am looking for some acquaintances of my brother. He has passed, and I have something he wanted them to have. He told me to look for a bar named Poor Joe's."

"I go there sometimes on my nights off! You will love it. Try Dora's clam chowder on Friday nights…the best ever. It is on Grant Street, right before you get to the river."

"Thank you."

"Who is your brother's friend?"

"Timothy Fife."

"Oh, Timothy is the owner and bartender. He's kind of tall and very good looking; you can't miss him. He is real nice. I wish I worked at Poor Joe's."

Machete finished eating everything on the plate while Nancy watched and sipped her coffee.

"That was very good," Machete said, wiping his mouth on a paper napkin. "How much?"

"Ten dollars and ninety-five cents."

Machete slid a twenty-dollar bill across the table.

"Maybe I will see you again, Nancy," he said.

"Which way is that Grant Street?"

CHAPTER 19
FROM THE OLD MAPLE TREE

Machete walked in the fog and darkness for twenty minutes, stopping when he reached the river. He sat on a granite rock extending over the river from the bank and listened to the wet tinkling sounds moving past and a distant rumbling of water spilling through a dam's turbines, ending forty feet below in a frothy pool. He walked along the riverbank for one block then turned west.

"There is that Poor Joe's," he whispered out loud. Machete walked along Grant Street using the sidewalk across the street from the bar. He pulled himself into an old maple tree and climbed through the branches until he found a comfortable crotch, thirty feet above the ground and listened to the piano music coming through the screen door and the laughter.

At midnight, the music stopped. Machete looked down from his perch, watching the people leave the bar, some driving away but many walking in three directions. He watched the lights shine for a short time through the six windows under the eaves then go out one by one.

From the street lamp yellow light, Machete could tell the lady beside the tall man had blonde hair. The tall man pulled the front door shut but did not lock it. They walked directly under Machete.

"That was the best Tuesday we've had," the man said.

The lady laughed. "I'm glad we bought that old piano," she said.

They stopped for a brief pause directly under Machete's tree and turned back, looking at Poor Joe's.

"I'm really happy," the tall man said. He hugged the blonde lady and then they walked away down the sidewalk.

Machete watched and listened for a very long time. A cat found a lover under his tree and they fought a good fight for several minutes before they ran off together.

About 3 a.m., Machete climbed down through the branches of the old maple tree and scurried across Grant Street to Poor Joe's front door. He opened the screen door and turned the wobbly brass doorknob. The door opened, and he entered.

He stood next to the popcorn machine and felt its warmth. The big room with little round tables, one long table next to the bar, and booths along the outside wall, was faintly illuminated by a neon Schlitz Beer clock above the bar. The only sound…*tic…tock…tic…tock*…came from a Martinek's clock on the far wall.

Machete walked closer to the bar and looked at himself in the mirror that had GOEBEL inscribed in big gold letters.

What is this Goebel…?

With sliding steps, Machete moved behind the bar. He looked up at a framed document above the cash register with a black and white picture near the bottom. Gently, he placed a tall chair next to the wall and stood on it.

TIMOTHY FIFE.

"That is the tall man under my tree," Machete whispered, squinting in the dim light at the document. "Very soon we meet, Timothy Fife. Perhaps even tomorrow you will meet Machete."

He climbed down from the chair and glanced up one more time.

"Perhaps tomorrow, I think, or next week," he whispered up at the picture.

Carefully, he closed the front door. His grip on the screen door frame slipped, and the stretched spring slammed it shut. He froze and listened to a dog bark a single bark from upstairs, then silence except for the crickets.

At the bottom of the cement steps, Machete pressed his nose flat against the wood structure and inhaled deeply.

The old wood will burn very easily.

For almost two hours, Machete wandered the dimly lit web of sidewalks in Big Bay. He stopped in front of a two-story house with a For Sale sign in the front yard and walked around back and opened an unlocked garage door.

No car.

The walkout basement door would not open. On the third attempt, sliding his jackknife into the crack between the door and the frame, the lock surrendered. Machete walked up the cement steps, feeling the wall with his left hand and the next step with is right. A dim nightlight in the day room illuminated a rocking chair and short sofa. He plopped on the sofa, rolled to his back, and closed his eyes.

Soon brother…Perhaps tomorrow or the next day.

Machete opened his eyes wide in the darkness, startled awake by his recurring dream. He looked at the dark ceiling from the sofa, watching his mother and sister looking down. His sister then came close, her nose nearly touching his, and she smiled with her blue eyes.

Machete reached above his head with both hands and grasp only air.

Maria giggled.

CHAPTER 20

PARTY INVITATION

The teenage couple cuddling in the end booth next to the restrooms did not look when Machete entered Jen's Diner. The girl shoved a spoon heaped with jiggling flan into the boy's mouth and laughed when some of it dribbled down his chin.

Nancy carried a large cup of café con leche to Machete and smiled.

"Would you like the special again?"

"Yes, and talk again. I have more questions."

"When they leave," the waitress said, nodding in the direction of the teenagers. The girl wiped the boy's chin with a napkin and laughed again.

Machete attempted to stand, and Nancy pushed him down.

"I will give them their bill; be right back."

Machete stared at her feminine shape in the tight, light pink waitress dress, walking away toward the young lovers.

She must have a new boyfriend...beautiful like Rosa.

The little bell activated by opening the diner's front door resonated its irritating sound. Machete watched them walk away, holding hands, until the young lovers disappeared into the darkness.

Nancy slid a plate on the booth table, leaving a trail of brown gravy. She wiped the table with a towel and sat across from Machete, holding a glass of raspberry lemonade.

"Did you find Poor Joe's?"

"Yes. When I got there, it had already closed. Perhaps I will go today."

"You will like it."

Machete ate two forks full of mojo marinated pork.

"You have more questions?" Nancy inquired, looking over the rim of the plastic diner glass.

"Brother has a friend. He wanted me to thank a Stanley Mc-Millen. Have you heard of Stanley?"

"Stanley is a nurse at the hospital. Was he a patient of Stanley's?"

"Yes."

"Everyone in Big Bay knows Stanley. He's in charge of the critical care unit at the hospital. He comes down to Poor Joe's often and every Friday night for the fish fry with his wife, Danielle, who used to work for him in the heart unit...that's where they met. She moved up from New Orleans. They are both nurses, and she worked for him until they got married and then she transferred to the emergency room. Everyone likes them. They had a baby girl two years ago; her name is Chloe."

Machete watched Nancy's brown eyes glisten while she spoke.

"You really like that Stanley."

Nancy grinned.

"If he wasn't married to Danielle, I'd be camped on his doorstep."

"They live close to Poor Joe's?"

"Nope. They have a condo on the bluff above the city. I've never been inside, but I hear the view from the deck is beautiful. The road just west of the hospital leads right up to their house."

"Thank you."

"Saturday night there's going to be a surprise welcome home party for Timothy. You should come and meet everyone."

"Welcome home?"

"He's just back from the Mayo Clinic hospital, had an infection in his heart after he got shot, lost part of his right arm. Stanley saved his life. Everybody is going to be there. Danielle and Wendell made everyone promise to make it a surprise. You should have seen the helicopter they flew Timothy home in."

"Saturday night?"

"Seven o'clock."

"How did he get shot?"

"Rescuing Wendell who was tied up and terribly abused by two bad men in a cabin in the woods behind Benjamin's Seafood Restaurant—two guys sent by a Mexican godfather looking for Timothy. No one knows why. Timothy was in Nashville with his wife, Carla. She was recording a new album. Carla has a wonderful voice. Timothy flew home and a bunch of guys found the cabin and rescued Wendell. That's how Timothy got shot. I hear he would have bled to death if Stanley had not been there; he put some sort of clamp into the bullet hole and plugged a major artery."

"What happened to the men?"

"They got what they had coming. They both got shot to death."

Machete nodded and pushed his empty plate toward the window.

"Thank you, Nancy. I will see you again, I hope."

Machete placed a twenty-dollar bill on the table. He stood. Nancy leaned forward from the booth seat, and he kissed her on the forehead.

Nancy smiled, listening to the little doorbell tinkle.

CHAPTER 21

LITTLE MYSTERIOUS FIGURE

"I think we should get a babysitter," Danielle said to Stanley. "Don't want to take Chloe to the party Saturday night."

"Why?" Stanley inquired, closing the dishwasher door and pushing the start button.

"I don't know."

"The guys are looking forward to babysitting her at the party. Wendell and Pete are all excited, planning on taking turns."

"Just a feeling."

"It'll be fine. If she gets fussy, we have an excuse to leave."

Danielle sighed. She poured a full glass of Pinot Grigio and walked out on the deck. She stared down the steep hill at the city far below.

If I still smoked, I'd light one right now.

From the corner of her eyes, she watched movement far down in the dusky light, a figure. Quickly, the man moved past the big trees in a row.

Stanley put his arm around her waist and pulled his wife close.

"Want a puff on my Fuente?"

Danielle grinned and took the cigar. She pointed with the cigar down toward a short man walking up the hill.

"Don't recognize him, do you?" she asked, taking a single puff.

Stanley sipped on his glass of Basil Hayden's.

They watched until the figure disappeared where the pavement curved into the woods.

"Nope," he replied.

Stanley reached for his cigar, then said with a grin, "Keep it."

CHAPTER 22

MARIA!

Machete watched the glass front door of the hardware store for twenty minutes through the window from his table at Jen's Cuban Diner.

"Where is Nancy?" he asked the middle-aged waitress with a single butterfly barrette in her gray hair. Her white apron pocket held seven ballpoint pens in a neat row.

"Day off, what you want to eat?"

"Eggs and the bacon. What time does that hardware store open?" Machete nodded at the store.

"Ten. How you want those eggs?"

Machete stared at her.

"Scrambled or what?"

"Yes, and café con leche."

She shook her head and walked away.

The red *OPEN* sign above the door flickered on at the hardware store.

"Are you going to that party for Timothy tonight?" Machete inquired, watching the waitress return with two scrambled eggs, three slices of crispy bacon, and one slice of limp, buttered, whole wheat toast.

"You talking about that Poor Joe's Bar? Absolutely not; only heathens go there. No Bible-believing folks would be caught in such a place."

"Perhaps you would not be caught," Machete said, and he smiled. He piled the eggs and bacon on the toast and folded it into a sandwich. With each bite, the sandwich dripped juices down his wrist.

"Six dollars," the waitress said, tossing the bill on the table.

Machete wiped both hands with a wad of brown paper napkins then counted out six dollars. He glared briefly at the waitress before tossing the dollar bills into the bacon grease puddle. The little bell above the door tinkled then the restaurant wooden screen door slammed shut, and Machete walked to the hardware store.

"Camping?" the old man with disfigured arthritic fingers muttered when Machete lifted the tin of kerosene to the checkout counter.

Machete smiled.

"You camping down at the river?"

"Yes."

"Black flies will eat you alive this time of year."

"Knife...need one knife," Machete said.

The old man tipped his head down a little and peered over his reading glasses.

"Anything particular in mind?" he queried, staring at the scar on Machete's right cheek.

"Camping knife," Machete retorted.

The man nodded. He walked to a glass display case behind the cash register, opened it, and returned with a hunting knife in a leather sheath.

"*Imperial,* made in Providence, Rhode Island, right here in the good old U. S. of A. Father gave me one for my thirteenth birthday. Still have it, sharp as ever."

 Machete fingered the blade edge.

"Very sharp, amigo."

"It holds a good edge," the hardware man commented. He

punched numbers on the cash register with his crooked forefinger and pulled the tally lever.

"Forty-eight dollars and ten cents."

• • •

From the crotch in the old maple tree, he watched and listened to the laughter and music coming through the open windows at Poor Joe's. The Saturday sun had set two hours ago. Machete glanced in all directions then climbed down and walked to the bar. He hid the gallon of kerosene behind a white spirera bush next to the side door.

Machete pushed his nose against the clapboard siding and inhaled then ran his hand along the dry wood. *It will burn fast.* He walked up the three wood plank steps and pushed the narrow side door into a large lady. He scrunched into the crowd. The swaying mass forced him against the wall, and he sat on a folding chair next to a green waste basket.

"FOR HE'S A JOLLY GOOD FELLOW," the crowd sang loudly while three men hoisted Timothy to the countertop.

Machete felt the knife under his shirt and tilted the handle forward.

A man carried a young child on his shoulder, holding her in place with a hand consisting of a thumb and forefinger. They squeezed past Machete.

A baby…Maria would be in her bed at this time.

The little girl snuggled her head against the man's head and twisted just enough to look at Machete.

Tetchy sensations spread over his body, and he listened to himself taking rapid, little whistling breaths.

She smiled at Machete with pure blue eyes.

Maria.

Dumbfounded, Machete stood and took several steps into the crowd then walked backwards, feeling for the folding chair, volcanic memories erupting into each other, scrambling his thoughts pell-mell.

No slapping...stop...do not hurt the baby.

The old lady with hollow brown eyes is walking, bent over from the green couch. She places the baby on my lap.

"Keep your little sister safe. We will call her Maria in honor of the mother of Jesus. You keep Maria safe."

She is sticky.

My sister stops crying when I touch her forehead.

Blue eyes...

The pounding piano music resumed.

Machete stood and pushed through the throng.

Someone joined the piano player with a harmonica.

"Hi," said Nancy, "let's dance."

She pulled Machete close.

"What's this?" Nancy asked. She reached under his shirt and wiggled the knife handle.

"My camping knife. I always have it."

"Oh."

"Who is that little girl?" Machete asked. He pushed against Nancy toward the child.

"That is the baby I told you about, Stanley's and Danielle's Chloe. Isn't this a great party? I'm so glad you came!"

They were now directly behind the man and the child on his shoulder. The little girl turned her curly head and stared at Machete then reached towards him. Machete stretched out his left arm and touched her hand.

And he knew.

She looked back and smiled.

"Isn't she just the sweetest little thing?" Nancy said.

The song ended.

"I go now," Machete said.

"So soon?"

"I do not like the crowds. See you at the diner."

Machete left through the side door. He grabbed the can of kerosene and walked down Grant Street to the dark river.

Doug, one of the Usual Suspects, sat at the top of the stairs with his German Shepherd. They watched Machete touch Chloe and then leave.

"Malcolm," Doug said, scratching him between the ears, "we need to keep an eye on that guy."

CHAPTER 23

BABY SISTER

Before the Monday morning sunrise, Machete walked from the river up the hill to the McMillen condo and climbed the sycamore tree at the end of the cul-de-sac. For five mornings in a row, Machete watched. Like clockwork, at 6:30, the black Avanti started with a rumble. Stanley backed the car from the garage while Danielle, with Chloe in her arms, stood on the porch and waved goodbye. Next, the babysitter arrived just before 7 a.m., driving a yellow car with a dent in the driver's door; it sputtered and rattled every time she turned off the ignition. At 7:15, Danielle would leave for her morning shift in the ER.

• • •

Squeak...lub...squeak...lub.

The old rocking chair had a flat spot on both runners, and the dry wooden joints wiggled with each movement. Chloe sat on Machete's lap, staring up and listening. He spoke in Spanish while he rocked.

"The old lady, on the day you were born, told me to take care of you. I failed that night in Mama's shack. Then you left into the smoke with the angel. The angel winked at me. It was a sign. You are back, and this time I will do better. I love you, Maria."

Looking through the sunroom windows, Doug watched the little black-haired man rocking back and forth in a rocking chair, Chloe sitting on his lap.

Doug briefly considered shooting through the window.

Nope...can't...shit...she'll get hit by glass.

For six minutes he carefully worked his way into the house through the basement, up the cement steps, through two more doors, until Doug and Malcolm were directly behind the rocking chair.

Doug stepped on the back of the chair's runner, stopping it. He pressed a .38 Special hard against the man's left ear.

"One move, I will kill you."

"This is my baby sister."

"I don't care if she's Mother Theresa. Put her on the floor... RIGHT NOW!"

Machete gently placed Chloe on the hardwood floor and leaned back with his eyes closed.

"Get her," Doug softly commanded.

Malcolm gently grasped a pajama sleeve and pulled Chloe behind the rocking chair.

"Good boy, Malcolm. Good boy"

• • •

Now there he sat in the Big Bay Police Department interrogation room, dressed in an orange jump suit, his left ankle shackled by a short chain to an eye bolt in the floor, his long black hair pulled back into a ponytail.

"She is my sister. Maria has come back to me."

Machete Juarez answered every question asked by Chief of Police Strait with that same answer until Chief Strait asked, "Why are you in Big Bay?"

CHAPTER 24

THE DEAL

They sat in a semicircle facing Chief of Police Larry Strait, behind his desk, Timothy Fife, Wendell, Stanley and Danielle.

Danielle trembled.

Stanley clenched his fists, over and over.

"The little Mexican tells me he was sent by a Mexican cartel godfather, name of Veracruz. Something about revenge for the killing of his son, Diego, in Saint Paul. Tells me that the fellows who beat the crap out of you, Wendell, were also sent by the godfather, looking for you, Timothy."

Timothy leaned forward, resting both elbows on his knees, and studied the chief's floor.

"You need to get this carpet cleaned, Larry."

"He had a knife on him, big *Imperial* hunting knife. He planned on cutting your throat then burning Poor Joe's. Had a gallon of kerosene outside. Says he threw it in the river after he saw Chloe riding around on your shoulder, Wendell. Says that your little girl is his sister—Maria, he called her—that Chloe is his baby sister, reincarnated, and that's when he called the whole thing off."

"Well, he's bat-shit crazy," Stanley said.

"Oh my God," Danielle whispered.

"We have him for kidnapping," Chief Strait continued. "But, we need to think about this real hard. He intended no harm to Chloe. And, he's providing important information about the cartel.

The problem isn't going away simply because we have thwarted the godfather for a second time."

Timothy looked up. "What's his name?"

"Machete Juarez."

"Oh my God," Danielle looked at her husband.

"What are you suggesting, Chief," Stanley asked.

"Nothing lost by having a conversation with him, all of us, same room," Larry Strait replied, watching Danielle's face.

"If I thought the worst of this nightmare was over, I would say send this Machete to hell, but I feel it is NOT over. I don't want to live in fear."

Stanley watched his wife's lips move, amazed by the sounds coming out.

"I'll call Victor," Timothy said. "You guys need to meet Victor Bonifacio. He's got a history with the Mexicans."

Stanley said, "I'm calling Quinn O'Malley. You need to meet him, Timothy."

"I've heard that."

●●●

Machete shuffled, each step resulting in a musical cadence of chains clanking from the ankle shackles, into the interrogation room. He stopped briefly, studying each face around the table.

The jail guard directed Machete to the empty chair between Quinn O'Malley and Victor Bonifacio.

Machete sat directly across from Danielle.

"Mister Juarez has agreed to help us in our battle with the cartel. He has only one request, for his cooperation," Chief Strait announced. He paused then continued with hesitation, watching Danielle and Stanley.

"He wants to see his baby sister first."

Stanley stiffened. Danielle reached under the table and patted his leg.

"That's it? That's ALL he wants, to see my precious daughter; that's all? I'll go home right now. I'll get her right now. You sure that's all, Machete?"

Can't believe what I'm saying.

Machete quietly said, "She is my sister."

"Oh, you mean your sister, Maria, the baby girl murdered by the cartel, along with your mother, Lilliana, the night your shack burned to the ground?" Quinn O'Malley said in Spanish, looking to his left.

Machete glared at Quinn.

"He's correct about that scenario, there, Machete Juarez, or should we call you Marco; that's how it went down," Victor Bonifacio said from the other side. "Seems your Veracruz friends were engaged in a turf battle; shit happens."

"You both are telling lies," Machete said, looking desperately at Danielle.

Quinn pushed a manila folder to Machete.

"Take a look."

Danielle watched Machete's face. With the turn of each page, with each picture, the little Mexican's scowling face softened and then his brown eyes melted with tears, dripping on the black and white photos.

"I'll go get Chloe."

• • •

I can't believe I'm doing this.

Danielle walked in Machete's direction, holding Chloe.

Nearly transfixed, Chief of Police Larry Strait, Timothy, Stanley, Wendell, Quinn O'Malley, and Victor Bonifacio watched Danielle approach Machete. They watched Chloe extend both arms and wrap them tightly around the little Mexican's neck. They watch Chole's mother step back and then lean forward and embrace her daughter and Machete.

Then Danielle looked at the pictures spread on the table in front of Machete.

"We are not going to press any charges, Chief," she said softly.

CHAPTER 25

CARTEL REVENGE

"The news is bad from Big Bay. Mostly bad, Grandfather," Cesar reported to Raul Veracruz.

The old man tilted his head back to better focus on his grandson sitting across the big oak desk.

Cesar continued, "It appears Machete has failed. Roland returned from that city last night. He reports that Machete has become friendly with these people."

"'Mostly bad' indicates there is good news with such disappointments," The Godfather replied. He stood and walked to the liquor cabinet. "We have learned that Timothy has a son."

The old man continued to pour bourbon into a glass, handed it to his grandson, and filled his own favorite crystal glass, without ice, overflowing.

"Get Roland. We have a mission." He took a long drink of Blanton's from his dripping glass. "Get him today."

● ● ●

Timothy had missed ten months of the Wednesday poker nights at Poor Joe's, preferring to stay home with his wife Carla and their new son, Charles Dwight. The guys looked up from the long table with surprise when Timothy joined them.

"Carla left for Nashville yesterday…recording sessions; took Charles with her. Deal me in."

One week earlier, Roland Chanchez stood in Raul Veracruz's Mexico City living room.

"I want them brought to me," Raul said, poking his finger in the air at Roland. "That Timothy Fife has destroyed my family. I want him to suffer a most terrible pain worse than death. Bring me his wife and son. I will make him a dead man in his soul when he sees the pictures I send him."

•••

Carla returned to her studio condo following a long recording session.

"How was Charles today, Latraia?"

"He is such a good boy."

Carla smiled, handed the young lady a fifty-dollar bill from her purse, saying, "See ya in the morning."

"You are too kind."

Three minutes later, the doorbell rang.

"Latraia?" Carla unlocked the door and opened it.

Roland Chanchez pushed the door open and quickly closed it.

•••

Timothy sat at the long table in front of the bar with Pete, Ralph, Wayne, Stanley, red-haired Katie, and Machete. They looked in the direction of the front door when Victor Bonifacio walked in.

"Timothy, we need to talk. In private."

Timothy shrugged.

"No secrets here, Victor. Talk."

Victor sat.

"We've been advised by our friends in Cuba there is an imminent threat against your family by the Mexican Cartel."

Timothy stiffened.

"Carla and Charles are in Nashville."

"We know; have a team headed there now. Spoke with O'Malley. The team is gathering."

Timothy's entire body shivered. Katie reached under the table and held his cold hand.

Victor's yellow satellite phone vibrated.

"We're too late, sir," the young voice on the other end said. "Here is the video we have from the studio's security camera. Stand-by."

Timothy and Victor watched the small screen. They watched Roland Chanchez with his arm around Carla, holding Charles tight against her chest, walk down a hallway and out the door.

"Roland Chanchez!" Timothy shouted. "I arrested him in St. Paul for human trafficking."

"We just received word that a Lear jet left the Nashville airport two hours ago, headed for Mexico City, sir," the young man said.

"Thank you," Victor replied. "Tell everyone good job."

Timothy grasped the table and sat, looking up. Victor leaned close to Timothy's pale face. "We'll be in the air soon, Timothy, we can save them."

"I must go as well," came a voice from the end of the table.

They all looked at Machete, shaking his head up and down.

"I have the promise to keep, and I know that place."

●●●

The Sukhoi-Gulfstream S-21 flies at Mach 2. Originally designed in Russia with the help of Gulfstream, plans to mass produce the sleek plane with a needle nose were scrapped because of massive cost overruns. One plane was eventually built, ordered by a Saudi Prince as a gift to Quinn O'Malley. Quinn and the True Believers had rescued his family being held by terrorists.

・・・

Quinn O'Malley entered Poor Joe's and walked directly to Timothy.

They were the same height, six-feet two-inches.

Quinn reached for Timothy's left hand and shook it with both hands.

"Victor has told me much about you, young man. We didn't have a chance to talk at the chief's office. Sorry to meet like this."

He paused and glanced at everyone else in the room, stopping for a second on Machete, then continued, "I lost someone I loved long ago at the hands of Batista. Know how you feel inside. We'll get them back."

Victor nodded at Machete.

"So, you want to come along?"

Machete nodded yes.

"Let's go," Quinn said.

・・・

At ten minutes after noon, the windows in the City of Big Bay and bottles resting against Poor Joe's Goebel mirror rattled. The S-21's three turbines roared down the short Big Bay Airport runway, assisted by twin rocket thrusters. From the tarmac, the Usual Suspects watched the plane climb steeply, almost straight up, and then out of sight.

"Thank you for joining us," Quinn said loudly to Machete, leaning close.

"I have the promise to keep."

"May I ask what?"

Flying at 63,000 feet in the direction of Havana, Cuba, Machete told Quinn.

"When we get to Havana," Quinn said, "We'll take our helicopters to Mexico City."

"Why?"

"They are very special helicopters," Quinn smiled. "Hold all the men we need for today, fly at four-hundred, and invisible to radar. The Mexicans will never see us coming."

"Bueno."

CHAPTER 26

A PROMISE KEPT

Roland pulled Carla's left arm toward the desk then pushed her spine, in the direction of The Godfather. Caesar handed a bolt cutter to his grandfather. Raul Veracruz grasped the red handles in each hand, opening and closing the tool slowly, watching Carla's face.

"Give me the boy," Raul growled, from his chair.

A hollow point bullet struck Roland's skull. It exploded, splattering Carla and Charles with bloody matter.

Carla collapsed to the floor. She protected her screaming child with her quivering body.

NO......NO...NO.

Raul Veracruz studied Machete's face for three seconds. Machete shot him twice in the forehead.

Caesar pointed his gun at Machete. "Traitor! Burn in hell!"

Machete shot Caesar in his screaming mouth.

Two young cartel lieutenants pulled their pistols then tossed them on the floor. Seconds later, Quinn O'Malley and five men dressed in black shot them dead.

Outside, a strange looking helicopter idled in the courtyard, its twin turbines whining. An identical machine circled above the compound, making dull chop-chopping sounds when it banked. Two Mexico City police cars pulled up to the locked wrought iron front gate, overhead lights flashing red and blue. The car doors opened and four policemen began shooting at the helicopter. The black machine rotated as it hovered above and with the roar from its Gatling gun, reduced both cars to bloody metallic rubble.

From his pilot's seat, Richard Elmore Fortin watched twelve men dressed in black, Carla holding little Charles with Quinn on one side and Machete on the other, run across the compound and into his waiting machine. Side by side, the two stealth flying machines flew just above the treetops in the direction of El Paso.

From the helicopter floor, Carla stared at her rescuers. Machete reached over and wiped the blood from Charles' face then hers. She looked up at a banner hanging above the men's heads on the bulkhead.

Stenciled in bold red letters she read, *TRUE BELIEVERS*.

● ● ●

"Timothy!" Victor rubbed his hand on Timothy's head which rested on the bar table.

Timothy's red eyes looked up at Victor.

"They're on the way to El Paso. O'Malley says they are safe."

Katie squeezed Timothy's hand and bowed her head. Everyone around the tabled bowed their heads with her.

● ● ●

"When we get all these dropped off, will you give me a ride back to Mexico City?" Machete asked Quinn.

"I'd like to ask for what reason."

"I must visit with Miguel Fausto."

Quinn smiled, revealing a missing front tooth.

"Yes, we will do that for you."

"What happened with your front tooth?"

"Lost it in an explosion, saving a good college buddy."

"Who?"

"Fidel Castro."

"Oh."

●●●

The children playing in the street outside Fausto's Market stared at the sky in amazement. They watched a sleek helicopter circle three times before landing in the intersection between Amigo's Cantina and the grocery store.

The back door to Fausto's office opened, and Rosa peeked out.

The children gathered all around the machine, pointing up, wide-eyed, at the rotor slowly circling over their heads. The black helicopter door opened.

All alone, Machete walked down the ramp toward the produce stand.

Rosa and Machete embraced next to the melon and avocado table—a simple, long embrace, silent.

"Uncle Miguel is in his office. He has been very worried for you."

Machete held Rosa by the shoulders. The children surrounded them, chanting, "Kiss…kiss…kiss." Rosa held up her left ring finger and waved it. The chant grew louder. And it happened to clapping and cheers.

"Let's get you inside," Rosa said. "You have new teeth!"

"The people in Big Bay sent me to a kind tooth doctor."

Miguel Fausto stood when he saw Machete.

"You look good, Marco. I have worried since you left for the States. You look good and healthy. Are you back to stay?"

"No, sir. I came to tell you I have kept my promise."

Rosa's head jerked a little, and she stared at Machete.

"The promise you made the very first day I hired you, that you would someday find the ones guilty for killing your mother and sister?"

Machete nodded *yes*.

"Then justice has been done," the old man said. "Would you tell me who?"

"The Veracruz family."

Cloudy alarm formed in the old man's eyes.

"Do not worry," Machete continued, "they are dead."

From his shirt pocket, Machete retrieved a small colored picture and handed it to Rosa. She walked to Miguel, and they looked at the little girl with blue eyes and curly hair.

"She is back. Maria came back for me."

The young lady and old man looked up from the photo.

"They call her Chloe, and she lives in Big Bay. I am going back."

"You should," Miguel said softly. "You need to look out for her."

"I see my lean-to is still against the wall."

"Yes," Miguel Fausto said, "I just had a new canvas put over it."

"Thank you."

CHAPTER 27

TIME EVAPORATING

"**S**tanley called last night," Timothy said, walking around the Poor Joe's long table, pouring coffee for the Usual Suspects. "He said the doctors are planning to remove Machete's breathing tube tomorrow."

"Hard to believe it's been twenty years since he showed up," Pete said.

"Gonna burn this place down, he was," Wayne added, "had a can of kerosene and a knife in his belt."

Timothy made a cutting motion across his neck with his left hand.

"Doug and his dog—what was his dog's name—remember the day they tracked Machete to that vacant house and then marched him down Front Street to Chief Strait's office?" Ralph asked.

"Malcolm, his dog's name was Malcolm," Pete replied.

"I miss Doug," Timothy said. "That was his place on poker night," he continued, pointing at the empty chair next to Pete.

"That night after he died, we had his jacket draped on the back of his chair, talking and telling stories about Doug and how lucky he was to be married to Katie. None of us believed it when he told us they were engaged. Then Katie walked in, sat in Doug's chair, rolled his jacket into a pillow, and buried her face in it for a long time," Timothy mused. "I will never forget that night for as long as I live."

"Time has a way of evaporating," Wendell commented, feeling the disfigured remains of his right hand with his left thumb.

"Damn, it's been nearly six years since we all went to Cuba for protection from that so-called *committee*," he said with disdain. "Relieved they got their just rewards...in hell. Glad we're back and Poor Joe's is open again. Think Katie and the McMillens will ever move back to Big Bay?"

"I've asked Stanley. He says they're talking about coming home after Chloe graduates. He said the hospital in Cardenas is running smoothly, Doctor's Smith and McCaferty are retiring and moving back in December, and that he's proud of the Intensive Care Unit. I think they'll move back. I heard through the grapevine that the couple renting their condo up on the hill are looking for a new place."

Timothy sipped on his coffee then blew on it.

"Machete and Moses have been talking, too. Stan laughed and said Moses wants her bar back." Timothy smiled.

"That's right, you gave Poor Joe's to Machete and Moses as a wedding gift!" Pete said.

"Yup, and I hope they come back and run this place. I want them all to come home. It'll never be the same without Dora in the kitchen, but she's a happily married lady now and has Fidel wrapped around her little finger."

"Hear things between your son and Chloe are kinda serious, there, Timothy," Wayne said while walking to the coffee pot. He watched Timothy's face and missed the mug, pouring coffee on the floor.

"The mop is in the closet next to the telephone booth," Timothy said.

Everyone waited.

"To answer your question...yes."

"Yes, what?" Wayne asked walking back with the mop.

"Yes, they're in love. Every time Carla and I see them together, it reminds us of when we were young and couldn't wait to be married. Charles told me he's waiting to pop the question until after

Chloe graduates next month. He still has one more year at Harvard."

"What kinda doctor is he gonna be?" Morris inquired.

"Heart doctor. We're all flying together to Havana for Chloe's graduation. She's giving the commencement speech. The first student to ever have that honor. Stanley and Danielle are very proud of her."

"Hard to believe it was twenty years ago when that little Mexican kidnapped her and changed our lives forever," Wayne said.

"Lots of water over that dam," Pete said to no one in particular. "Machete shot in the head by a drug crazed kid hiding in the men's room." He pointed toward the hallway. "Blind ever since, except somehow Little Miss can see for him. Some friends gone, too: Chief Johnson, Norma, that young couple murdered—she got thrown down the mine shaft; can't remember their names, and Doug…you remember, that nice nurse from Michigan and her boyfriend, killed by that crazy pastor…her ex-husband."

"Ric and Michelle," Wendell stated.

"What?"

"Their names were Ric and Michelle."

"Right."

"Buried up in the hill alongside of Chief, Norma, and Doug," Timothy added.

"Twenty years. Someone should write a book," Wendel said.

Timothy grinned. "Our lives would not be plausible, Wendell. No one would believe the plot."

"Good point."

"Anyway, life goes on," Timothy said. "Tomorrow they remove Machete's breathing tube, and next month we're all headed to Havana for a graduation."

CHAPTER 28

THE COMMITTEE

The mussed-haired man sitting at the head of the table lit a fresh Camel, using the nearly spent butt of the previous cigarette, and squinted through the smoke at the people around the long office table. He pushed the butt into a second ashtray next to the full one.

"Now that we're all here, I call this meeting of The Committee to order."

He took a long drag on the unfiltered cigarette and continued, smoke puffing from his lungs with each syllable.

"Please meet Evan from the United States. He is assuming the responsibilities of Jon, whose Armani suit has several holes in it. Unfortunately, Jon was wearing it at the time, thanks to that damn O'Malley. Evan comes from the Windy City and is accustomed to the affairs on streets. Welcome, Evan. This is Ronald from Cape Town, Joan from Toronto, Ahuja from Calcutta, Tan from Singapore, Matthew from St. Kitts, Veronica from Mexico City, and Caswell from right here in London.

They looked at the little fellow wearing a red, white, and blue Evil Knievel leather motorcycle jacket with white stars sewn on the blue sash. His left eye wandered independently of his right. Hanging from his mouth, lodged in the space formally occupied by a tooth, was a little brown cigarillo.

"Hello, everyone," Evan said, looking from face to face, searching into the eyes staring at his cigarillo wagging up and down with each word. "My birthday is January 8th, same as Elvis. I like these Al Capone cigars. They're soaked in Cognac." He lit the cigarillo, puffed twice, and smiled. "My mom named me Evan. Never have liked that name. Evan got the shit kicked out of him in grade school."

He relit the cigarillo, flicked the smoking ash dangling, and held the end in the lighter's flickering flame for several seconds.

"You will call me Ace."

"Evan...Ace...joins this committee with high recommendations from our friends in Mexico." The mussed-haired man continued, "His resumé includes surviving the attack on the Veracruz compound years ago and having considerable knowledge of tactical warfare. He served in the French Foreign Legion for five years and has a mighty hatred for Quinn O'Malley and his True Believers."

"Welcome," those around the table, each wearing a custom-made suit, uttered in unison.

"While we are safe here in London with the tightened security," Ahuja said, "it is when we leave for our respective duties that we are in much danger of having our suits damaged as our friend, Jon, discovered."

"True," Ace replied. "I know that your predecessors, when this organization was based at Fort Willoughby, all died in a mysterious explosion aboard a Suriname Navy Destroyer." He replaced the cigarillo and continued without lighting it.

"I knew your predecessor." He nodded in the direction of the mussed-haired man. "His name was Robert Cash. We served together for several years. I have taken an oath to avenge his death. There was never anything on radar. Means it was either O'Malley with one of his damn invisible 'copters or his buddy, Castro. Word has it the Germans built Castro a plane they call the Ghost Wing. Either way, the mistake here is that you are cowering like a bunny trying to elude the fox."

Ace reached over the table and took the mussed-haired man's lighter. He flicked it several times before it ignited then slid it back. "Needs some lighter fluid. It is time for the bunny to attack the fox."

The mussed-haired man lit another Camel using a match, reached into a worn brown leather briefcase, and plopped several pictures on the table.

"Five years ago, I showed you the picture of a young lady by the name of Chloe Norma McMillen, the apple of Fidel Castro's eye and goddaughter of Quinn O'Malley. You remember?"

Everyone except Evan nodded yes.

He passed the pictures around.

"Here she is at Habana University last week. She graduates in a month. Bright young lady, with a Ph.D. in economics, and a Master's in philosophy."

"Bright young thing," Ace said, studying a color photo. "How old?"

"Just turned twenty-two."

Ace pulled at his ponytail, several strokes, then looked at the mussed-haired man.

"How is she going to help us?"

"O'Malley and Castro will agree to anything when they listen to her sob over the phone."

CHAPTER 29

EVEN MORE BEAUTIFUL

The waiting room door opened. Doctors Gonzalez and Congdon entered, wearing green scrubs.

"I have something for you," Doctor Congdon said. He held out his right hand toward Moses.

Stanley leaned close to her and whispered, "It's the bullet, Moses; they got the bullet."

"My man be alive?"

Doctor Gonzalez nodded *yes* and smiled. "He is. We fixed the weak spot in the blood vessel which gave your husband the head-aches, and while we were in the neighborhood, we removed the bullet."

"PRAISE JESUS!"

Moses hugged Doctor Gonzalez then Doctor Congdon then Doctor Gonzalez again.

Chloe, Dora, and Danielle stayed with Moses in the waiting room, huddled close on the couch. Moses swayed side to side, sing-ing a hymn, almost whispering. Soon they stood, arms around each other, humming the tune as one.

Fidel and Stanley walked into the hallway with the doctors.

"That was a close one," Doctor Gonzalez said. "The aneurysm burst when we touched it. He's a damn good surgeon; cool as a cucumber." He nodded toward Doctor Congdon, walking in the direction of the nurse's station.

Dora left to open Dora's Place restaurant. Moses walked meekly into the Intensive Care room with Danielle on her left and Chloe holding her right hand.

Oh, da tubes…so many tubes…you feel like ice, me darlin'…why you be dis cold?

Danielle held the cardiac monitoring cables and subclavian intravenous lines above Moses' head. The lady from Guadeloupe leaned down and kissed her husband's pale, cold lips through the tape securing the endotracheal tube and then his nose, protruding from the layers of gauze wrapped around his head.

"Why he be so cold?" Moses asked, looking up at Danielle.

"He's on a special cooling blanket to help keep his brain from swelling."

Danielle watched terror cloud Moses' eyes.

"He's doing just fine," Danielle continued, pointing at the numbers on the monitor. "His ICP—the pressure in his brain—is perfectly normal."

•••

The headache…gone…no more headache…Moses…Moses…

Machete raised his right hand in the darkness. Moses grasped it tightly.

Damn this hose in my mouth…

"Machete, this is Doctor Congdon. Let's take that breathing tube out, and this afternoon, get those dressing off your head."

Machete raised his left arm and waved it.

And then the endotracheal came out. Machete gagged once, took a deep breath, and smiled.

"The headache is gone," Machete uttered with a gravelly voice.

"Good. We found the problem and fixed it. And your wife has a gift for you," Doctor Congdon said.

"Da bullet, darlin'…dey found da bullet dat boy shoot into your head. I made a hole an' put it on da chain for you. Today I put it 'round your neck."

"How long have I been sleeping?"

"Seven days, honey."

• • •

Stanley, Danielle, Chloe, Quinn and his wife Debra, Fidel and his wife Dora, gathered at the foot of the bed. Moses held Machete's left hand, squeezing it. They watched the white gauze unwind from Machete's head and then the gauze pledgets from both eyes.

Moses slid into bed next to her husband. Gently, she pushed Doctor Congdon away. She grasped each side of Machete's head with her hands, pulling their faces close until their noses merged, and she kissed him. She pulled back just a little and stared into his eyes.

"You are even more beautiful than I imagined," Machete whispered very softly.

Moses moved her lips to his right ear.

"What dat you say?"

"I love your blue eyes…our secret."

Moses extended her arms around Machete's neck and closed the clasp, securing the necklace holding the bullet. She leaned back and gazed into Machete's brown eyes. He made a quick wink with his left eye and then resumed a blank stare into the room.

She winked into his gaze, leaned close, and began humming her favorite hymn.

Everyone in the room joined her, humming *What a friend we have in Jesus.*

CHAPTER 30

THE GREATEST GIFT

Stanley drove past Hospital de Cardenas, out the peninsula to their house on the sand dunes.

"The first time I saw that hospital, Daddy, there were bullet holes in the wall, and the glass doors were shattered. It had just rained when Richard drove Mom and me back to get you, and the curb water ran a pale shade of red," Chloe said from the back seat.

Stanley looked into the rearview mirror and smiled. "That, Chloe, was the worst day of my life. But I'd do it again in a heartbeat if my friends were in danger."

"Mom said you were wounded. I never knew."

Stanley, Danielle and Chloe got out of the car and stood together, looking from their deck at the Atlantic waves lapping and the several palms swaying.

"You miss Big Bay?" Chloe asked her parents.

"It's been a long time since we called that home. Sure do," Stanley said.

"Someday we'll go back, honey. I miss it," Danielle said.

They went inside. Stanley left them in the living room and returned with a grin on his face.

"A graduation gift." He handed his daughter a bottle wrapped in thin white gift paper.

"Basil Hayden's!" Chloe exclaimed. "How'd you get this?"

"Timothy sent it down with Quinn O'Malley."

"Oh Daddy, you remembered your promise!"

Chloe glanced at her mother.

"Dad and I had communion with this when I was fifteen, in the den. I walked in and he had a water glass nearly full on the desk. He looked so sad and angry, and I sat in the chair and we talked and then I wanted a sip, and he gave me a shot glass. It burned all the way down, but I loved the way it tasted. Then he took the copper band off the bottle and made me a bracelet. He promised me a bottle when I turned twenty-one. Thought you forgot, Daddy."

"Better late than never." Stanley grinned.

Danielle said, "I heard all about that and wasn't happy."

Chloe opened her purse.

"I still have it. I'm wearing it for the graduation!"

"You be careful with that stuff," Danielle said. She shook her head and looked at her husband with the sideways look he understood.

"Oh Mom, I'll save it for times when Dad and I need a little communion."

"Did you see the way Little Miss reacted when they wheeled Machete out to the car?" Danielle queried.

"She climbed up onto his lap and kept licking his eyes," Chloe answered. "When they drove away, she was still licking at his eyes."

Stanley nodded yes. "She's been his eyes for a long time. They have a powerful bond. I think they read each other's thoughts."

"She kept licking his eyes, and her tail wagged like crazy," Danielle said, standing and walking toward the kitchen. "Light the grill, Stanley."

Stanley and Chloe walked to the deck.

"Have you finished writing your speech?" he asked.

The grill ignited with a *PUFF*.

"I started then tossed it in the wastebasket. I'm just going to stand up there and talk from my heart. Whatever comes out, you'll hear."

"Can't wait; so proud of you."

"Thanks, Dad."

Danielle watched her husband and daughter through the screened open window.

There's a rip in the screen, no wonder we have flies in here...she's as tall as I am...people think she's my younger sister.

Danielle smiled, rubbed three steaks with olive oil, salt, and coarse pepper and listened.

"When you and Mom move back to Big Bay, would you be upset if I stayed here for a few years?"

Danielle walked from the kitchen, carrying three thick streaks on a plate.

Stanley tossed the steaks on the grill, leaned back from the smoke, and turned the center burner down.

"Still like your steaks medium?" he asked Chloe.

"More medium-rare, now."

"You're growing up!" He paused. "I remember when you wouldn't touch steak unless it resembled leather."

"I really want to go back to Nueva Gerona and teach. When I was a student there, when we first moved to Cuba, they treated me with so much love, Dad. They laughed a little while I learned their way of speaking Spanish. I thought I knew Spanish. Then they wanted me to teach them English. I'll remember for the rest of my life, my sixteenth birthday, when all the kids, the entire school, came with presents I knew they couldn't afford. Felt like crying."

"Why?" Danielle asked.

"I watched them excitedly gobble the food and ask for seconds," Chloe answered, "and I watched you tell uncle Fidel to send the left overs home with them. I love those kids. I want to go back and teach there. They have so little...except love."

Chloe leaned close, hugged Danielle, and whispered, "You think I'm being silly?"

Stanley flipped the steaks.

The ladies simply hugged.

"Time to get your VW out of storage," Stanley said, taking the steaks off the grill and wrapping them in foil.

Chloe smiled. "I love that little yellow car. Hope she still runs."

"The truth is, Fidel already had it tuned. It's waiting for you at the Nueva Gerona compound. Mentioned last week that he had your room repainted."

Chloe smiled. "Well, I did ask if he thought there would be an opening for me."

Stanley shook his head and carried the steaks to the table.

"Let's have a toast."

Chloe and Stanley turned to see Danielle holding the golden bottle of Basil Hayden's and three shot glasses.

"To my parents, two amazing human beings. You have taught me many things, but mostly you have taught me that love is the greatest gift."

Stanley took a deep breath through his tight throat. Danielle simply touched her daughter's hand.

"A toast to love," Stanley said.

"To love eternal," Chloe responded.

"Whew, still warm, Dad," Chloe said, pulling her chair away from the table and sitting.

"The university president asked if I needed anything," Chloe said. She cut the steak, then rested the knife on the salad plate.

"I told him," she continued, staring at the palm trees, "that I would like the front row reserved for my parents and our friends, the people who have looked after me and have cared about me since I can remember." She took a bite of steak.

"President Garcia smiled when I said that. He said, 'The President of Cuba has already taken care of the seating arrangements, Chloe.' Then he looked at me really seriously, and said, 'He never wanted you to know, but he checked on how you were doing every week. He is so very proud of you, young lady.' I'm going to miss Doctor Blue. He was a precious man. What he did for all of us, especially Norah Chase. Poor Norah has never been the same since St. Kitts, but I heard last week she is back in college and going to be a veterinarian. I'm looking forward to looking out and seeing Fidel and Dora, side by side, and Uncle Quinn with Debra, and you two, holding hands like you always do, and Timothy with Carla."

She paused and smiled. "And, Charles Dwight, sitting with his parents. You know he's going to ask me to marry him when he finishes his cardiology residency...and I'll say yes. Chloe McMillen Fife, I like that. I've invited Belvia Chase and Norah; I hope they come. Ralph said all the Usual Suspects are flying down with Timothy. Wendell, he'll be staring at me the entire time, and Pete, Wayne and Rose—she's sad since Jonathon died—Victor Bonifacio, Richard Elmore Fortin, Machete, and Moses. I love that little lady from Guadeloupe; she told me one time her mouth cannot tell a lie."

"I heard Dad ask you if you'd finished writing your speech. I'm so proud of you. Didn't hear your answer," Danielle said.

Chloe grinned at her mother.

"I'm going to stare at Little Miss sitting on the floor next to Machete and just start talking, Mom."

Chloe took another bite of steak. "This is delicious."

"Dry-aged," Stanley replied.

"Did you know that Fidel has bodyguards assigned to me?"

Stanley and Danielle shook their heads *no*.

"Didn't pay much attention at first then I noticed these three buff guys were in all my classes and one girl about my age—a real knockout—no matter which subject. When I started my doctoral studies, there they were, rotating through my classes, glassy-eyed. Then one night a bunch of us went out to celebrate a birthday, and the one guy asked me to dance. I had my arm around his waist and felt a gun under his shirt in the small of his back, so I led him out to the veranda and asked him why he was stalking me with a gun under his shirt. Dad, he looked terrified. 'I am with Cuban Special Forces,' he said. 'Part of President Castro's Secret Service. You are my assignment. Please, this must remain a secret. I am sorry. I just wanted to be close for a moment. You are amazing.' I hugged him tight and promised to keep his secret."

"You're very special to Fidel. Doesn't surprise me at all, Chloe," Stanley said.

He reached for the Cuban bread and ripped the end away.

"What happens if Little Miss isn't at the graduation?

"Big trouble, Dad."

CHAPTER 31

THE COLOR OF LIFE

Richard Elmore Fortin pulled the 1960 Checker cab, with thick glass windows, up to the hospital's entrance and waited. He watched with his good eye while a nurse pushed Machete in a wheelchair down the sidewalk toward the car. The nurse paused when Richard climbed out and opened the rear passenger door. She stared at the white scar, which extended from near his chin up his right cheek, over his forehead to the cowlick hairline. She shuttered a little and stopped walking.

The glass eye is creepy.

Moses placed her hand on the nurse's back.

"He be a friend, dearie. Dis be Richard…he once saved President Castro's life."

Little Miss climbed on Richard, her body wiggling in all directions, before she jumped into the back seat.

Richard grasped Machete's arm. He pulled his friend out of the wheelchair.

Quietly, Machete said, "Good to see you again, my friend."

Moses and the nurse, and Little Miss from the back seat, watched the friends with a bond forged by death, hug. Looking down, Richard watched a twinkle form in his friend's eyes before resuming a blank blind man's stare.

Richard nodded and helped his friend into the back seat, and then Moses.

Green…green…forgot how beautiful the green is.

Moses sat in the jump-seat, facing her husband, her eyes not leaving his eyes. He stared back. Then, Machete slowly turned his head and watched the palm trees pass by.

"Green. I forgot the color of green," he said.

His eyes returned to her blue ones. "How beautiful green is."

"Dat be my favorite color," Moses said. She leaned forward in her seat, close enough that he could feel each word she breathed.

"It is the color of life," Machete continued. "Green is the color of life, and white is the color of pain."

Moses touched her nose against her husband's.

"And, I think blue is the color of love," he whispered. "I did not know that until now."

He kissed her on the lips. They stared into each other's souls, never blinking.

Little Miss licked Machete's hand. He patted her golden head.

"I know," he said, "you are my eyes. Still, you see their souls; you can pick the evil from the good. You will always be my eyes to their souls."

Little Miss licked at Machete's eyes again.

"How we keep dis da secret? Why dis be a gud idea?" Moses asked.

Machete's eyes smiled.

"It is good to be underestimated?"

"What dat mean?"

"I want the bad ones to believe I am still a blind Mexican with a dog."

"OH, "Moses replied, "dat be a gud idea!"

Little Miss's tail thumped on the leather seat.

"Only our friends can know, Moses."

"Dat be gud," she replied. "Dey never see you comin,' da bad ones."

Machete chuckled.

"What be da worry? I feel your worry," Moses asked.

"I have an ache inside. I am worried for my sister at this graduation."

"We see her graduate dis next Saturday."

"Very proud of my sister. Very proud of Maria."

"Chloe?" Moses whispered.

"This time," Machete replied, "this time she is named Chloe."

Moses leaned close again and touched her cheek to his.

"Love you, sweet man. Dis time you will protect her. Dis time you have Little Miss and Moses to help."

CHAPTER 32

RECOLLECTING

"Red sky in morning, sailors take warning," Quinn O'Malley said.

Together they watched the red fog rise from the valley below until the yellow 1973 Volkswagen Super Beetle, parked next to the helicopter pad, appeared.

"Don't believe that crap and neither do you," Fidel Castro retorted.

"Have it looking new," Quinn said. "New top?"

"Had the canvas hand-stitched by two old ladies. The shop next to the old ferry terminal." Fidel nodded down the hill.

"That little car has been part of historic turmoil over the years," Quinn chuckled.

The two friends, bonded by scars and salvation, stared in silence for several minutes at the evaporating fog. Sitting in white wicker chairs on the brick patio, they looked down the hill from the east side of the Presidential Villa.

"What did Chloe name it?" Quinn asked, pointing at Chloe's car.

"Can't remember," Fidel answered. "That is the problem with being our age, knowing we know something and cannot remember what."

"Think she named it Charles," Quinn replied.

"You are just making that up. That is her boyfriend's name; Timothy's son."

"Oh, right."

"Well, my friend, at least we are here. Many of our brave companions from our college years—the brave ones who followed us to the mountains—never got old like we have," Fidel said.

"'All the brave soldiers that cannot get older,'" Quinn said softly.

"Stephen Stills wrote that: *Daylight Again,* Crosby, Stills and Nash," Fidel said. Not bad, huh, Quinn. Did you know who sang that?"

"Yes."

"We all acted brave, daring death and at the same time fearing it, so we fought even harder, proving to each other we had no fear. The bullshit of young men, Quinn. The only people I have known without such fear are my mother—it was her absolute faith—and then there is Richard Elmore Fortin as well as Machete Juarez. Absolutely no fear in either of those men."

"Well," Quinn replied, "first of all, Richard has an advantage, he's died already at least once. He told me that he has met God, and He is very kind. He told me that when you are with God, all the colors in the universe make beautiful music, and there is no sorrow, only joy."

Fidel stared at Quinn.

"What about Machete?"

"You know his real name is Marco?"

"Did not."

"As a young boy, he watched his mother and baby sister murdered in their shack—shot through the wall—then the place burned. That's how he got the scar on his right cheek. He was on a cartel hit, to kill Timothy, when he saw Chole being carried around Poor Joe's by Wendell. He's convinced Chloe is his baby sister, reincarnated. Moses brings joy to his life now, but I can tell you, Chloe's safety is what drives him. He would sacrifice himself without hesitation to keep her safe."

"Wish I could remember that car's name," Fidel muttered. "I love that Poor Joe's."

"Think it's been worth the effort?" Quinn asked. He poured a second cup of coffee and splashed two sugar cubes into it. He wiped at the coffee drops with the back of his hand then poured too much cream, causing the cup to overflow.

"Shit," Quinn muttered. He lifted the saucer and slurped it empty.

"Yes!" Fidel answered emphatically. "Yes, we eliminated some of the evil in the world. Batista is gone and his corrupt government. We did that, my friend. We have rid the world of the scourge...*The Committee*...the human trafficking and drug smuggling."

"And their damn engineered, disease-carrying mosquitoes," Quinn said.

"But mostly," Fidel continued, "mostly it is the friends we have made over the years. They have made these trips around the sun worth living. We have wonderful friends, thanks to each other, amigo."

"Like your wife." Quinn laughed.

"My point!" Fidel laughed. "I would never have met Dora if not for the people living in Big Bay. He lit a cigar. "Would have never met Stanley and Danielle if not for you."

He puffed the big cigar and watched the smoke drift down the hill toward the car.

"I would never have met Chloe, either. Her sixteenth birthday, when I had that car brought up the hill on a flatbed during the party, how excited she was, jumping up and down and dancing all around and her parents looking at me like I was insane or something."

"You blamed me," Quinn chuckled then snipped a cigar and licked the wrapper around and around.

"Then you put me in charge of teaching her how to drive a stick shift. Going through the roundabout actually frightened me more than busting you out of that prison." Quinn pointed down the hill toward the dilapidated, round, cement building in the distance.

"I am fondly watching the damn place fall apart," Fidel replied. "I hope it falls down completely before I die."

"You could bomb it."

"I just might, someday, after a few mojitos."

They smoked the cigars and sipped hot coffee, waiting for breakfast.

"Saturday will be the highlight of my life, I think, Quinn."

"Chloe's graduation."

Fidel shrugged and continued, "For some reason, that event holds much anticipation for me. He relit his cigar. "Even more exciting, I think, than when I rode through Habana on the captured tank, compliments of President Eisenhower," he said with sarcasm.

"We are looking at the future, Fidel. The future that we will be part of, long after we are gone."

"Maybe that is it. That, and that I love that young lady," Fidel replied.

"You and Machete."

Fidel smiled. "And Charles."

"Who do you suppose will take over? Who will lead the True Believers when we are no longer in the picture?" Quinn asked.

"I think Richard," Fidel answered. "Machete is handicapped by his blindness or he would, also. I think Richard. What do you think?"

"I think you're right. Maybe Timothy, too, with his military experience; hard to say, he's getting older. He will help, though, along with Bonifacio, but they're all getting older. Maybe someday, Chloe."

They looked at each other through the cigar smoke swirling in the heavy morning air.

"Wish I could remember that car's name," Fidel said, scratching his beard and rubbing his right ear.

"Ask her Saturday."

CHAPTER 33

STICKS AND STONES

"There's good news and bad news," Ace said.

The mussed-haired man smashed a mostly consumed Camel into the ivory ash tray and fumbled for a fresh cigarette from a new pack.

"Start with the bad news," he muttered, flicking the lighter several times before the flint ignited the wick.

"Needs lighter fluid," Ace said.

The mussed-haired man squinted through the smoke at the committee members on either side of the table then back at Ace.

"Well?"

"There's no way in hell we are going to get close to that Chloe McMillen," Ace said.

The mussed-haired man's cold eyes stared at Ace.

Ace stared back.

Damn…which eye IS he using?

The mussed-haired man looked away for an instant.

"The Cubans have layers of security around her, tight as a cocoon. Fidel must really have something for that girl. Not kidding, her security is every bit as tight as his. I mean, we could probably get to her—not sure we'd get her alive—and pay plenty for our effort. There are secret agents under the guise of students, professors, janitors, taxi drivers, street beggars, bartenders, prostitutes. Damn, I've never seen anything like it. That's in addition to the uniformed special forces everywhere she goes."

Ace smelled a cognac-soaked cigarillo and lit it. "Warm in here," he said, unzipping the red, white, and blue leather jacket.

Ronald from Cape Town cleared his throat and asked, "That the only coat you possess?"

Ace shifted in his chair to look directly at the South African and said nothing.

"Would you care to share your good news?" Joan from Toronto asked.

Ace smiled at Ronald and turned toward Joan.

"She has a boyfriend by the name of Charles Fife, studying to be a heart doctor at Harvard. He's flying from Boston to Havana on Thursday—flying first class. I have the seat next to him on the first leg, to Toronto."

"How'd you manage that?" Matthew from St. Kitts inquired.

Ace shifted in his seat again, wedged the burning cigarillo in the tooth gap, and exhaled.

"You all need me. I'm here simply because we have a common hatred; different reasons, same goals. I can take the sticks and stones from your simple minds; have at it. Just remember, you're all hiding up here like the cowards you are, afraid you'll end up like your predecessors, room temperature, or in their case, chum for the bottom feeders. You need me more than I need you."

"I apologize," Ronald said.

"And, yes, I'm wearing my jacket on first class," Ace said, twisting back in Ronald's direction.

From each side of the table in their plush room, they watched the Al Capone sweet cigarillo wag up and down with each word.

Ace twisted back in his chair to face the head of the table. He watched the mussed-haired man light a new cigarette. "Those things are going to kill you," he said.

"If O'Malley doesn't first," the mussed-haired man said, tossing the lighter on the table.

"You let me worry about O'Malley," Ace replied.

"What?"

Ace smiled.

"Fidel's helicopter is always escorted by three MiG fighters, one in the lead, and two trailing, one above and one below."

The committee watched the short glowing cigarillo growing shorter with each word.

Ace snatched the cigarillo and rubbed at the burn on his lower lip then continued, "The pilot flying below owes me."

He lit a new cigarillo.

"That is the good news," Ace said, looking at the mussed-haired man with his left eye. He turned in his chair to face the entire committee.

"You see, my myopic friends, we never needed Chloe," Ace said. He stood, wedged the little brown cigarillo in the tooth gap, and nodded at Ronald.

The committee watched Ace adjust his Evil Knievel jacket while walking toward the door. With his left hand on the door knob, he turned just a little and pointed his outstretched right arm at Ronald with a pistol pointing finger.

"He's one scary fellow," Ronald muttered.

"Yes," the mussed-haired man replied.

"He is our scary little man."

CHAPTER 34

NOT WASTED LIVES

The palms created strange prehistoric animal shadows on the pale patio brick, the light shining through the branches, coming down from a yellow moon.

"Beautiful moon," Quinn said; "supposed to be a full moon on Saturday."

"Saturday is our reward for not living a lie," Fidel replied.

Quinn studied Fidel's eyes in the moonlight.

"We have not always been right," Fidel continued, "but my friend, we have been honest."

Quinn smiled. "Some of us have been more stubborn than others."

Fidel grinned. "Those who live a lie will someday regret it. I have peace in my soul."

"Listen to you, talking about souls. I remember a time when you claimed that all to be rubbish."

"If a person lives as long as we have, Quinn, and learned nothing, if life does not change a person, it has been a wasted life."

Quinn leaned over and patted his old friend's knee.

"Ours have not been wasted."

"And," Fidel said, looking at the animal shadows moving slightly in the breeze, "Saturday we watch something few would have dreamed possible, a young lady from North America, from the City of Big Bay, giving the commencement speech at Habana University."

The old man, the President of Cuba, rubbed his beard and smiled.

CHAPTER 35

COMRADE'S DEBT

Ten years ago, José Aguilera fought alongside Ace, against the Columbian rebels and drug dealers. Contracted by the Columbian government, his French Foreign Legion battalion, commanded by Ace, waded through the jungle marshes, chasing the rebels, burning their camps and destroying vast stores of cocaine.

Rat-a-tat...bang...bang...rat-a-tat...BOOM.

In the jungle darkness, nineteen Foreign Legion soldiers formed a tight circle, firing back into the black, interrupted only by flashing from the attacker's guns.

"Shit," José muttered, reloading his gun. He rolled against a mossy tree and against a dead comrade. "Shit...shit...shit!"

The jungle became quiet.

"One minute you surrender," a voice shouted in broken English from the darkness.

"Go to hell," José shouted back.

"You go first, amigo."

And the dark jungle suddenly became bright with artificial white light from three flares.

"Thirty seconds."

José's eyes went from body to body, counting. Only he and a wounded man from Nigeria remained. José stood and faced a bright light.

For three hours, tied by their wrists, joined together with hemp rope, José and his Nigerian comrade walked through the jungle barefooted in front of thirty rebels who would take turns poking at them with sharp bamboo sticks when they slowed.

Can't breathe.

José opened his puffy eyelids, his left eye mostly closed. On the right, his wounded comrade dangled from a post in the ground, tied like he was, with their arms behind their backs, wrists bound tightly and suspended off the ground by a nail, allowing only the tips of their bloody toes to touch the dirt. They were naked.

Lines of fire ants marched up their legs, nibbling and stinging.

"WHO ARE YOU?"

José focused on a tall man, dressed in camouflage, standing ten feet in front of him.

"Who are you?" the tall man said again, and he nodded at a rebel who poured wild honey on both men and smirked, "Just wait until they reach your genitals."

José watched his comrade's head slump forward and to the side, red drool dripping from his open mouth and dribbling down his bare chest. The tall man walked close to the unconscious man and stared at José.

"Who are you?" he asked again.

Staring at José, he pulled the trigger of his handgun, blowing the back of the unconscious man's head against the post. The red speckled clumps of white matter attracted swarms of black flies.

The burning bites from fire ants climbing José's legs no longer hurt.

"You are next!" the tall man screamed into José's face.

"Your breath stinks like pig shit," José sneered.

"What?"

"I said your breath stinks; I think perhaps you have a rotten brain."

The tall man walked backwards several steps and raised his handgun. He pointed it at José's forehead.

BANG.

José stared directly at the tall man, not blinking at the sound; his body jerked just a little. Blood first appeared from the tall man's nose, then gushed from his left ear, and he crumpled.

The jungle erupted in gunfire from all around before silence, except for the squawking of birds from the tree canopy.

"That was a close one," Ace said while lifting José a little to free the rope away from the nail in the post. Then Ace cut the rope from his comrade's bloody, blue wrists.

"Thank you, Ace," José said. He watched a large contingent of Foreign Legion soldiers walk from a semicircle around the rebel's camp and a young boy with a dog on a rope.

"The boy's dog has some Bloodhound in him," Ace said.

"Good tracker, thank God," José replied.

"The boy's mother is a good friend," Ace said, "and a kilo of cocaine sweetened the deal."

José rubbed both sticky legs, brushing away fire ants with his fingers.

"I owe you, amigo."

Ace nodded *yes*.

● ● ●

One year to the week of the jungle rescue, both Ace and José's five-year contracts with the French Foreign Legion ended.

"Come to Cuba with me," José said to Ace in a Paris café.

"Why?"

"It is a beautiful place, especially Santiago de Cuba."

"Never been there."

José shrugged. "You will agree with me, I am sure. There are openings in the Cuban Air Force. Did you see that poster?"

"You can fly a plane?" Ace queried while waving at a waitress. "More coffee please for both of us."

"I flew crop dusters…nothing to it. Come with me."

Ace blew on the fresh coffee and smiled.

They sat in a small, humid office with faded, green wallpaper and waited, listening to a slow typist in the next room.

"Havana is a bigger city than I thought," Ace said.

"The other side of Cuba is more beautiful."

The typing stopped, and a slender young lady entered through a side door.

"The lieutenant will see you now," she said, looking at a paper in her hand, "José Aguilera?"

José walked with her.

Ace smiled.

The ladies here are beautiful.

Ten minutes later, José walked through the side door, smiling.

"I start next month," he said.

The young lady appeared and waved Ace to follower her.

The young man behind the desk motioned for Ace to sit on a green, metal, folding chair in front of his metal desk.

"Where were you born?" the young officer asked.

"Chicago."

"Chicago, Illinois, United States?"

"Yes."

"José tells me that you are very brave, that you fought next to him in the jungles of Columbia and that you saved his life."

"He is brave as well, "Ace said.

"You speak adequate Spanish for a North American."

"José taught me."

The young man looked at Ace then down at the papers on his desk. He stamped the top paper with a rubber stamp.

"I am sorry, President Castro will not permit North Americans to enter his military."

"Why?" Ace asked, standing.

"North Americans are not to be trusted."

"Well?" José asked when Ace joined him in the waiting room.

"No go, José. North Americans cannot be trusted."

"I am sorry, amigo. I tried."

"It's OK. You have a fantastic time, flying those Russian planes."

José reached and shook Ace's hand.

"I'll be in touch," Ace said when they reached the street, and he walked away toward the shipyard.

CHAPTER 36

HONORED

José flew old propeller planes for the first three years after enlisting. He loved flying propeller planes which had been part of Batista's Air Force before the overthrow. The planes made sputtering sounds sometimes and leaked oil on the hot cylinders which resulted in smoke blowing back into his face.

"Reminds me of the crop duster," he said one day when questioned about his enthusiasm.

He was promoted to first lieutenant and given a MiG fighter jet on his 30th birthday.

• • •

He had patrolled the coast for three hours, just south of Santiago de Cuba, watching for drug cartel submarines and cigar boats coming from the various Caribbean islands, flying his MiG 21 just above the stall speed.

"I need to refuel," the pilot flying off his left wing radioed to José.

"Go ahead. One more pass, then I will refuel as well."

"These damn things fly like a barn when the tank gets low."

"They put the tank in the wrong place," José replied. "The weight becomes unbalanced. Helps to keep the nose up a little."

"Thanks."

José watched his wing man bank sharply and accelerate away, then banked himself and descended to 300 feet, traveling west.

BAM…

Fuel sprayed from under the MiG's right wing.

Damnit…what the hell?

José reached to his right, feeling for the fire extinguisher in the cramped cockpit and then pulled the throttle to maximum thrust. He banked tightly and descended a little more, scanning the beach.

WHOOSH!

Where'd that come from?

José watched a small rocket fly past the cockpit, igniting the fuel spewing from the MiG for an instant until he barrel rolled twice.

There!

A small group of men stood next to a rubber dingy. One had a rocket launcher on his shoulder, the rest had machine guns, firing up in his direction.

Damn…where is their sub? José banked the fighter and pointed the nose directly at the group, firing the plane's machine gun.

Whap…whap…whap…whap…Bullets hit the glass canopy over and over. José stared at the muzzle flashes coming closer and closer until there were only bodies on the beach. He pulled up and circled, looking for the sub.

"THERE!" he shouted into his radio. "Air Force recon 212, engaging cartel on Romance Beach. I am hit."

"Rescue equipment activated. Runway three is all yours. Altimeter three-zero-three-two. Wind west at twenty with gusts to twenty-eight," the tower answered.

"See their sub, be back shortly."

Damn submarines.

His MiG 21 had a single rocket under each wing.

José smiled and pulled his fingers away from the starboard trigger.

That would have been stupid. Watching the wafting fuel blow away.

"Bye bye," he said into the mic, watching the rocket from under his port wing streak away and make a direct hit on the sub's conning tower.

"What?" the air traffic controller asked.

"On heading for runway three. Landing gear failure light…on. Low fuel alarm sounding. See you soon."

FOAM!…great…great…They put down foam.

S C R A P E…CRUNCH…crunch…crunch…poof.

The plane came to a stop, twisting on its belly, flames all around.

José pulled the ejection lever and rocketed from the cockpit.

All black.

From his back, still strapped in his cockpit seat, José looked at three men gazing down. Two were cutting his shoulder straps while the third watched and finally said, "Are you hurt?"

The bearded man reached his right hand down, and José grasped his wrist.

"No, I'm fine for the shape I'm in."

The tall man helped José stand.

José shook his head and looked up at the tall bearded man wearing a green military hat with a bill then took a deep breath.

"I am fine, Mister President."

"I listened in the tower. You are very brave, Lieutenant."

"Thank you, Mister President. I hate drug dealers."

Fidel Castro nodded *yes.*

"As do I. I hear you are a very accomplished pilot, one of the best in my Air Force, that you make planes do what your fellow pilots dream about."

"I love flying."

Fidel took a handkerchief from his pants pocket and turned José enough to see a wound in his pilot's neck.

"And," he said while wiping the blood away, "you continued to fly while wounded, in a plane that looks like a swiss cheese."

José grinned a little.

"Grilled cheese, Mister President."

"I have no idea how you kept this thing in the air."

"Had too. I don't like crashing."

"Cuba recently received three new MiG 29s, in the opinion of many, the best fighter plane in the world. Would you like to fly one, Lieutenant, and be part of my personal escort?"

"I would be honored, Mister President."

CHAPTER 37

SMART BABIES

"I miss him," Carla said to Timothy.

"He's making us proud, honey,"

"My son, the cardiologist."

"Just making his mama proud."

"I see your chest swell when you're talking about him, don't give me that."

"He's smarter than me, got that from his mother." Timothy leaned closer and kissed Carla.

"What?"

"Thinking how this nearly didn't happen. The Godfather," she whispered.

"But it is," Timothy said. He wrapped his arms around his wife and squeezed her close; his chin on the top of her head.

"It's happening."

"We have angels all around us," Carla said. "You know that, don't you? We have angles guarding us."

Timothy smiled. "Like Machete?"

"Like Machete and Quinn and Bonifacio. I would…Charles and I would not be here now if they hadn't rescued us."

"Yup," the old Vietnam war vet said, "we have angels looking out for us. That notion would have Quinn laughing."

"It would, wouldn't it?" Carla said. "Doesn't change my mind."

"Quinn is a lot of things; not sure he'd make the angel list."

Carla looked at Timothy's face and he looked back.

She's serious.

"Our son was about to die. That man had a bolt cutter, making it open and close over and over. He had hatred, red hatred, in his eyes. Then Quinn and Machete walked into that evil place, calm. Honey, they had a protective glow all around them. I will never forget Quinn's eyes. His eyes were fearless. And then Machete walked past Quinn and right up to that Godfather like he knew him and shot him in the forehead. They are angels, honey, protective angels."

Timothy hugged her close.

"I wish Charles could have come home and flown to Havana with us on Quinn's plane," Carla whispered into her husband's shoulder.

"That's what happens when you're a resident. He did manage to swap next week with somebody. He's flying to Toronto tonight for a direct flight to Havana."

"He's going to ask Chloe to marry him while he's in Cuba," Carla said.

Timothy smiled. "What makes you think that?"

"Just a mother's intuition."

● ● ●

Chloe Norma McMillen and Charles Dwight Fife grew up together in Big Bay. Chloe was two years old when Charles was delivered at Big Bay General. Chloe's mother helped with the delivery. By the time Charles reached twelve, it became obvious the two were enamored with each other. Frequently they would be found in the corner booth at his father's bar, Poor Joe's, next to the popcorn machine, their bare feet rubbing each other's legs while they studied.

Then came her family's evacuation to Cuba. Chloe attended the high school in Nueva Gerona, and Charles went to a private school, located in New Hampshire. He graduated at age fourteen, before attending the Citadel Military College, then transferring to Harvard Medical School.

They never lost touch.

Every week they would receive each other's letters regardless of events taking place in their lives. With a great distance between them, they grew closer.

"I love you," Charles wrote at the close of each letter. "More than you know."

Chloe would end each letter with, "Not true, honey. I adore you just as much."

He now stood one inch taller than his father, Timothy, who is six feet two inches tall. He looks very much like his father, with blue eyes always smiling. He has curly blond hair, like his mother, long enough to cover his ears. And, he is smart, with a photographic memory.

"I am so very proud of you," Chloe wrote when Charles graduated from Harvard Medical School at the top of his class and started his Cardiology Residency.

He wrote back, "I wish I was as smart as you, honey."

Chloe smiled when she read that and wrote back, "We would make smart babies, I bet."

Charles read that line over and over. He lay in bed, smelling the paper, searching for her perfume.

CHAPTER 38

FRIDAY CONVERSATIONS

"How old be Chloe da day dat boy shot your brain and made de eyes blind?" Moses asked.

"Five, I think," Machete replied.

"Oh, dat be so long. She be beautiful lady now."

Machete smiled.

"I see her face every day."

"When you gonna tell your sister dat you see her widt your eyes again?"

"Tomorrow."

● ● ●

"Dora and Deb have Dora's Place all decorated. I saw the menu; it's going to be a glorious party," Danielle said.

"It doesn't seem like this should be happening so soon," Stanley said, "that she should be all grown up and everything."

"She got her brains and determination from you, Stan."

"She's a whole bunch smarter than I am. She inherited your beauty and your heart. She loves life and people."

"I feel so proud when I watch her in a crowd," Danielle said, "watching people come up to her like they want to touch her or see her smile."

"Tomorrow will be the second-best day of my life." Stanley said.

"The second?"

"Right after the day you said you would marry me."

"On Mallery Square," Danielle said, "and we've never looked back."

●●●

"Our wives will meet us at the graduation," Fidel said to Quinn.

"Deb told me Monday they were flying here and we would all fly to Havana together," Quinn replied.

"Better talk to her again. Dora called last night and told me they still have things to do before the party, and they would meet us at the auditorium."

"Oh." Quinn shook his head.

"Still have some decorating or something."

●●●

"We are part of a brotherhood," Ace said, staring out the window into the darkness with just a hint of sunrise.

"Yes, sir, we are that," José said, looking at Ace sitting across the café table. "We are, and I am grateful."

Ace looked around the café and studied two young ladies at the far end before speaking again.

José glanced into Ace's blue eyes then looked at the unlit cigarillo wedged in the gap.

"What is it you need, commander?" José asked. He looked down at his mug and watched two brown sugar cubes dissolve in the black coffee.

Ace watched José stir the coffee.

"I have an important mission for you."

He lit the cigarillo, inhaled deeply, and glanced at his watch.

Ace handed José a small piece of yellow paper and watched José turn pale. Ace put a finger to his lips.

"You understand?" Ace asked.

"Yes, sir."

Ace took the paper from José, crumpled the frail parchment, and placed it in the ash tray. Together they watched it burn into nothing.

CHAPTER 39

COG IN THE WHEEL

"Whoa there, Evil Knievel, no smoking on planes."

Charles looked up from seat 3B. He watched the matronly flight attendant stop a man wearing a leather motorcycle jacket, red and blue with a white sash hosting several blue stars. She held her right hand out, wiggling her fingers impatiently.

"Give it here or turn yourself right around and get off," she said.

"It's not lit," the man replied.

The attendant stared, blocking the entrance, wiggling her fingers. The co-pilot stuck his head out from the cockpit. "Trouble Gertie? Want me to call security?"

Charles watched the man remove the cigarillo from his bottom lip and flick it through the opening between the plane and the passenger boarding bridge.

The flight attendant rubbed her forehead. With an incredulous look, she said, "You DO KNOW they are FUELING this plane."

"Said it wasn't lit." He looked at his boarding pass and attempted to push past the lady who outweighed him by 20 pounds. She muttered something in a foreign tongue and stepped aside, looking at the next passenger with a smile.

Ace stopped at row 3.

"I have 3A," he said to Charles.

Charles stood, and the man moved past and sat.

American Airlines flight 3722 lifted from the tarmac and pointed northwest.

"Business in Toronto?" Charles asked the man to his left.

"Could say that, Charles," Ace replied, "or would you prefer to be addressed as Doctor Fife?"

What the hell?

Ace watched Charles' face. It showed him nothing. He watched Charles open a book.

"What ya reading?"

"The Old Man and the Sea."

"Ernest Hemingway wrote that."

Charles smiled. "You've read it?"

"Yup, his best book."

"Wrote it to prove he still had it in him," Charles replied. "His previous novel was a disaster."

"Oh."

"He wrote *Across the River and into the Trees* while distracted, probably his worst. Had to prove he could still do it, as much to himself as the world. What's your name?"

"William Roberts."

"Well, William, how is it you know my name, or would you prefer I call you Bill?"

"You want to go by Doctor Fife or Charles?"

Charles closed the book and shoved it into the seat-back area with the magazines. He turned in the seat, just a little, and stared down at the man.

"Is this some sort of game, or are you simply a strange little man wearing a dirty Evil Knievel motorcycle jacket...Bill?"

• • •

William Roberts owns a successful Citroën auto dealership in Montreal, Canada. Seven days ago, he flew from Montreal on a business trip to the Peugeot-Citroën headquarters in Paris, France. The following day, he did not keep an appointment with the Citroën vice-president for sales, who notified security.

"I watched that man leave with three men—one of them black," replied a waitress at Café de la Palx, when shown a picture by the police. She pointed north. "They went that way, on Rue Auber, in a Mercedes, a silver Mercedes. That is all I remember. Oh, he had not eaten his breakfast yet when he left with those men."

● ● ●

Ace had traveled back to the United States on a plane owned by The Committee, arriving at Newark Liberty International Airport at midnight. The Customs Agent smiled at Ace.

"Nice jacket," the agent commented, reaching for Ace's passport.

"Thanks, Evil was amazing," Ace replied.

The agent looked at the passport, then Ace's face, then the passport.

"Everything seems in order," and the agent winked. "I trust everything went well in France."

"It did." Ace said.

● ● ●

"ID," TSA agent demanded when Ace approached the airport security screening corral.

Ace produced his ticket and passport.

The TSA lady placed the passport picture under a light and moved it in various positions.

"Reason for travel to Canada?" She asked

"Business."

She picked up a clipboard and ran her finger down a list of names. Then she picked up the phone. She held her hand up and looked at Ace while talking.

"Yes, sir. Standing right here. Yes, sir."

She put the phone receiver down and said, "The computer has you listed as a missing person in Paris."

Ace smiled.

"Don't you love computers? Well, tell the computer here I am, in Boston, alive and well. Don't know what to say. Probably a virus or something. You can check with Newark Customs."

The TSA lady scowled, looked at the passport and boarding pass one last glance, and handed them back.

"Have a good day, Mister Roberts."

Ace smiled, again.

●●●

Ace smirked. "Oh, I assure you this is no game…Charles."

Charles watched the flight attendant making coffee in the galley, then leaned close, smelling the old leather odor. "This conversation is over. Do not bother me again, understand?" He reached for the book.

"When we land, you walk out with me. There's a vehicle waiting."

Charles opened the book.

"I'm serious, there, Doctor Fife. You need to come with me."

"Or what?" Charles snapped, slamming the book shut.

Could snap this shrimp's neck…Can't be armed.

Ace watched Charles' hands clinch into fists. Then he reached inside his jacket, removing a glossy 5 x 7 black and white and extended the picture toward Charles.

"Name's Chloe, right? Graduating in Havana tomorrow. Chloe McMillen. She's a beautiful young lady, Charles."

He extended the picture across the arm rest.

"I bet she is even more stunning in true color."

Charles looked but did not touch the glossy. He simply stared.

"Who are you, really?"

Ace smirked a little.

There…got 'um.

"Not important who I am, Doctor Fife. Just a cog in the big wheel of life; part of something much bigger. Now, hand me your phone. If you make a commotion here, doctor, I have a friend that'll take care of your sweetheart in ways you will find disturbing."

Ace paused.

"These are people who are accustomed to having their way," he continued. "Now you be a good boy and come with me when we land…phone, give it here."

Charles looked down at the closed book on his lap.

Snap his neck like a pretzel.

"Think about it doctor, I knew you were on this plane, in this seat. Do not disappoint these people."

"I have friends, as well."

"We will see about that," Ace replied.

Charles handed Ace his phone.

CHAPTER 40

TINY GREEN SMITHERS

José sat on a brown, metal folding chair in the small Quonset hut, alongside two other MiG pilots. The morning air, while walking to the briefing hut, seemed cold.

"Papa One will lift at 0930 for Habana. There are no complicating weather conditions forecast. Anticipate the usual altitude of fifteen thousand feet with the total flight time of thirty-five minutes," said the Air Force General. "Once Papa has landed, assume the seven-mile Universidad de la Habana pattern. Expected departure from Habana is 1300. Your axillary fuel tanks are attached and filled. Any questions?"

"Do we know who is traveling with President Castro?" José inquired.

"He will be accompanied by his friend, Quinn O'Malley."

José nodded, retrieved his sunglasses from his pocket, and cleaned them.

• • •

Fidel and Quinn walked down the hill toward the idling Mi-17 helicopter, watching several doves swoop through the warm exhaust coming from the turbines. The blades began to slowly turn.

Both men looked up at the sound of jets above them.

"Aren't they beautiful?" Fidel said.

"They are," Quinn replied. "I still think we should be flying in the XS-1."

Fidel shook his head while entering the Russian helicopter.

"Any excuse to mobilize the True Believers, huh Quinn?"

Quinn stood inside the door, watching his old friend buckling the seatbelt, before saying, "No safer ride in the world, you know."

"Amazing flying machine the Germans built for us," Fidel said, "for missions Quinn, not joyrides to Habana."

"You're right."

Quinn sat and fastened his seatbelt.

The helicopter lifted and ascended rapidly to 15,000 feet, traveling north at 162 miles per hour toward Havana 90 miles away.

The helicopter pilots smiled when the lead MiG 29 flew over, wagging its wings, then moving into the lead position.

José took his trailing position behind and below the helicopter. The third MiG flew above José.

José took deliberate deep breaths, over and over. He reached down and yanked the seatbelt tighter, then slowed his jet just a little, just slow enough to see the MiG above him for a few seconds.

Forgive me, mother...forgive me, Jesus...very sorry...I will be banished to hell...Forgive me, Mister President...I am sorry...sorry... Forgive me.

His helmet face-shield fogged over, and he pushed it up.

Then José pushed the MiG's throttle to full thrust before moving his right hand, putting his forefinger on the rocket launch button. He clinched his jaw.

Very sorry.

Two heat-seeking rockets launched, one from under each wing.

He watched both rockets being swallowed into the helicopter's exhaust, followed by a brilliant explosion, leaving only tiny green smithers in the air.

● ● ●

Quinn and Fidel watched, from their new dimension, the twirling downward metal confetti. Both pilots emerged from the debris and waved at their passengers before disappearing through the veil.

"Ready?" Quinn asked.

"Have a choice?" Fidel replied.

Three smiling, glowing beings drifted through the veil and toward the two souls.

"Lina...Naty," Fidel whispered.

Quinn grinned. "There is hope for you; your mother and your lover."

The third angel moved closer, and Quinn recognized her.

"Janet Sue!"

The glowing ones touched the souls and then lead them through the veil and into the brilliance.

Just ahead the Watchman's Son stood with arms outstretched.

"Come meet your Father." And they moved with Him toward the sanguine eyes shining brilliantly in the center of it all.

Fidel said to Quinn, "Now I understand."

"Richard Fortin is right...AMAZING LOVE!" Quinn exclaimed.

Bathed in love, Quinn and Fidel were absorbed into the complete joy.

• • •

José ignited both afterburners and pointed the nose of his MiG straight up. He leveled at 59,000 feet and made a tight turn to the south, in the direction of Air Base Paramaribo in Suriname.

It took the pilots flying the other MiGs several seconds to comprehend what they had just witnessed.

"Security One, what the hell?" the pilot stationed behind and above radioed to the lead plane.

José listened.

"Get him!" the lead pilot screamed. "I am too far away to catch him."

"Security Two in pursuit. You copy central?"

"Tracking Security Three...headed southeast at Mach 2. Did he shoot Papa down?"

"Yes," replied both pilots.

"Jettison your auxiliary tank," the lead pilot advised the second pilot. "You can hit two-two-five without it. If you run out of fuel, eject, and I'll stay with you."

José listened, *Didn't think of that,* and pulled the tank release lever. The tank remained affixed. He pulled it twice more. The tank remained. He watched the second MiG, now traveling 191 miles per hour faster than he could, slowly close the gap on his radar screen.

Ten minutes later the alarm indicating a radar lock on his plane screeched loud beep-beeping sounds. José took a deep breath and did the Valsalva maneuver while putting his MiG in a steep downward evasive spiral, then straight up before pointing the nose downward again. The combination of the Valsalva and G forces made his vision gray.

José watched the first air to air rocket miss his plane by 20 yards.

Then the flash.

●●●

On the dark side of the veil, José hesitated, dreading with his entire being to proceed. He had turned his back to the veil when he felt Fidel's arm wrap tightly around him, pulling him through into the brightness.

"Forgive me."

"Father wants to see you."

CHAPTER 41

FORTY-FIVE MINUTES PAST

Machete moved only his eyes, watching Chloe, dressed in a graduation gown and cap, climb the seven steps and walk across the stage. She stopped, briefly, and looked to her right at the crowd then sat next to the President of Universidad de la Habana.

"She is more beautiful than I imagined," he said, leaning close to Moses.

Moses smiled.

Little Miss looked up at Machete. Her tail swished back and forth on the polished hardwood floor.

"My sister is a beautiful lady."

"Yes, she be beautiful all da way from her soul. She loves da peoples."

"Wish my mother was here to see this."

Moses moved even closer to her husband.

"She be here, wit us, honey, at dis moment, and she be happy."

Machete looked at Moses.

"I talked wit Lilliana last night, in da dream," she said.

Machete nodded.

"I have dreams about her, too."

Chloe looked out over the great auditorium. The bleacher seats on either side, from the hardwood floor to the ceiling beams, were filled with people wearing festive clothing. So too, were all the brown folding chairs assembled on the basketball court.

She took a deep breath and looked at the front row.

Mom and Dad. God, thank you for my beautiful parents and my friends; they never left my side. There are Timothy and Carla. Where's Charles? Dora and Deb—Dora makes the best hot chocolate. Uncle Quinn must be with Fidel, running late as usual. God I love Katie. There they are, the Usual Suspects. I so miss Poor Joe's. They helped raise me, especially Wendell. Where's Richard? Good, Belvia made it and Norah, too; she looks old. Where's Charles? Machete and Moses—he still believes I'm his little sister. Little Miss—he'd be lost without Little Miss. Here's Victor Bonifacio.

Chloe scanned to the far end of the front row.

Doctor McCaferty and Kathy. Doctor Smith and Mary. Wish Doctor Blue was still alive; saved Norah. Where's Charles?

She smiled, looked down, and twisted the copper Basil Hayden's bracelet around and around on her left wrist.

Dad was so sweet when he gave me this.

Chloe looked down at her father, holding Danielle's hand, then shifted her gaze to Machete.

Machete looked up at Chloe's hazel eyes looking down directly at him.

He winked at her.

The President looked at the empty chairs reserved for President Castro and Quinn O'Malley and glanced at his watch.

"It is thirty minutes past, Miss McMillen."

Chloe looked at the empty chairs for several seconds before replying, "May we wait fifteen minutes?"

President Garcia nodded *yes.*

Dora Castro moved over one chair and sat next to Debra O'Malley.

"Where the hell are they?" Dora said to Debra.

"I don't like this, Dora. They both adore Chloe. I don't like this."

The University President stood and walked to the podium.

"Ladies and Gentlemen, students, and those graduating today, welcome. I will have a few closing comments later, but first, it is with great pride that I introduce the first student to give this university's commencement speech. Chloe Norma McMillen accomplished in less than six years what would take most of us twice that time, and she graduates with the highest honors. Miss McMillen exemplifies the finest that Cuba sends out into this world."

He turned and held out his right hand toward Chloe. She shook his hand and adjusted the microphone closer.

"Thank you for your kind words, President Garcia."

Chloe spoke in perfect Spanish with a Cuban dialect. President Garcia smiled.

"Thank you all for being here. This, for those of us graduating today, is the reward for years of hard work. Without the support and love of those close to us, helping and encouraging along the way, some of us would not have been able to climb this mountain.

My father asked if I had finished writing my speech for today. I told him I tried but threw it away and that I would say whatever came from my heart."

She paused, looking down at Stanley.

"You getting any of this?" Danielle asked.

"Most of it," Stanley replied, smiling up at his daughter.

"I have met many great and famous people in my short time on this earth, very brave people, people who try hard to do the right thing, who see wrong and try to make it right and make this life better for others. They have set the bar high for those of us who follow. They have set the example. My daddy...."

She paused again and stared at her father.

Out of the corner of her eye, she saw Timothy looking at something yellow in his hand.

He looks pale.

Chloe watched Victor Bonifacio take a yellow phone from his pocket, glance at the screen, then at Timothy.

"...My daddy shared with me, when I turned fifteen, this quote, his favorite quote by his favorite United States president, Teddy Roosevelt, and I share it with you today. 'Far better is it to dare mighty things, to win glorious triumphs, even though checkered by failure, than to rank with those poor spirits who neither enjoy much nor suffer much, because they live in that gray twilight that knows neither victory nor defeat.' My hope for each of us here today is that we have no gray twilights, that we endeavor to persevere, regardless of what life throws at us, and that we love each other."

In unison, the crowd stood and applauded.

The great auditorium roof began to pulsate with a rhythmic chop-chop-chopping sounds. The applause faded to silence, and the percussive sounds above became more intense. Then came additional sounds, distinctive helicopter sounds, the sounds of helicopters landing on the San Lazaro traffic triangle, one helicopter and then a second.

The people driving outside stopped their vehicles and watched, and the people on the sidewalks backed away, watching two sleek, strange-looking helicopters land in the intersection while a third helicopter hovered, slowly rotating above the building, a Gatling gun protruding from its belly.

Chloe spotted him first.

Richard Elmore Fortin ran down the center aisle, his long hair bouncing. At the same instant, twelve men dressed completely in black walked calmly down the side aisles with automatic weapons.

The University President stood to shield Chloe when Richard bounced up the seven steps. Chloe whispered. "It's OK," and reached for Richard's hand.

Stanley stood then ran. He met his daughter and Richard coming down the steps.

"We're under attack, Stan. You, Victor, and Timothy get everyone together, and go with them." He nodded at the approaching True Believers.

Richard turned Chloe toward the side exit and walked directly into Machete and Little Miss.

"What is happening, amigo?"

Richard stared directly into Machete's eyes and moved just a little.

Machete winked.

"Answer my question."

"We're under attack."

"I am NOT leaving my sister's side," Machete replied, watching Moses, Debra, Dora, Stanley, Danielle, Katie, and the remainder of the front row being ushered through the side door by Timothy and Victor.

Chloe bent down a little then hugged Machete.

"Let's go!" Richard commanded.

Chloe turned, watching her mother walking in the opposite direction toward the west exit. Danielle held Stanley's arm, looking back at her daughter.

Richard took a firm hold of Chloe's arm.

"We'll catch up with them soon, Chloe. Come with me."

She pulled back just a little and looked Richard in the face.

"Why?"

Richard pursed his lips.

He's not saying.

Machete moved closer, almost between them.

"Amigo, we have never kept secrets," Machete said, staring at Richard's glass eye.

Richard exhaled a deep puff.

"They want you, Chloe. Plan to kidnap you."

She leaned down to eye level with Richard.

"Who?"

"Bad people; call themselves The Committee. Now let's go."

"Give me a gun," Machete said, trotting beside Little Miss in the bright sunlight toward the XS-1 stealth helicopter.

CHAPTER 42

THE TRUE BELIEVERS

The True Believers conjure fear and great respect from agencies such as the Central Intelligence Agency, and the Federal Security Service of the Russian Federation.

The idea to form a rapid response team capable of traveling worldwide was born one night in Havana's Sloppy Joe's Bar at the intersection of Animas and Agramonte streets, three years after the Cuban Revolution.

"I cannot bring myself to believe my trusted friends, the very ones at my side in the mountains of Santiago de Cuba, would do this," Fidel said.

"Greed is a powerful thing," Quinn replied, "and they were never friends."

"This is everything we fought to free Cuba from. Batista must be laughing wherever he is hiding."

"The Mexican drug cartels have ways of persuading. You know this is the cartel's doing."

Fidel lit a fresh cigar and stared up at the white ceiling then shrugged a little.

"I suppose there are always the weak ones. How do we deal with the cartels?

Quinn scratched the hair above his right ear and looked down the long dark bar before saying, "Let's have our own private strike group. I know men who would be delighted to join."

He rubbed his beard and looked at Quinn.

"Can't afford it," Fidel replied. "Cuba is broke."

"This will not be a Cuban thing, Fidel. This will be international. The bad guys will have no place to hide. I have friends in Spain, France, Germany, Minnesota, Nevada, Angola, Ghana, and Australia."

Quinn paused and waved at the bartender and pointed at his empty glass.

"…And I know wealthy men in Texas and Saudi Arabia. They worry about their families and would exchange protection for funding."

"Could have used that support during the revolution," Fidel muttered.

"This will be bigger," Quinn said, "than any revolution."

Fidel looked surprised.

"Governments come and go, have throughout recorded history, my friend. This is about the fight between good and evil."

"Do it. Contact your friends," Fidel said.

●●●

"Why do you call yourselves the True Believers?" Debra asked Quinn during their first flight together, astonished by the airplane.

"Because," Quinn answered, "that name scares the hell out of the bad guys and because we believe we can, no matter what needs done. We believe."

Financed with Saudi oil money as well as "private donations" from the Minnesota Godfather, Victor Bonifacio and his friend, Rose, a madam in Nevada, the True Believers were born.

Quinn O'Malley's friends at Berlin Technical University worked with Akaflieg Berlin Aircraft to secretly design and build a high-speed, stealth helicopter, capable of traveling 400 miles per hour. After three helicopters were built, all plans were destroyed, and everyone involved denied any knowledge, scoffing at the very idea.

After the True Believers traveled over the Atlantic to a remote site, using commercial airlines, to rescue a Saudi sheik's family from a terrorist compound, the sheik had a prototype of a supersonic private aircraft built. Designed in Russia with the help of Gulfstream, the needle-nosed Gulfstream S-21 flies at Mach 2. The plane was equipped with the latest military radar and secret avoidance software. Only one was built and given to the True Believers.

Five years later, the same German group, now financed by the Saudi Prince, built a "Flying Wing," invisible to radar and capable of speeds up to Mach 5. The only one to exist is hidden underground in a bunker near Havana. It has been used only twice, to sink a Suriname Naval Destroyer, and to destroy a lab in Nicaragua. Aboard the Suriname ship was the original group known as The Committee.

There are on average, thirty members that comprise the True Believers. There are no papers ever signed. The only requirement to join is a commitment to relieve the world of evil and a promise to never acknowledge they did. The members are comprised of former special forces from six countries and former French Foreign Legion members.

And their final commitment is a willingness to die.

It was the True Believers who rescued Timothy's wife and son Charles from the Mexican Godfather's compound. They also rescued Beliva Brown's daughter, Norah, after being kidnapped while walking to school on White Street in Key West and taken to St. Kitts to be sold to a Saudi Prince.

And now, the True Believers rushed the Universidad de la Habana auditorium. The lead XS-1 hovered over the building, slowly twisting around and around, clockwise, with a Gatling gun lowered, protecting while first one, then the second, helicopter landed, each with six True Believers aboard, allowing room for passengers.

The True Believers flew to Universidad de la Habana, knowing their leaders had been blown out of the sky.

CHAPTER 43
VERY BAD NEWS

The people watched.

From their open car windows and old Chevy and Plymouth convertibles and from the sidewalks they watched with astonishment.

They watched two groups of people walk with men dressed in black, carrying submachine guns, to the strange-shaped helicopters, painted a dull black color.

An old man leaned close to a little boy and shouted over the noise, "It is the North Americans. Another Bay of Pigs is beginning, I think."

The first helicopter lifted from the Lazaro traffic triangle. A Gatling gun emerged from its belly while it gained altitude. It circled while the second helicopter lifted to a higher altitude and hovered.

The people watched the third helicopter, which had been above the auditorium, now descend and land on the grass between the building and the parking lot. From the sidewalk they watched a man with long hair, holding the arm of a young lady two inches taller, and a short Mexican with a dog on a leash, trot from the building and enter the helicopter, which lifted immediately, even before the door had closed.

Then all three helicopters departed in a triangle pattern, noses pointed slightly down, their twin turbines roaring, headed north in the direction of Key West at 400 miles per hour.

Chloe pulled the seatbelt tight while looking at the *TRUE BELIEVER* banner affixed to the bulkhead.

Machete reached to his right and grasped her left hand.

He is so cold...shaking.

Richard looked at the floor, bent over, silent for several minutes.

Finally, Chloe bumped Richard with her shoulder.

"Hey, you!" she said above the roar.

He turned his face toward Chloe and Machete, and they saw his absolute agony.

"The last time I flew this helicopter," he said, "Fidel and Quinn were sitting in your very seats. It was for your sixteenth birthday party. Quinn was mad as hell when he found out I was flying."

He gulped twice and took a deep breath.

"Now they are watching us fly from heaven."

Chloe felt Machete's grip tightening, tighter and tighter.

"What did you just say, amigo?"

Richard sat back and looked at the ceiling.

"They are dead. Their helicopter was shot down on the way to the graduation."

Chloe watched his lips move, absorbing each sound.

Richard Elmore Fortin unbuckled his seatbelt so he could turn in his seat and face Chloe.

She watched his face distort with each word.

"They have Charles, Chloe."

Chloe looked away from the pain, slowly turning her face to the left, looking past Machete toward the tail section and the six True Believers seated in the canvas seats, looking back at her.

"Why?" Chloe asked. "Why is this happening?"

"They want you, your safe return in exchange for ignoring their enterprises, you as their bargaining chip. They knew how much Fidel and Quinn loved you. When they discovered your security, they settled for your boyfriend."

Chloe's body stiffened.

"Do Timothy and Carla know?"

"Not yet."

"I WILL be the one to tell them."

She paused and thought for a brief period.

"Have Debra and Dora been told?" Chloe asked.

"Not yet. Victor wants to wait until we're on the ground and their friends are close."

Chloe nodded before asking, "How'd they pull this off? Who shot them down?"

"We think, from the radio traffic we've intercepted, a Cuban Air Force pilot working for a group known as The Committee."

Chloe's eyes widened just a little, and her voice changed. Richard watched her pupils dilate.

"Do we know where they have Charles?"

"No, only a terse message and his social security number."

She nodded at the True Believers seated in the back and waved her left arm up at the *TRUE BELIEVER* banner.

"With Fidel and Quinn gone, who's in charge of all this?" Chloe asked.

Richard shrugged a little.

"Right now, I am, Chloe, and Victor. We'll get it figured out."

Chloe took Machete's hand in hers, grasped Richard's left hand, and squeezed hard.

"Damn right, we're going to figure it out," she said.

After several shallow breaths, Chloe continued, "When we land, let's get with Bonifacio and Timothy."

Only Machete heard his sister's sad sigh.

"To plan a reckoning. I'll tell Dora and Deb," she said. "They should hear it from me. Then we go find the man I'm going to marry."

"You do not have to do this," Machete said. "We will find him."

She looked at Machete with an expression he remembered from long ago.

Richard and Machete looked at each other and nodded. Then Richard looked forward and up at the banner and smiled, just a little. He pointed to headphones hanging behind their heads.

Richard unbuckled his seatbelt and opened the cockpit door. He buckled into the navigator's seat behind the pilot and co-pilot and tapped the pilot on the shoulder, pointing at a red dashboard switch. The pilot flipped it up.

"Naval Station Key West…Naval Station Key West, this is X-ray Sierra One on your scrambled frequency alpha."

"This is Naval Station Key West. Repeat."

"This is stealth helicopter X-ray Sierra One. Our beacon is activated."

"We have three on radar."

"Yes, sir, that is correct. Three. This is team True Believers arriving from Havana, requesting air support and permission to land."

"Copy that. Two F-35s will be over you in five minutes."

"Is this Lieutenant Richard Fortin?" queried the tower.

"Yes, sir."

"It's been a long time, sir. Altimeter is twenty-nine-zero-niner. Wind out of the east at twelve. Visibility ten miles. Proceed on current course to runway twenty-five."

"Thank you. We have precious cargo aboard."

"Understand that. Two planes on the tarmac awaiting your arrival."

Richard's eye twinkled.

Bonifacio.

Machete and Chloe listened in their headphones.

Chloe leaned close to Machete and lifted the headphone from his right ear.

"Dad told me that Richard was once one of the best helicopter pilots in the US Air Force before he was shot down and lost his eye," she said, watching Richard remove his headphones and release his seatbelt straps.

He stooped down, coming through the small cockpit opening. And then Richard winked at Chloe with his good eye.

● ● ●

"Why have you separated me from my daughter?" Danielle shouted over the turbine whine in XS-2.

"Just worked out that way," Victor Bonifacio shouted back.

Stanley leaned past his wife toward Victor.

"Today is not the time, Victor. We want the damn truth."

Victor left his seat and crouched in front of Stanley and Danielle.

"We have intel that Chloe is in danger of being kidnapped. We have a team dedicated to her specifically. Machete is a bonus if he doesn't get in the way."

Danielle's body shivered.

"Why would anyone want to kidnap her?"

"Planned on using her as a bargaining chip to extract an agreement from Quinn and Fidel to stay out of their businesses."

Stanley studied Victor's face.

"Who, Victor?" Stanley asked.

"The Committee."

"Thought they were dead. Quinn told me they were all on that Suriname Navy Destroyer."

"Those men were eliminated; the conglomerate persists: Oleson Pharmaceuticals in England, Cover Pharmaceuticals in Nicaragua, Holy Adoption in Brazil and St. Kitts, the human trafficking in Bangkok, Toledo, Chicago, Flint, Cape Town, and Moscow. And in Xiamen, China, they have a lab. Evil is pervasive, Stanley."

Victor paused, looking up at the McMillens' stunned faces.

"What did Richard mean, we're under attack?" Stanley asked.

Victor never took his eyes from their faces while he spoke.

"They shot down Fidel's helicopter. Fidel and Quinn are dead."

Stanley and Danielle stared back.

"They have kidnapped Charles Fife."

Danielle unbuckled her seatbelt and melted into Stanley. He felt her body convulse with sobs.

Danielle wiped at her nose with the back of her hand and twisted her head, looking up at her husband's face.

He looks older today.

CHAPTER 44

LIKE THE KENNEDY THING

*C*hloroform...trichloro methane...damn.

Charles shook his head, gagged on the oral airway, and moved the hard rubber to one side with his tongue.

Both cheeks stuck to the black hood over his head, and vomit plugged his right nostril.

Damn...stuff smells like sweet piss...Glad they used an airway... damn.

The vibration from two reciprocal engines caused the metal pushing against his forehead to hurt. He felt warm blood oozing around his left eye, and his eye felt stuck shut.

Seaplane...must be a seaplane...old seaplane...Hands are numb.

He squirmed and wriggled his arms tied behind his back, trying loosen the tight ropes binding his wrists.

That's worse.

Charles gagged again. He felt a big hand clamp tight over his face, holding a sweet-smelling cloth.

Chloe...they're killing me...Chloe...Chloe.

The pain in his forehead drifted to black.

• • •

A polished black London taxi stopped in front of the tall, brick building on Moorgate Street. Ace climbed out and handed the driver a crisp one-hundred-dollar bill. He placed an Al Capone cigarillo in the gap and glanced up, looking at the sunlight reflecting from the golden windows on the top floor.

The mussed-haired man looked up from the head of the table then stood when Ace entered the room.

Joan from Toronto pushed her chair back and stood. So too, did Ahuja from Calcutta, Tan from Singapore, Matthew from St. Kitts, Veronica from Mexico City, Caswell from London, and finally, Ronald from South Africa.

Veronica began clapping. She was joined by everyone around the table except Ronald who simply glared at Ace.

"Job well done," the mussed-haired man proclaimed while shaking Ace's hand. "Have a seat," he said, pointing to the chair immediately to his right.

Ace lit the brown cigarillo and sat.

"You accomplished more in one day then we have in three years," Ahuja proclaimed with a big smile.

"Have them right where we want them," Caswell said.

"Yes, on their heels, dazed and confused," added Joan.

"I admit quite a feat, that," Tan said from the other side of the table. "Taking Fidel and Quinn out with their own security, damn good move."

"And the pilot who shot them down eliminating the evidence, brilliant," the mussed-haired man commented while lighting a fresh Camel.

"Like Oswald after the Kennedy thing," Caswell smirked.

"You think this is over?" Ronald said. "You think the True Believers are going to roll over and wave a little white flag? Idiots. Just because two old men are dead? Really, you think they will not come for us now?" He shook his head and glared again at Ace, before continuing, "I wanted to have a summit meeting with them, but no, you had to kill them. About as brilliant as shooting down a hornet's nest. Just brilliant."

Ace twirled a silver Zippo lighter on the wooden tabletop and watched it slowly twist to a stop, pointing at Ronald.

"You win," Ace said.

Ronald watched the cigarillo wag up and down with each syllable.

"Win what?"

"Haven't decided, but you're the winner, guaranteed," Ace said, while replacing the cigarillo.

"Before you arrived, Joan told us you have a hostage," Ronald said.

"Doctor Charles Fife. Son of Timothy Fife—a True Believer—and boyfriend of Chloe McMillen's."

"Brilliant, just brilliant," Ronald said, snapping his thumb nail on his front tooth.

"Where do you have this Charles Fife?"

Ace looked around the room before answering.

"Wawa."

"Where?"

"Wawa is in Ontario," Joan said sarcastically, "Canada."

"He's all tucked in at the Bristol Motel," Ace said, "in the company of three big fellows, old friends of mine, from Nigeria."

"I want him moved here," Ronald said, looking up and down the table. "Get him here, however the hell you do these things. Right here. We're going to need a shield…idiot."

The mussed-haired man fumbled for his cigarette lighter, watching Ace stare death at Ronald.

"Splendid idea, this," Caswell said, "best we have our asset close by to do our bidding."

"Such as?" Ace snapped.

"Such as, Evan, having him writing letters back to the folks at home," Caswell smirked.

Ace removed the smoldering Al Capone cigarillo from the gap, placed it on the table, and with his right forefinger, flicked the sweet smoke at the Englishmen.

"There was this tough kid in the twelfth grade, quarterback for the Panthers, real good-looking guy, all the girls fluttered their eyes around him. I believe he was the last one to call me Evan. Yup, pretty sure, his name was Mark. Died, he did, Caswell, when his Corvette brakes failed. Brand new red Corvette his rich daddy bought him as a graduation gift. So much sorrow."

Ace wedged a fresh cigarillo in place and smiled a cold smile at Caswell.

"Enough!" the mussed-haired man said.

"My point being, if we have our hostage here on the premises, we can more easily convince his cooperation, and if need be, he will be available to donate various body parts for the cause," Caswell retorted.

"Right!" Ronald agreed.

"Ace," the mussed-haired man said, blowing a fresh cloud from his lungs, "let's get young Doctor Fife here."

"Where do we keep him?"

"Your apartment," the mussed-haired man replied. And then he smiled at Ronald and Caswell.

Ace light the cigarillo.

"Take your best shot," he said in the direction of Ronald and Caswell.

He inhaled.

"Mark the quarterback did," Ace said, smoke puffing out with the words.

CHAPTER 45

EVIL WITNESSED

The XS-2 with Stanley, Danielle, Victor, and some of the Usual Suspects landed first, followed immediately by the XS-3 carrying Timothy, Carla, Moses, Debra, Dora, Katie with her four children, and the remainder of the Big Bay friends. They had been escorted by uniformed naval officers to an office building just north of the white fuel depots when XS-1 flew over and landed.

"Take a seat," Victor shouted, "I'll explain what's happened and our plans soon as Richard and Machete join us with Chloe."

Moses jumped from her seat first and ran, leaping at Machete. He caught her.

"How'd he do that?" Pete said to Wayne.

"Little Miss sees for him. Amazing."

"Do not eber do dat again, mister," Moses said, her nose pushing against Machete's nose, "never leave me alone like dat."

"I promise," Machete replied.

Chloe walked straight to Stanley and Danielle. They hugged for several seconds.

"I know what's happened," she told her parents, in a tone neither recognized.

"They'll find Charles," Stanley said.

"We sure will, Dad. And then all hell is going to break loose."

Mother and Father felt the transformation. The softness evaporated from her hazel eyes. The soft whispering quality of her twenty-two-year-old voice grew firm and chilled.

"Mom, they've killed my precious mentors, and they have the man I love. They've picked the wrong girl to mess with."

Chloe spotted Timothy and Carla standing near Debra and Dora.

"Be right back."

The whispering conversations stopped. Everyone in the room watched Chloe Norma McMillen lead her four friends to the far corner by themselves. The people from Big Bay watched the young lady they had known from birth put her arms over her friends' shoulders while she whispered. They watched Dora slump to her knees and Debra's body stiffen. They saw Carla bury her face on Timothy's chest and saw absolute anger streaming from Timothy's eyes as he looked out over his wife's head.

"Wonder what she said to them," Wayne said to Pete.

"Don't know, but by the look on Timothy's face, all hell is about to bust loose," Pete said.

Katherine Kennedy McGinnis sat in the back row, looking down the row at her children.

Doug would be so proud. We did the right thing. You were right, honey, they have been a joy from the very day we adopted them. Miss you so much.

Katie closed both eyes, her memory searching back to that awful afternoon, finding her husband, the man her parents never liked—*He's too old, what are you thinking? You're a Duke graduate, top of your law class. You and Garrison are a perfect couple. An alcoholic war vet; what are you thinking? This a Methodist preacher thing you're going through?*

She found Doug in the garage, slumped over the old rototiller.

'Auld Lang Syne.' We sang 'Auld Land Syne' at Poor Joe's…his favorite song.

Katie felt a deep aching growing in the center of her chest and the urge to stand. She stood, watching Dora slump to her knees.

Oh Jesus…please…please.

Chloe watched the red-haired lady from Boston walking toward her. Katie locked eyes with Chloe and felt the agony grow.

"Quinn and Fidel are dead," Chloe whispered.

Katie waved to a uniformed young man.

"Need a room," she said to him.

He pointed at a white door with a little window, and she said, "Thanks."

Dora looked up at Katie. She took Katie's hand and stood. The three widows, with Katie in the middle, her arms on Dora and Debra's shoulders, walked toward the white door.

"I think I'm going to throw up," Dora whispered.

The uniformed Navy person opened the door and saluted when the ladies walked past and then closed the door.

Help me, Jesus. Help me comfort my friends. I know the pain they have.

The big room became silent, except for the sounds of jet fighters taking off and landing.

Timothy and Victor met near a lectern in the front, by a big blackboard.

"We need to fill everyone in," Timothy said. "You do it, I can hardly talk."

"I'm sorry, Timothy. We'll find your son."

Timothy walked back to join his wife, and Victor went to the lectern.

"Today is a very sad day," Victor said; his voice cracking with each word. He paused, gripping the top of the lectern tightly. His eyes followed Chloe walk near from the far corner. She came close and hugged the Italian Godfather and gently moved him to the side.

Danielle squeezed Stanley's hand hard.

Chloe's hazel eyes glistened.

"Today we have witnessed evil. We have each seen it before, but today it is personal. Katie is with Dora and Debra in that room over there because their husbands were murdered today. Fidel's helicopter was shot down on the way to my graduation. Uncle Quinn was with him. We will never see them again."

Chloe paused and looked to her right, at her pale parents.

"My boyfriend, the man I have dreamed of marrying since the third grade...."

She stopped and looked at Timothy with his arm around Carla.

"...The same evil ones have kidnapped Charles."

She paused again and gulped a little before continuing.

"We will find him. The evil people who have done this have no idea."

Chloe stopped and looked searchingly at Victor.

Victor said, "Now we will grieve the loss of our dear friends. There will be a day of reckoning, and we will bring Charles home. Right now, I have associates from my many business connections...."

He paused.

"Well, to be honest, I have my personal security force headed to Big Bay. This afternoon a contingent of True Believers will arrive in Big Bay as well. I have spoken with Chief of Police Strait. By tonight, that city will be the most secure place on earth. There are two planes waiting outside, Quinn's Gulfstream and my Lear, fueled and ready to fly us all back to Big Bay. We will say goodbye as best we are able to Quinn and Fidel. Then we find Charles. We leave here at 3 p.m."

He turned just enough to hug Chloe and whispered, "We'll find him."

CHAPTER 46

HOLE IN THEIR WORLD

Stay close to me today, honey.

Katherine Kennedy McGinnis looked at her reflection in the mirror and adjusted her clerical robes. She closed her eyes, recalling Doug's hug before each Sunday sermon.

Doug...Janet Sue!

Katie reached forward and touched their images in the mirror before they faded.

Thank you, Lord.

• • •

Big Bay Central Methodist Church is a large, red, brick building. It was constructed in 1901 by German and Irish bricklayers from brick made at the Big Bay Brickworks. The clay came from the banks of the river near Poor Joe's Bar. The church provided an alternative, during the city's early years, for those immigrants not Catholic. Katie found that history amusing during the time she pastored Central Methodist.

"A Boston Irish Catholic girl turned Methodist."

• • •

Katie opened the side door and glanced to her left at the empty choir loft before walking to a chair behind the pulpit.

Katie watched the young lady with shoulder-length brunette hair walk down the center aisle, looking straight ahead, then up at Katie while climbing the steps. Chloe bent close to Katie.

Chloe is radiating.

"You go first, Katie. I'm still thinking."

Chloe sat in the upholstered chair next to Katie. Together they looked at the crowded pews, both in front and in both balconies, and at folks peering through the main entrance door and open side doors, standing in a cold October rain.

A distant siren sound ebbed and raised, over and over, vacillating through the fog.

Katie sucked in a deep breath and stood.

"I have no words. There are no words. No words exist which adequately describe the horrid blackness of grief and loss we feel here today."

Katie looked to her right, up into the balcony. Her Harvard Law School boyfriend (and former fiancé) sat in the front row, staring down at her, sitting in the very same location when he interrupted one of her first services, shouting, *"You could have been a renowned Wall Street lawyer. Look at you now; aren't you grand-looking in your robes, engaged to a worn out drunk!"*

Garrison.

Katie glance back at Chloe, panic in her blue eyes. Chloe stood, moving close to Katie, grasping her left hand behind the pulpit.

"The light and joy has been sucked from our souls," Katie said.

With her free hand, Chloe moved the microphone closer and began speaking.

"They are gone from our lives and we can hardly imagine the future without them here. Quinn and Fidel helped form my life and touched the lives of many here today. Our lives are better because they loved us."

Chloe paused while looking at her parents sitting in the front row.

"One of my father's favorite bands is the Eagles. After the horror of 9/11, that band came out with a special song and I remember my daddy sitting in his den, playing "Hole in the World," over and over. We are gathered in great sorrow today with a hole in our worlds and our hearts."

Chloe stepped back, staring at the packed sanctuary, before moving forward and putting her lips close to the microphone. Softly she sang,

"There's a hole in the world tonight.
There's a cloud of fear and sorrow.
There's a hole in the world tonight
Don't let there be a hole in the world tomorrow."

She paused and glanced toward Katie on her right before continuing,

"Amazing Grace, how sweet the sound,
That saved a wretch like me."

Katie moved close to the mic and sang harmony.

"I once was lost but now I'm found.
My chains are gone
I've been set free.
My God, my Savior has ransomed me
And like a flood His mercy rains.
Unending love. Amazing grace."

Many in the old brick church looked up toward the choir loft, convinced there was a third voice harmonizing. Wendell smiled, hearing Janet Sue's voice.

"That is Uncle Quinn's favorite verse. He's smiling, right now." Chloe looked out at the faces. "I asked Uncle Fidel one day while I drove him to Nueva Gerome for pizza in the Volkswagen he gave me for my sixteenth birthday, if he believed in God. 'How else do you explain all this beauty and wonder, Sis?' He called me Sis when we were alone. 'Yes, I believe in God, and Sis, I hope you love Him, too.' He told me it was all the religions fighting with each other that he despised."

She stared at her parents.

"They are with God now, free from time and religion. Our dear friends are where the colors have sounds and the sounds have colors. Richard Fortin told me he didn't want to come back; the sounds astounded him with the amazing feeling of love wrapped all around. Janet Sue said it is true. Our time will come. Our friends are waiting to greet us."

Chloe stopped speaking and looked at Charles' parents.

Richard Elmore Fortin winked at Chloe with his good eye from the second row.

"They are waiting to welcome us, and that is the only comfort we can take from this awful…."

Chloe looked to her left and then all around the massive sanctuary packed with faces looking back up at her.

"For now, all we can do is hug each other," Chloe concluded.

Chloe stepped back from the pulpit, then stepped close again and leaned down, her lips nearly touching the microphone.

"One of my favorite authors is C.S. Lewis. In great anguish following his wife's death, he wrote 'There are far, far better things ahead than we leave behind.' I believe that."

She stepped back and reached for Katie's hand.

Hand in hand, Chloe and Katie walked down the steps from the stage toward the entrance door.

Katie glanced to her right.

Garrison waved a little wave.

"I'm so happy you know Janet Sue," Katie said. "Not sure how many know who you were talking about."

"They can ask," Chloe said.

The ladies released hands, stopping at the main entrance. They turned to greet the mourners lining up to leave.

"You know she was Wendell's girlfriend."

"Wendell told me about her, that she died in a car accident—he was driving her home on Prom night—and that he enlisted with the Marines one month after graduation. He told me she saved his life while he was in Vietnam."

Katie smiled at the parishioners approaching.

"She saved Doug's life in Vietnam, too. He told me Janet Sue wrapped her arms around him during a vicious ambush. Most of his platoon died that day," Katie said. "He never understood why she protected him. I did."

"I think we are her assignment," Chloe said. She paused then said, "The eighth of November, 1965."

Shivers, for a second, traveled Katie's skin.

"I listened to Doug and Wendell talk while I did my homework in the corner booth."

Katie watched Chloe shake hands with a stooped-over old man, depending on a cane. She watched Chloe take the cane from his boney hand and while they hugged, Chloe kissed the top of his head.

CHAPTER 47

A NEED

Moses and Machete sat on the edge of their wrinkled bed in their apartment on the second story of Poor Joe's bar.

"I need something," Machete said quietly, "in Mexico City."

"What be dat?"

Machete hesitated.

Moses scooched closer until their naked thighs touched.

"We promised dere be no secrets," she whispered firmly.

"When I was young, I lived in a lean-to I built on the back wall of Fausto's Grocery store."

"You told me dat."

"I buried a cane knife under it…wrapped a machete in burlap and buried it. I need it."

Moses studied her husband's face.

"It be rusty now."

Machete nodded *yes*.

"I need it."

"How we get dere?"

Machete turned his face toward Moses.

"Yes, I be going wid you."

"I will ask Victor Bonifacio in the morning for help."

● ● ●

"That was the shortest funeral I've ever attended," Stanley said, standing on the condo deck, looking down in the darkness at the lights shining in Big Bay. He turned enough to watch Danielle walking from the kitchen with a glass of red wine in one hand and a golden glass of Basil Hayden's, with one large ice cube, in the other hand.

"It was a memorial service, honey."

"Right." Stanley took a long sip and looked at the glass.

"Chloe astounds me, the way she connects with people," Stanley said. "I think she hugged everyone going out that door. They lined up for a hug. Damn, we have a special daughter, Danielle."

"I'm worried about her," Danielle said.

"About what?"

"Don't know if you noticed, but after the sanctuary emptied, I watched Chole and Machete walk to the balcony and sit alone. They talked for at least ten minutes and then they stood and shook hands. Why would they shake hands, Stan? A hug, I'd understand, but they shook hands."

Stanley took a long sip, emptying his glass.

• • •

"MY BABY...THEY HAVE MY BABY!" Carla screamed up at Timothy, pummeling his chest with both fists, over and over. Timothy's jaw muscles quivered. He pulled her close with his left arm and rubbed her back with his right arm stub, staring over her head at the black and white picture on their wall, the three of them, taken last Christmas next to the tree.

Year and a half, eighteen months before I had her back. Thank God for Machete driving her around, her body guard. Call Danielle... and Katie. Help us Jesus, help us.

Timothy leaned back a little and peered into his wife's searching eyes, her pupils dilated, only a tiny ring of blue around the circumference.

He sighed a deep sigh and emptied his lungs through pursed lips.

"Meeting Tuesday morning, honey, Bonifacio, Rose, and the guys, the True Believers, will all be here. We're going to find him. Going with them. I'll find our son."

"I love those guys," Carla said, wiping at the dripping from her nose with her forefinger and thumb.

"You find my baby and then you kill the bastards."

"Yes, dear."

● ● ●

Timothy stood next to Dora in Poor Joe's kitchen, relighting the gas pilot lights, when Victor Bonifacio entered through the front door with a younger man following. Timothy walked past the cash register and extended his hand toward the younger man.

"Arturo Rossi! It's great to see you!" Timothy said.

Arturo smiled and extended his hand. "Didn't know that you'd remember me."

"Never forget that night. I was a new patrolman and you a scared seventeen-year-old driving around St. Paul using an Italian driver's license in a Camaro with a tail light out."

Victor listened and smiled.

"I have never forgotten your kindness, Mister Fife. You took me to the Minnesota Secretary of State office the next Monday and vouched for me passing a driver's test. I have never forgotten."

"Call me Timothy."

"Yes, sir."

"Arturo is my chief of staff," Victor said.

"Congratulations, Arturo. The last I knew, you were a busboy at The Sicilian."

"Thank you, Timothy. I am honored and fortunate."

Timothy and Victor turned, watching Machete walk down the stairs, followed by Moses and Little Miss.

"His vision is back, since the operation," Timothy said, "it's not public knowledge."

"Miracle; praise Jesus." Victor said, turning to Arturo. "You are about to meet a miracle, in more ways than you can imagine."

Victor embraced Moses and then Machete.

"I have a need," Machete said.

"I'm listening," Victor replied.

"Need to get me back to Mexico City for something before we rescue Charles."

Moses stepped closer and grasped Victor's hand.

Victor pondered with a quizzical scrunched expression.

"What?" Victor asked.

"Da machete he used," Moses said, pulling Victor closer. "He be *sans peur* wid dat machete."

Victor glanced at Arturo.

"French for fearless," Arturo said.

"Speaks seven languages," Victor said.

Timothy smiled.

Victor shook his head and replied, "Fearless, I like fearless. We'll need to refuel in New Orleans down and back."

He glanced at the Martinek's Jewelers clock in the far wall.

"If we leave at ten, we'll be back tonight."

Arturo shook Machete's hand then nodded at a gathering of men standing on the sidewalk, six men wearing black berets embossed with a golden lion.

"We trust them with our lives, every day. Hope you don't mind if they travel with us."

"Dat be jus fine," Moses said.

Arturo turned enough to look at the little lady from Guadalupe. Moses released Victor's hand and stepped toward Arturo.

"My name be Moses," she said, shaking Arturo's hand.

Arturo's brown eyes twinkled.

"Never met a Moses before," he said.

"Just wait until you know her," Timothy said.

"Yup," Victor said. He glanced at the wall clock again. "Let's get to the airport."

• • •

"Danielle, please look after Carla while I'm out of town." Timothy said, standing in Poor Joe's red phone booth.

"You're going with the True Believers?"

"Yes."

"Stanley said he's going, too. I'll try to convince her to stay with me, but no matter what, between Chloe and Katie, we'll never leave her alone."

"Thank you, Danielle. I love you."

"Love you, Timothy. Go find your son."

CHAPTER 48

LEGEND FROM IZTAPALAPA

Moses watched the expressions change on Machete's face as he gazed through the black GMC Suburban's thick glass windows, driving past the main Big Bay airport entrance to the private terminal.

We be blessed by de miracle. I love you, Jesus.

Next to Victor Bonifacio's Lear Jet, the True Believer's XS-1 helicopters idled.

Surrounding the plane and the helicopter stood twelve men dressed in black, wearing red berets embossed with golden lions. More men stood around a large Quonset hut, holding automatic weapons, wearing black berets.

"Did not mean to be such a trouble, amigo," Machete said to Victor, in the front seat.

"This is not a trouble, my friend. We are about to embark on a mission with heart-breaking consequences should we fail."

Victor shifted his eyes to Moses' proud face then at Little Miss's head on Machete's lap.

"You need this special machete, well, we get your special machete, simple as that; not a problem."

The Suburban came to a stop ten yards from the sleek, wide, stealth helicopter. A tall young man with a submachine gun strapped to his back opened Machete's door and stood back, saluting.

"Going in the helicopter?" Machete asked.

Victor nodded *yes*.

"We'll be in and out, and they'll never know; Mexican Air Force would see our Lear."

Moses smiled. "Imbissable. I like dat," she said to no one in particular while entering the flying machine. She hesitated just long enough to run her hand on the soft, black surface, rubbing it and then patting it several times.

"Imbissable."

●●●

They listened while sitting on the smooth, wooden bench beside Amigo's Cantina's rusty screen door, two old men smoking cigars, leaning over a little green metal table, playing dominos and five young men, passing a bottle of El Toro back and forth. They listened to the *chop…chop…chopping* sounds growing louder and then feeling the concussive vibrations before the afternoon sunlight was momentarily blocked.

The old men stopped the domino game, and one reached for the El Toro. The young men stood and watched with their bravest faces.

XS-1 gently landed at the intersection of San Lucas and Victoria Streets between Fausto's Grocery Store and Amigo's Cantina.

The side door lowered into a puff of dust.

"That is Machete Juarez!" shouted one old man.

"You are right, I think!" shouted the other old man, watching Machete walk down the incline, flanked by Little Miss and Moses, with twelve men following, some with red berets and some wearing black berets.

The helicopter rotors slowed to a gentle turning, and the twin turbines idled to a whispering whine.

"Who is this Machete?" asked one young man.

"Perhaps you will meet him and perhaps not. He is a legend from Iztapalapa," the old man holding the El Toro said.

"Yeah, right."

"Perhaps your fortune will hold young man, and you will not meet Machete," said the other old man, reaching for the nearly empty bottle of tequila.

Fausto's back door opened.

"Who be dis woman?" Moses asked, watching the lady with long black hair walking rapidly toward them.

"Rosa Fausto," Machete replied.

"Oh, dat be Rosa! Da friend of dat girl you married for a while."

"Rosa is my best good friend. She taught me much."

Moses stood aside and watched her husband silently embrace the tall, slender lady with shoulder-length black hair.

Without speaking, Rosa released Machete and leaned down, hugging Moses.

"My Uncle Miguel died three months ago with a cancer," Rosa said.

"I am sorry," Machete said. "He changed my life."

"He helped many," Rosa replied, "but he was proud of you, Marco. He loved you, I think. He spoke of you often and wondered why you did not visit."

"My husband do da best he can," Moses said.

They walked together to the lean-to.

"It has a new canvas!" Machete exclaimed.

"Yes, Uncle had the canvas replaced twice a year. He told me you may need it someday."

Machete smiled.

"I am here for my machete."

Rosa's complexion blanched pale.

Machete pushed aside the canvas hanging over the lean-to entrance and crawled inside.

"Why does he want that cane knife?" Rosa asked Moses.

"He call it de reckoning. Dere 'bout to be de reckoning."

Rosa nodded. "I understand."

Machete came out on his hands and knees. He stood.

The twelve True Believers surrounding the helicopter watched. Both helicopter pilots watched from their cockpit. Victor Bonifacio watched from the open 'copter door. The two old men and five young men watched from Amigo's bench. Slowly Machete unwound the layers of dusty, brown burlap, around and around. Then he held the shining machete high above his head and smiled.

Rosa smiled a little painful smile.

The curly-headed bastard who raped me met his reckoning.

"You see that cane knife?" the old man said to the young men. "Trust me, this is as close as you want to be."

"Right," slurred the young man at the very end of the bench.

"His given name is Marco, son to Lilliana the prostitute," the old man holding the empty bottle of 80 proof El Toro said. "He earned the name Machete; that is all I will tell you, young Raul. He earned that name."

Machete turned and hugged Rosa.

"You render justice, my friend, and then you come back for a visit. We will go to Uncle's grave and you apologize for not visiting him."

Machete nodded and reached for Moses' hand.

Rosa watched Machete, hand in hand with Moses, walk up the ramp and into the helicopter with Little Miss following.

Marco always has loved dogs.

The men from the bench protected their faces from the dusty wind, watching the helicopter rise straight up above the trees then point north and accelerate out of site, the *chop...chop...chopping* sounds becoming faint and then fading away completely.

CHAPTER 49

SCARED AND HUMBLE

"I was engaged once, before I met Quinn," Debra said.

"What happened?" Chloe asked.

"Johnny was a med student. We met in college. I loved that man."

Kind blue eyes wide open…curled on the floor.

"He died from a drug overdose. I believe he was murdered. Never could prove it and I don't know why. I'm certain he never used drugs until that day. I quit college and drove to Seattle and joined the D.E.A. Told the mousey little fellow behind the desk I hated drug dealers, and I passed all their tests. Would never have met Quinn if I hadn't been with the D.E.A.; met in Alaska, helping Belvia get out of a bad situation, her and her children. I was investigating Belvia's husband, who it turns out was a big-time drug dealer and scumbag."

"What happened to her husband?"

"Dead in a cartel submarine. The Gulf of Mexico."

"Every time I watched you and Quinn together, I felt love."

Debra smiled.

"I adored Quinn, and he adored me. He was the most honest human being I've met, and kindest. Under his crust, Quinn was a marshmallow. He loved you, Chloe, and was so very proud of you."

Debra stood.

"You want a warm-up?"

"Sure."

Chloe watched Debra walk to Poor Joe's big silver coffee urn then return with both mugs spilling over the lips with each step.

"Quinn dragged me back from the brink of deep depression and despair," Debra continued, "and that's the reason I'm going to be at the meeting Tuesday night and the reason I'm going with them to find Charles."

Debra raised her sweatshirt just enough to expose a .38 Special holstered on her belt.

"I'm going to shoot the bastards that killed my husband."

Chloe dropped her chin and stared at the gun.

"What?" Debra asked.

"Like you did to the guy Doctor Blue called Wire-rim on St. Kitts?"

"Like the guy Doctor Blue called Wire-rim."

"Sitting next to Katie, looking out at the grief, and trying to come up with the words to say…I watched my grieving parents holding hands. I saw the fear and agony in Carla's eyes and felt the anger coming from Timothy," Chloe said, stirring cream into her coffee.

"The coffee is better in Cuba," Chole said, and then continued. "It's all I can do to keep my mind from imploding, Deb. They've taken the only man I've been in love with, and it's my fault, they wanted me."

Chloe sipped from the coffee mug and looked over the brim at Debra.

"So, I've decided I'm going with them. I'll go to the meeting with you. And I'm going with them to find my Charles."

"Chloe, you don't realize how this can go down. You really don't. And, to be honest, you really don't know this evil world."

Chloe smiled.

"This is the first time I have said this, Deb. I was raised to be humble, but this is the truth. I have a Ph.D. and a Masters. I studied military tactics for four years and marveled at the stupidity and occasional brilliance."

She paused.

"No offense intended."

"None taken, but you need to know there is no substitute for flight time. Richard told me that and it's true."

"And besides," Chloe continued, "Machete and I have a plan."

"Figured Machete was going."

"Yup, poor blind Machete," Chloe said softly, "and I'll have you at my side with your thirty-eight."

"That's a guess," Debra said.

Chloe grinned. She lifted her blouse a little.

"Gift from Fidel on my twenty-first birthday. Guess who taught me to shoot it."

"Quinn."

"I practiced every day for months. You know what he told me a couple of weeks ago…that the only person he knew better than me is you."

Chloe looked at the dark stain on the hardwood floor then pointed.

"Dad told me that is blood from the night Machete shot a cartel hitman planting a bomb under the cash register."

"Quinn gave me a tour one night, pointing out the buckshot holes over there by the bar and the stains in the hallway by the men's room where Machete was shot by a deranged high school boy hiding in the bathroom," Debra said.

With her head still facing down, Chloe moved her eyes up to Debra's face.

"To be completely honest, Deb, this stuff makes me sick to my stomach. I hate violence; it's so senseless."

Debra nodded.

"I've never seen my parents fight. I've never been in a battle, except in debate, and that was easy. I need your help."

"There's the humble girl I know," Debra said.

"I want the man I adore safe, and I want to be there when he's rescued."

Chloe paused.

"I'm scared to death."

"We'll go to the meeting together," Debra said.

Chloe straightened up in her chair and watched her reflection in the Goebel mirror.

"How'd you feel after you shot Wire-rim?"

"I felt grateful for the opportunity to destroy evil." She sipped the hot coffee before continuing, "the secret, Chloe, is never let them know you're scared."

CHAPTER 50

LET'S MAKE A DEAL

The wooden chair back rested against the head of the long table in Poor Joe's bar, tilted forward with a worn, brown fishing vest draped over it. Quinn O'Malley's favorite cigar, a HOYO de MONTER-REY lay beside a polished white ashtray. And next to the ashtray, an open matchbook from his favorite restaurant, El Siboney.

A *CLOSED* sign dangled from Poor Joe's front door, flapping around in the chilly evening breeze.

Pete, followed by Wayne, walked down the worn wooden stairs from their apartments. They hesitated, touching the fishing vest reverently, before taking a seat. Seven minutes later, Victor Bonifacio entered through the side door, followed by Arturo Rossi. Victor's jaw muscles tightened when he glanced at the head of the table then walked to the far end and took his customary seat, motioning Arturo to sit on his left.

Rose Jackson opened the front door. She stopped at the shrine, placed both hands on the chair back, and stood, looking down the table at Victor, for several silent minutes. Then she took her seat on the right of Victor, next to the chair used by Fidel the few times he had been in Big Bay.

Richard Elmore Fortin entered Poor Joe's with the sound of a helicopter pulsating above the old building. He approached Quinn's chair, leaned down, and kissed the vest.

Timothy and Stanley arrived together. They touched the ragged vest on the way to their chairs. Big Bay Chief of Police Larry Strait followed, pausing at the chair, making the sign of the cross before sitting.

Everyone looked toward the back, up at the stairs, and watched Moses then Machete walk down from their apartment. Moses stood back a little, her brown eyes observing her husband approach the vest. Machete leaned over and pressed his forehead against the vest. When he rose, a red impression in the shape of a cross appeared on his skin.

"Just received this letter twenty minutes ago," Timothy said. "Delivered by a private courier; no return address."

He opened a manila folder and fingered a white envelope.

●●●

Debra drove east past Poor Joe's and at the Grant Street intersection made a U-turn, parking on the opposite side of Union Street.

"What have you told your mom?" Debra asked Chloe.

"That building has been part of my life for as long as I remember," Chloe said. "It's the place Machete saw me riding on Wendell's back. Poor Joe's is the place I fell in love with Charles. We made a pact in the corner booth when I was thirteen to someday be married."

Chloe stared through the car window at the white, clapboard, two-story building, and the rusty white metal sign suspended above the front door.

"Can hardly read the sign," Chloe said, looking at *POOR JOE'S* faded green letters, the P hidden in the rust.

"You didn't answer my question."

Chloe shook her head *no.*

"Your dad is going to be in there."

"I know."

"Excuse me ladies, Poor Joe's is closed this evening," said the man dressed completely in black. He walked toward them from the shadow of a big Sycamore tree.

Chloe looked at his Thompson submachine gun and tilted her head a little, listening to the circling helicopter.

Debra nodded in the direction of the parking lot and seven black SUVs.

"Look down Basswood," she said, pointing at twelve armored SUVs all in a row, blocking both lanes at the intersection.

"Thank you, sir," Chloe said to the young man. "My name is Chloe McMillen. This is Debra Jean O'Malley, wife of Quinn O'Malley. We are attending this meeting of the True Believers."

The young man stepped back and studied Debra's face, briefly.

"I apologize, Mrs. O'Malley, didn't recognize you in this light. I am sorry for your loss."

The young man escorted Debra and Chloe to the front door. He walked up the steps and opened the door with the *CLOSED* sign and saluted a stiff salute.

●●●

"It's a note from Charles," Timothy said.

"Had it analyzed for prints, paper type and ink analysis. No prints. Ink is from a typewriter ribbon commonly used in Europe. The paper was manufactured in Poland," Chief Strait said.

The front door opened. The people at the long table watched a True Believer enter, hold the door open with his back, and salute while Debra and Chloe walked past.

Stanley started to stand. Rose firmly pulled on his shirt, sitting him back in the chair.

Dora entered Poor Joe's through the kitchen entrance. She and the True Believer who had escorted her watched from the kitchen.

They approached the shrine, side by side. Debra ran both hands down the back of the chair, feeling her husband's vest. She pushed her shoulder against Chloe and looked up at her.

The eyes around the table watched Debra's lips move next to Chloe's right ear, but their ears heard not a sound. Chloe's youthful jaw clinched.

They watched, from both sides of the long table, Debra pull her husband's chair back and remove the vest. Debra gently kissed the vest and then took Chloe's right hand and slipped the vest over her arm and then the left arm. Then Debra pulled the chair back and sat in it. She motioned for Chloe to sit in the chair immediately to her right.

"Ladies and gentlemen, Quinn knew this day would come," Debra said. "He told me several times he believed Chloe to the best hope for leading the True Believers into the future. I plan on teaching her everything I know. Victor and Rose agree."

Debra paused, and her eyes darted to Chloe's face. The astonished expression made her smile a little.

Victor Bonifacio nodded to Chloe from the opposite end of the long table.

Rose Jackson reached under the table and grasped Stanley's hand, feeling cold, trembling fingers.

The sound of Dora clapping in the kitchen drifted into the bar, at first a soft, timid clap, then firm and confidant. Richard Elmore Fortin stood and joined Dora.

Then everyone at the table stood and clapped.

Stanley stood, clapping, looking at his daughter sitting next to Debra.

Chloe looked all around, at each face, then fixed her eyes on Stanley, and she winked at her father.

Ring-ring…ring-ring…ring-ring…ring-ring…ring-ring…ring-ring…ring-ring.

Dora pushed the red phone booth's folding-door open.

"Hello, Poor Joe's."

"Yes. I'll check."

Leaning out, holding the door open with her thigh, Dora shouted down the hall.

"Some guy is asking for Chloe."

Debra's body stiffened.

Chloe looked at her father.

"Take the call," Victor said. "Mostly just listen."

Chloe took the receiver from Dora.

"Hello?"

"Chloe Norma McMillen?"

"Who's asking?"

"You can call me Henry," the mussed-haired man replied.

"Why are you calling me, Henry?"

"Wondering how I knew where to find you?"

"I've always been amazed by the ingenuity of perverts. I assume you are a pervert, Henry. This conversation is over."

"Hanging up will be Charles' death sentence."

Chloe struggled to gasp air. She looked through the smudged phone booth glass at the faces from the table and at her daddy.

Dad…help.

"You know that would be your death sentence, Henry."

"How 'bout we play *Let's Make a Deal,* Chloe. Here's how it works. I make an offer and you find out which body part your boyfriend donates should you refuse."

The mussed-haired man listened to Chloe breathing in the mouthpiece.

"You still there, Miss McMillen?"

"I'm listening."

"I want you to arrange a meeting with Victor Bonifacio. He trusts you. Tell him The Committee wants a summit meeting. Tell Victor I'll have a representative meet him next Wednesday in New York at the hot dog stand outside the Grand Central Terminal on 42nd and Park Avenue. High noon. Alone."

"Guess what, Henry, I'm not playing your game."

"You're going to do exactly as you're told, Miss McMillen. Guess which body part your sweetheart will be donating next Wednesday? You do this or get ready for a penis on ice."

Her lungs again refused to suck air, except in little gasps.

"That, Henry, will be your death sentence. They never saw us coming on the Suriname Destroyer. Trust me, that was a pleasant way to die."

Click.

Chloe walked down the hallway, stepping over the faded, dark blood stain in the hardwood floor and over the buckshot holes never filled, toward the wondering faces. She sat next to Debra and exhaled.

"That was from someone on The Committee." Chloe said. "He seemed to be in charge. Called himself Henry."

"What'd he want?" Victor asked.

"He wanted to play mind games. I told him to go to hell," Chloe answered, staring at Victor's face.

CHAPTER 51

THEY DON'T USUALLY KILL NUNS

Doctor Charles Fife watched Ace squeeze a cigarillo into the gap and wiggle it up and down with his tongue before lighting it.

"Smoke bother you?"

"Not at all. Just picturing you on your death bed, gasping for a satisfying breath," Charles retorted.

"Well, Doctor, we're all gonna die. 'Pick your poison,' my grandpa always said. He lived to be 94, hating the last four or five. He shouda' enjoyed these."

He flicked some ash, watching it drop to the floor.

"We're in London," Charles said, looking out the window, down at the city below and Big Ben on the horizon.

"Very good, Charles. You don't mind I call you Charles, do you?"

"Charles is my name. What name are you using today?"

"Ace. You should call me Ace."

"That's about right, kidnapped by a degenerate, being held prisoner in a London skyscraper. Kinda sounds like a James Bond movie, Ace."

"You think about death much, there Charles. I mean, you being a doc and all, seeing all sorts of ways to die; you ever think about your demise?"

Charles shook his head *no*.

"More focused of the joy of living, Ace."

"Well, Charles, you might want to ponder the alternative in case this adventure goes south and we start sending your body parts back to the States in baggies."

Charles shrugged.

"Just keep writing those nice little notes to Big Bay, and we'll see," Ace sneered.

"Mind loosening these handcuffs?"

"Yup."

"You have no idea what you have unleased."

"That's what I've been told. Now, be a good boy and write me a nice note, expressing your great love and concern for Chloe."

Ace replaced the cigarillo.

"And, never call me a degenerate again," Ace said, pointing the flame from his butane lighter in Charles' direction.

"Want to guess what body part we'll send to sweet Chloe first?"

● ● ●

Timothy looked down the table at Chloe and opened the letter.

"This was dated yesterday," Timothy said. "Have no idea when it was actually written; there's no postmark."

Timothy took a deep breath then scowled. He read from the creased white paper, "'Dear father, Love to you, mother, and Chloe. On my way to the graduation I was kidnapped by an organization known to you as The Committee. Now I am being held, pending resolution of several ultimatums which will be forthcoming. Do not despair, father, these are reasonable people. Only when all of these demands are satisfied will I be released. Never fear, father; hopefully I will see you all soon.' It's signed Charles."

Timothy laid the white page on the worn, wooden table, rubbed at the paper creases tenderly before looking up.

"Not certain this was written by my son," he said.

"Why would you think that?" Victor asked.

"Has never addressed me as father," Timothy replied, "and it's not his style. He doesn't write like this. This is too mechanical or something. Doesn't feel like my son."

Chloe stretched her arm over the table in Timothy's direction.

"Let me see," she said.

"It's typed, Chloe," Timothy said.

Chloe smiled at Timothy.

"On a mechanical Royal typewriter, built around 1930, verified by letter indentation," Victor Bonifacio said.

Timothy passed the letter down the table to Chloe. She held it with both hands as if holding a holy scripture.

"He calls me Barbie…our secret. I'm Barbie, and he's Mister Dillon, after Marshal Dillon. Charles loves watching reruns of Gunsmoke," Chloe said to no one in particular. She held the letter gently.

From each side of the long table they watched her read the letter, put it down, then pick it up and read it again, twice more, before reaching in her purse for a blue ink pen.

The fourth time she read, she paused and made little circles on the paper. Then she looked up and exclaimed, "HE'S IN LONDON!"

Victor stared down the length of the table.

"How'd you know that?" Wayne asked.

"The first letter of each sentence," Chloe said, holding the letter up so everyone could see the circled letters. "The first letter of each sentence spells LONDON. That's why it feels mechanical, Timothy. Charles spelled his location."

Victor cleared his throat. Timothy simply started at Chloe.

Rose felt Stanley's subtle quivers.

"The Committee has been hiding in plain sight in London for five years," Victor said. "That syndicate built a new skyscraper on Moorgate Street, using the London security and street cameras as a shield. Amused the hell out of Quinn."

"You think they have Charles in that building?" Chloe asked.

"Most likely."

"How do we make certain?" Timothy asked.

"We have to get inside," Arturo said.

Victor looked at Arturo and nodded yes.

"I imagine that easier said than done," Timothy said, "and not sure an acceptable risk," the former Green Beret said, shaking his head back and forth. "I want my son back alive."

Silence in Poor Joe's Bar, except the *tick...toc...tick...*from the Martinek's clock on the wall and the hiss of steam escaping through the little hole in the top of the coffee urn.

"They have Mass every Sunday morning," Debra said. "It amused Quinn to no end that the scumbags built a chapel and hold Mass. When he and Fidel jousted about religion, Fidel would suggest they fly to London for Sunday Mass on Moorgate Street."

"How you know dis?" Moses inquired.

"Father O'Connor was a friend of Quinn's. They worked together as bouncers at a bar in Dublin. I think Quinn called it the Greene Dragon...many years ago. He told Quinn about the beautiful chapel on the 25th floor and the generous monthly tithing."

"Does that priest know who they are?" Pete asked, incredulously.

"Quinn never told him; thought it better. 'Might be useful to have inside eyes, someday,' Quinn said."

"Where be dis priest's church?" Moses asked.

"Holy Apostles. Archdiocese of Westminster," Debra replied.

"Den I need to be dar, dis church of de Holy Apostles. I be de nun and help de Holy Father wid de Masses."

Machete's dark pupils dilated.

No...no...no.

"You gid me to dis Holy Apostles an' make me meet dis Father O'Connor, I go wid him to da Masses an' see," Moses continued, now pointing at Victor.

"Moses, that's a high-risk proposition. They'll investigate everything about you...they leave no stone unturned," Victor replied.

"Let dem turn de damn stone dey like," Moses said. "I be Sister Mary Moses from de Holy Trinity of Guadeloupe. Dey can check dem records. An' raised by de holy nuns, too."

Machete's shoulders slumped a little, and his body shuddered. Moses slapped him in the middle of his back.

"Dey don't offen' kill nuns, honey."

CHAPTER 52

SEPSIS

"Ace."

"Yes, Doctor Fife."

"These cuffs are cutting into my wrists. Developing an infection here."

"Tough."

"Seriously, Ace, let me explain it to you in laymen's terms. The tight metal is cutting off the blood supply, and my flesh is rotting and there is puss. If you don't loosen these cuffs, I could lose my right hand."

"That'd be the first body part we send," Ace sneered.

"I need hands to type your damn letters."

"Use the other, you got two."

"It's infected, too. Won't be long and you'll be doing the typing.

"Can't type."

"Didn't think so."

Ace walked from the leather couch and studied Charles' wrists then bent over and sniffed.

"Jeeze, they stink."

"My point, exactly, Ace."

Ace retrieved a small handcuff key from his jacket pocket and loosened first the right cuff then the left.

"That better?"

"Hope so," Charles replied. "I need some hydrogen peroxide and betadine."

"Where the hell am I gonna get that stuff?"

"The drug store down there," Charles said, nodding out the window at the red neon *SUPERDRUG* sign at the end of the block.

"Oh."

"How's the committee you work for going to take the news their prisoner has died from sepsis."

"From what?"

"Infection…blood poisoning."

Ace unfolded a white piece of paper and pushed it on the table toward Charles.

"Tell the folks back home this stuff. Tell them it's not negotiable."

"Big word, Ace."

Charles read the note then scooted his chair to the typewriter.

Dear father, Seems there is only one demand. Only one, father. Seriously, the True Believers must promise to never interfere with The Committee's business enterprises again, or, regardless of the time lapsed, they will hunt me down and assassinate me. Charles. P.S.: reply by calling this cell number. Do not attempt a rescue. I will be executed.

"There you go, Ace," Charles said, pulling the paper from the typewriter roller.

Ace looked at a yellow smear on the bottom of the letter.

"What's this?"

"Puss. Get me these things at the drug store," Charles said, typing the words hydrogen peroxide and betadine. "I'm serious here, Ace. People die from infections every day, and I'm not feeling so good."

Ace pressed his nicotine-stained fingers against Charles' forehead.

"You're hot."

"No kidding. Your bosses aren't going be very happy when I'm a corpse."

"They are not my bosses."

"The Committee, then."

"I'll go tonight after dark."

"Sooner the better, Ace. I'm burning up."

"After dark. That's the rule; no one leaves until after dark."

"Hope I make it that long."

"Me, too, there Doctor Fife," Ace replied, squeezing a fresh cigarillo into the gap.

He flicked the lighter six times. On the seventh time Ace looked through the yellow flame at Charles' face. "Me, too."

CHAPTER 53

SATURDAY NIGHT

"I lose our son," Timothy said, "if we fail."

Chloe's eyes stared, without blinking, at his mouth when he said the words.

"If we fail, I lose the man I adore and have loved since seventh grade," Chloe said.

Timothy gulped.

Stanley swallowed hard several times.

"We need a plan A and plan B, Victor," Chloe continued. "Let's start with plan A."

Chloe nodded at Moses and said, "Debra has met Father O'Connor on several occasions."

Debra looked down the table at Moses and Machete. "I'll introduce Moses to O'Connor and share with him the nature of our mission."

"You trust him?" Victor asked.

"He was a good friend to Quinn. I do."

"Then what?" Richard Elmore Fortin inquired.

"Then we have Moses assist the good Father with the weekly Masses. Maybe she learns something, maybe not," Debra said resolutely. "It's a start, Richard, and low risk."

"They have a confessional in that chapel?" Arturo wondered out loud.

"Don't know. Wouldn't that be nice," Debra replied.

"Dat I find out!" Moses exclaimed.

"Team Alpha will accompany Moses, incognito," Arturo continued. "Except for the time she is in the committee's building, they will have eyes on her."

Machete stood and placed his right hand on Moses' shoulder and squeezed.

He be scared…de fingers shaky.

Moses looked up at her husband.

"I WILL be going with her, a blind street beggar with a leader dog on that very street," Machete said, looking at his wife's face.

"Not a good idea," Victor said.

Machete snarled, "Yes, it is a very good idea, amigo." He took his right hand from his wife's shoulder and reached down.

The cane knife made a soft metallic swishing sound coming from Machete's leg sheath. He placed the polished blade on the wooden table. The reflection from the bar lights illuminated his face when he tipped the blade toward him.

"It is a very good idea, Victor. It is for this reason Machete was born. This very time is the reason I still live…." And he made the sign of the cross.

Machete turned his face toward Chloe.

"…To bring him home to you, and to keep my wife safe," Machete said. He sat.

Chloe reached to her right and curled her fingers around Machete's forearm.

"You are going," she said, looking directly at Victor.

Victor stared back at her then mouthed a silent OK.

"We'll fly you to London tomorrow," Victor said, looking at Richard. "I'll make some calls to get you through Customs."

"What about plan B?" Stanley asked. He walked to the hissing coffee urn.

"Here's plan B." Victor looked at Arturo. "If things go south in London, should plan A implode, if Moses' mission is discovered, if Machete blows this blind beggar thing, if Father O'Connor is tight with The Committee and spills the beans…if Charles is executed… when we are certain hope is gone….”

Victor Bonifacio paused and glanced at Timothy's pale face.

“…plan B is flying the Ghost Wing from the Havana bunker and when we reach London, blowing that building on Moorgate Street off the face of the earth. That is plan B, Stanley.”

Chloe looked at Debra's face then her father's.

“What be dis ghost wing?” Moses asked.

“We have a plane, the only one, designed and built for us by a private German aeronautical engineering group. It is invisible to all radars and capable of flying up to Mach 5.”

“What be dat?”

“Five times the speed of sound,” Richard said. “Almost four thousand miles an hour, Moses. We can get to London from Havana in one hour and twenty minutes.”

“Richard named the plane,” Victor continued. “We used it to sink a Suriname battleship. No one saw it coming, no one saw us leave. Just like a ghost.”

“Oh, imbissable, like de helicopters.”

Victor smiled. “We keep it in a deep, secure, bomb-proof bunker. Only four people have the code to open the bunker door.” He took a deep breath. “Well, two of us now, Richard and myself,” he continued, looking at Chloe and Debra. He stood and removed a small slip of paper from his vest pocket. Victor walked to the bar for a coffee saucer. Carefully, he placed the slip of paper on the saucer and poured a tiny splash of vodka on the paper. Quickly, he returned to the table and placed the saucer in front of Chloe and Debra.

“Got it?” he asked.

“Got it,” the ladies replied in unison.

Then everyone at the table watched Victor walk to the kitchen and toss the wet slip of paper on the gas range, listening to it sizzle for an instant before it became nothing.

"Sorry Dad, I didn't know all that was going to happen to-night," Chloe said, riding in the passenger seat of Stanley's Avanti.

Stanley drove up the dark hill, staring though the wet wind-shield. He glanced in the rearview at the headlights following.

"You need a new wiper on this side."

"You're going to tell your mother...tonight...when she gets home from Carla's. No way I'm telling her."

"Mom reads you like a book, Dad."

"I know."

"I'll talk to her."

● ● ●

Danielle watched them from the living room for a short while. She poured a glass of white wine and watched a little longer.

"I think I'll join you," Danielle said, opening the sliding glass doors. She walked toward the gas heater. Danielle closed her eyes. The chilly rain splashed on her cheeks and trickled down her neck and between her breasts.

Chloe moved close, embracing her mother.

Stanley leaned against the railing and watched.

My God, they are nearly identical.

He watched their wet hair glisten in the living room light.

Chloe whispered in her mother's ear.

Danielle leaned back just far enough to look into Chloe's eyes.

"How'd your dad take it?"

"He's not talking much yet; you know how he gets."

"Not the first time you've done something that had him wor-ried. I'll talk to him."

"Thanks, Mom."

Danielle squeezed her wet daughter and this time whispered in her ear, "John Lennon was right."

"Life is what happens when you have other plans," Chloe said.

Goose bumps and shivers waved over Stanley's skin, everywhere, wave after wave. He gulped several swallows of Basil Hayden's until the glass was empty.

"I'll meet you in bed," he growled to Danielle, walking toward the living room.

● ● ●

Stanley scrunched the pillow to fit his face and turned the bedside light out, facing the wall.

Thirteen minutes later, Danielle crawled over the covers and snuggled her chin to the back of Stanley's neck so he could feel her breath.

"You want to talk about it?" she asked.

"Our daughter has the damn code for the Ghost Wing, honey. You know what kind of risk that puts her in? That, and she can order things blown to pieces. What the hell is happening to our lives?"

"Of course, she does, Stanley; you rather someone else have it?"

"Damn right I would. You seem to be taking this all in stride. Thought you'd be more upset."

Danielle blew on Stanley's neck several times and then said, "I've had a little time to ponder; Debra shared what she and Victor were thinking last Wednesday."

"And you didn't think this was important enough to share?"

He rolled over, face to face.

"Sometimes you astound me."

"Almost did, honey."

"Swell, thanks, Danielle."

"Are we having a fight?"

"Nope, I'm just pissed."

"Chloe is the exact age both Quinn and Fidel were when they conceived the True Believers," Danielle said, staring at the ceiling.

She rolled over and sat up on the edge of the bed and turned on the lamp.

Stanley started counting the freckles on her bare back. He watched her push her left arm down the sleeve of a pink bathrobe from the Don Cesar and over her back to the other arm. Danielle tightened the soft cloth belt and walked to the bar without looking back. She poured a full glass of Pinot. Deliberately, she removed several bottles of bourbon from the liquor cabinet and stretched to the back of the shelf.

Stanley watched his wife pull on the black wax seal tab and twist, exposing the cork top. Holding the bottle high over his favorite glass, she leaned her head to the right and watched the golden liquid pour from the bottle until it reached the lip of the glass.

"It's a no ice kind of night, Stanley," she said, extending the dripping glass.

"That is barrel proof Knob Creek you just poured; hundred and twenty proof."

"I know."

"Doctor Blue gave me that bottle two months before he died. Was saving it for a special occasion."

"Well, honey, tonight is that occasion. A toast...to the best lovers I know."

CLINK.

Stanley sucked down about half the glass.

"I didn't know about Quinn and Fidel, except for being roommates in college."

"Debra told me after they graduated Fidel ended up in the mountains near Santiago de Cuba, attacking Batista's garrison, and Quinn joined the French Foreign Legion, where he recruited the very first True Believers."

"Debra told you this?"

"She did, and that Quinn told her Chloe has the right stuff to succeed him."

Stanley finished the glass with a big swallow and set the glass down hard on the night stand.

"Danielle, she's our daughter. Our sweet, intelligent, charming daughter. You see the way people are drawn to her and the way she is drawn to people. People adore her. Can you really see her leading a band of mercenaries intent on killing?"

"Destroying evil, not killing, Stanley. That's how I look at it. It's the way our daughter looks at it, I'm sure, and how you look at it, if you think about it. You've spent your entire adult life working to heal the sick and injured, saving lives, and yet last week you told me you're going with the rescue party, that you are taking the pistol Fidel gave you at Hospital de Cardenas."

She finished the wine and set the glass next to Stanley's glass so they were touching.

"Checkmate!" she said firmly.

Stanley sat on the bed and pulled at Danielle's bathrobe. She fell on the bed beside him.

"I don't have to like it,"

"I don't either, Stanley."

CHAPTER 54

NOT HIDE NOR HAIR

An intoxicating vapor spread over the valley, covering the city of Big Bay. A combination of fear, excitement, doubt and curiosity bubbled in the diners, bars and the churches. Those once familiar faces from the past had reappeared in town: Victor, Moses, Machete, and Rose, in addition to occasional glimpses of those True Believers, driving big vehicles with darkened windows. The sound of their strange appearing helicopters; conjuring up memories. . . the night Poor Joe's was attacked, the mysterious explosion on the Seven Hills Highway, echoing through the valley, closing the road for nearly a week while the hole was filled with concrete. The question, 'Why did Quinn O'Malley insist that hole be filled with concrete?' had never been answered.

Sermons about the battle between good and evil were dusted off and recycled to nearly packed churches.

Tithing increased.

"I have not seen hide nor hair of that Quinn O'Malley," a man wearing a denim jacket said to the fellow sitting next to him at Jen's Cuban Diner.

"Me neither," replied the man. "Saw his wife, though, with that McMillen girl."

"Boy, has she ever grown up," the denim jacket man said. "Name's Chloe as I remember. Fifteen or so when they all took off for Cuba."

"Wonder why they're back?" the other fellow mused while pouring sugar in his black coffee and stirring it with his arthritic forefinger. He lifted the donut cover and speared a chocolate frosted one in the center using the wet finger.

"Probably the damn communists gave them the boot," the denim jacket fellow said. "Never did hear exactly why they all went down there in the first place."

The denim jacket fellow bit into a jelly donut, causing the raspberry filling to ooze out and drip on the table.

"Maybe the communists got Quinn held prisoner," the chocolate donut fellow commented between bites, "and those guys we see over to Poor Joe's are planning a rescue mission."

"By God, I think you're onto something there, Tom! I ran into Pete last week and said what the hell was going on and why was Poor Joe's closed so much. He told me 'private poker tournament,' when I asked him."

The vapor spread over the city from house to house.

The older residents worried and whispered about the forthcoming apocalypse.

CHAPTER 55

IN THE BLINK OF AN EYE

"**D**is plane be imbissable?" Moses inquired, rubbing her hand along the sleek needle-nosed jet.

Victor smiled. "No, but it is very fast."

Moses patted the nose of the plane. "Like a swordfish."

Little Miss trotted just in front of Machete, leading him up the ramp and into the Gulfstream S-21. Six True Believers entered and sat in the tail section.

Debra and Chloe entered and sat next to Moses.

Arturo entered and closed the door.

Victor, Stanley and Danielle, Timothy, and Carla stood on the tarmac, watching the plane taxi to the end of the runway, and then accelerate rapidly and lift steeply, banking to the right before heading east and out of sight in the evening darkness.

"This rescue mission stuff is a young person's sport," Victor said.

"There goes my baby girl. I hope I see her again." Danielle's voice quaked.

"Those six men are the very best in the world," Victor said, "and Arturo is better at this game than I ever was."

"We get even a hint that things are going wrong, we are going," Timothy said. "Pete, Wayne, and Wendell came downstairs last night when Dora and I were closing up. To be honest, they're a little pissed about not going. One single hint of things falling apart and we're going, Victor. I have connections, too."

Victor looked at Timothy for several seconds before answering.

"If things go wrong, Timothy, it will happen in the blink of an eye, just like St. Paul and Diego."

Timothy's eyes widened.

"Going right doesn't take long, either," Carla said. "Machete and Quinn saved me in the blink of an eye."

The gathering walked in the darkness from the hangar to their cars, saying nothing until Stanley muttered, "I wish Chloe hadn't gone."

• • •

Twenty minutes into the flight, they gathered around the round table located between the emergency exits on either side.

Chloe listened intently while Arturo spoke.

"Phase One is gathering intel," Arturo said over the roar of the 3 turbines, pointing at a map on the table. "We know the location of the building. We know their names and faces." He handed out, one by one, 5 x 8 color glossy photos.

"This one is their leader. Don't know his name." And he held up a picture of the mussed-haired man exiting a cab with a cigarette dangling from his lips.

This one is Ronald from Cape Town.

This is a picture of Joan Mercer from Toronto.

Here is an old picture of Ahuja from Calcutta.

Tan is from Singapore.

Matthew Benedict lives in St. Kitts. He is in charge of human trafficking.

Veronica is from Mexico City and is responsible for controlling the South American drug cartels.

This is a fellow named Caswell. He is, by all reports, a sociopath. He lives in London. He fed strychnine to his twin brother when they were teenagers because they wanted to date the same girl.

The newest committee member is a bit of a mystery. His name is Evan Crothers. He grew up in Chicago, joined the French Foreign Legion for five years, then worked for the Veracruz Cartel in Mexico. He was one of the few survivors from their Mexico City compound after Carla's rescue. More recently he spent time in Cuba. He goes by the name of Ace. We do know that he and the Cuban Air Force pilot that shot down Fidel's helicopter served together in the Legion."

Arturo held up a 5 x 8 color photo of Ace wearing his Evil Knievel jacket.

"He wears this jacket everywhere. Regardless of the weather or occasion."

"How do you know these things? Chloe inquired.

"It's what we do," Arturo replied, nodding at the rear of the plane. "Before we act, we have to learn what we don't know. We don't know who is actually in that building right now. We don't know where they are keeping Charles. We only suspect he's in the Moorgate building."

Arturo spread a floorplan of the Moorgate skyscraper over the map on the table.

"We need to know precisely where."

CHAPTER 56

FATHER MIKE O'CONNOR

"Father O'Connor will see you now," the young man with acne on his cheeks said, opening the large double doors to the parish office.

"Debra, how wonderful to see you again," Father O'Connor said, extending both arms. "I hope Quinn is well."

"Quinn is with our Heavenly Father, Mike."

"I am very sorry for your loss, Debra. Quinn was a good friend to me."

"He was murdered…helicopter shot down in Cuba. Fidel Castro died, too. They were flying to this young lady's college graduation."

Father Mike O'Connor looked at Chloe for an instant with his blue eyes before extending his right hand.

"I'm sorry, young lady. It is my honor to meet you. Mike O'Connor."

"Chloe McMillen."

Chloe shook his hand, their eyes fixed, his blue and her's, not blinking, just a nod. They stood the same height.

"You are the Chloe McMillen Quinn spoke of."

"Yes, Father."

"Mike."

"Yes, Mike."

"He adored you."

"I loved him."

"And now he watches over you from heaven."

"I hope so. We have a problem and need your help. Please meet my good friend, Moses."

"It is nice to meet you, Moses. Biblical name."

"I be leading my peoples to da promised lan', Father."

"I bet you are; honored to meet you. Tell me, ladies, how may I help?"

Chloe glanced at Debra.

"We believe Quinn and Fidel were murdered by a group head-quartered here in London. Are you familiar with the syndicate known as The Committee?" Debra asked.

"I am not."

Chloe moved closer to Father O'Connor and spoke softly, "You hold Mass for them in a private chapel on Moorgate Street." She watched the priest's pupils dilate.

"I perform Mass for a charity. Their tithes do much good in London."

"The Committee is a consortium with representatives from the USA, China, South Africa, Mexico, St. Kitts, Canada, India, Singapore, and right here in England," Arturo said. "This group is involved with human trafficking, sex for sale, and world-wide drug sales, both legal and illicit. They own pharmaceutical companies, banks, and casinos."

Mike O'Connor reached for the corner of his desk and leaned against it. With his left hand he reached for Chloe's hand.

"They give the church ten thousand pounds every month," he said, looking at Chloe's face. "Ten thousand pounds, the third Sunday every month."

Father Mike O'Conner's blue eyes moved from face to face.

Father, forgive me.

He steadied himself then let go of Chloe's hand and slumped back into the desk chair.

"I had no idea."

"Pocket change for them," Debra said.

The former bar bouncer looked at his big hands, opening them both over and over before rubbing the knuckles on his right hand.

"They seem so kind and concerned for the poor. Sorry, do you have PROOF?"

Debra and Arturo watched Chloe push a stuffed chair behind the desk and sit next to Father Mike O'Connor. She handed him five photographs.

"Do you recognize these people," she asked, leaning against his right shoulder.

"Yes, all except this one." He handed Chloe the picture of Ace.

"This is the leader," Chloe said, holding a picture of the mussed-haired man with a cigarette dangling from his lips. "We don't know his name."

"Nor do I. He comes to Mass."

"This is the woman who directs the drug cartel's distribution from Central and South America. This man is in charge of human trafficking; he is headquartered in St. Kitts."

She pointed to a black and white glossy on the desk next to the phone. "This man runs the syndicate's pharmaceutical enterprises.

This man, he lives here is London, is a psychopath; poisoned his twin brother over a girl. This man runs laboratories in China and Nicaragua. In the past, they have developed contagious diseases and hybrid mosquitoes."

"Father in heaven, please forgive me."

Mike O'Connor crossed himself.

"How may I help?"

"Moses was a nun in Guadalupe for many years," Debra said.

Moses leaned forward and silently kissed Father O'Connor's hand.

"It would be helpful if Moses assisted you at Mass. We need her inside that building," Arturo said.

The priest nodded his head *yes*.

"Do dey ever ask for confessions?" Moses inquired.

"Third Saturday of each month we have confessions." He paused. "I can't break that vow."

"But they never mentioned things that worried you?" Arturo asked.

"No, just the usual: girlfriends, sex, adultery, fornication, impure thoughts."

"That's smart of them," Chloe commented. "Just wait until they're face to face with the Almighty Father."

Mike O'Connor smiled and said, "Perhaps they will be forgiven, should they ask."

"I wouldn't count on evil requesting forgiveness," Chloe responded.

Mike O'Connor stared at the young face and her resolute eyes.

"I wouldn't either, Chloe."

Chloe stood and reached with her left hand and pulled Mike O'Connor to a standing position then leaned into him. Debra, Moses, and Arturo watched her lips whisper into his ear.

"This is very personal, Mike."

She pointed at the pictures spread out on his desk.

"These people have killed two of my precious friends. They are right now holding prisoner the man I am going to marry."

Mike O'Connor leaned away just far enough to search Chloe's face before looking down.

"Very personal," the big man said quietly, watching his hands open and close into fists several times. "Very personal. This one's for you, Quinn."

Then Mike O'Connor looked up at the bronze crucifix on the wall and winked.

CHAPTER 57

A FINE STOOP ON MOORGATE STREET

The man's cheeks appeared sunken in the red neon light, his earthly possessions piled in a grocery cart behind him, resting against the old brick building's fire escape door.

Machete walked under the illuminated *SUPERDRUG* sign overhead, turned left on Moorgate Street, stopping directly in front of a man wrapped in a gray army surplus blanket.

"MY STOOP!" the man sitting on a potato crate shouted.

The words made a whistling hiss through rotted teeth. He looked up at Machete while moving his dented Hills Brothers coffee can—containing a few coins—closer, with gnarled fingers.

Machete smiled at the man.

"Nice dog," the man said. "I had a dog once."

"What was your dog's name?" Machete asked.

"Bowdre. He liked that name. What's your dog called?"

"Little Miss. She's my eyes."

"You blind? Don't seem blind."

"I am, nearly."

"Sorry."

"Is your stoop for sale?"

"No."

"I will pay you well."

"This is the finest stoop. I like it here."

The man rubbed his hollowed cheeks and gray stubble with both bent hands, pondering.

"Then where would I go?" he asked.

"With the money you get for this beautiful stoop, you can purchase a fine new suit and stay in a nice hotel."

Fear and hesitation clouded the old man's eyes.

"Or perhaps you just purchase an even better stoop, one with shade in the afternoon and a street grate with steam for warmth."

The man pursed his lips and thought.

"I like Orwell's stoop on Hamilton Street. He stays dry and has steam for the cold days."

Machete smiled.

"Orwell will sell his stoop for one hundred pounds."

"How do you know that?"

"We had a discussion. He said one hundred pounds."

The old man shrugged.

"I have not had one hundred pounds in twenty years."

Machete fumbled with the clasp on his canvas satchel, opened it, touching around inside with his fingers. He extended his arm in the old man's direction, holding a thick bundle of paper currency held together with a wide, red rubber band.

"Here, amigo, is one thousand pounds."

The old man held the money with both hands.

Machete reached back into the satchel and retrieved a fifth of Bombay Gin. He placed the bottle in the Hills Brothers coffee can.

The old man studied Machete.

"How did you know where I moved the can?"

"Little Miss told me."

"And, I want your dog," the man said.

Machete stiffened, just briefly, before pulling his long coat aside, exposing his cane knife, the blade reflecting red light coming from the *SUPERDRUG* neon.

"Or perhaps, amigo, I will simply relieve you from your head and throw it in the Thames."

The old man involuntarily raised his hands to his neck.

Machete felt for the Bombay and unscrewed the cap.

"Greed is a terrible curse, my amigo, a poison, really. A toast to our agreement."

Machete handed the bottle to the old man who wrapped his lips tightly and pulled the gin down until the suction stopped the flow.

"You need your dog. I am sorry. I forgot you are nearly blind."

He handed the bottle to Machete.

Machete took a sip.

"Wise choice. What is your name, amigo?"

"Earl Carter."

"Goodbye, Earl Carter. When I am gone, you may have this stoop again, if you like."

"When might that be?"

"One never knows these things, do they. Leave the donation can."

Machete and Little Miss watched Earl Carter shuffle behind the grocery cart down the red foggy street until the darkness swallowed him.

CHAPTER 58

KEEP THIS DUDE ALIVE

"**H**ey, Ace!"

"Hey…what, Doctor?"

"Feel my forehead. I'm burning up."

Ace wiped his hands on the table cloth. Licking the remaining pizza sauce from his thumb, he walked from the kitchenette and cupped his hand on Charles' face.

"Kinda hot."

"I'm septic, Ace. If you don't get this stuff tonight," Charles said, pointing at the list on the table, "I'm going to die and your bosses are going to be really pissed."

"Told you, they're not my bosses."

"Right. Septic, look that up on your laptop, spelled S E P T I C."

Ace watched Charles' diaphoretic lips spell each letter.

"I can spell, Doctor."

"Just trying to be helpful, Ace. Google it. Read me what it says."

"Thought you already knew."

"Let's see if they have it right on the world wide web."

"It says, 'The presence in tissues of harmful bacteria and their toxins, typically through infection of a wound. Potentially life threatening.'"

"Serious stuff, this sepsis, Ace."

Keep working him. Keep 'im on the ropes.

Ace looked up from the computer screen.

Gotta keep this dude alive, damnit.

"Want a piece of pizza?"

"Nope, this sepsis is making me nauseated."

Ace, took the final slice of pizza and walked to the window, peering to the foggy street far below. He glanced at his watch.

"OK, come here," Ace said, pointing to the leather couch. He shackled Charles' left ankle to the metal leg support with handcuffs. He snatched the list from the table and without saying a word, left the room.

Charles twisted as far as the pain permitted, straining to watch the street below. He watched Ace walking quickly in the direction of *SUPERDRUGS* then slow his gait.

Careful. Watch this new dude.

Instinctively, Ace reached into his jacket pocket, feeling his German Luger, inserting his finger around the trigger while pushing the safety off with his thumb.

Blind bum…Keep moving…Nice dog.

"Good evening, amigo. Would you spare some change for a man on hard times?"

"You're new here; haven't seen you before," Ace said, taking several steps backward. He pushed the spent cigarillo from the gap with is tongue and replaced it. He watched Machete intently while flicking the lighter.

Damn his sunglasses.

"Yes, Earl Carter has moved on."

Ace moved closer and waved his hands in Machete's face.

Machete stared straight ahead.

One ugly jacket. Gun in right pocket. Keys on belt.

"Appreciate any help," Machete said.

Ace tossed coins into the dented coffee can and listened to the soft landing on a wad of paper money.

"Good night, bum."

"Thank you. See you around."

Ace's head snapped back at Machete, who waved in the direction of where Ace had been standing.

Ace walked backwards and reached into the Hills Bothers can, removing several bills. He walked to the drug store.

Charles watched Ace enter the drug store. He watched the dog circle the little man sitting on the potato crate then curl beside him. A car came from the east, and for an instant in the headlights glow, Charles saw a man standing in the darkness across the street in the narrow alley between buildings. The man wore black.

And then Charles knew.

CHAPTER 59

SISTER MARY MOSES FROM GUADELOUPE

Ace nodded at the big man wearing a shiny gray suit standing next to the closed mahogany door. The big man returned the nod and opened the door to the chapel.

What the hell's a nun doing here?

Ace hesitated, watching Moses light candles next to the altar and at the feet of Jesus. Then she turned and smiled a soft smile in his direction.

Dat's da man wid da ugly jacket.

Moses smiled again and bowed slightly toward Ace.

Ace walked to the far end of the chapel and entered the confessional booth.

"God bless you, how may I help?" Father O'Connor said through the veil.

"Hi there, Father. I ain't no Catholic and I ain't here to confess stuff."

"How may I help?"

"My mother was a believer in all this holy stuff. She was a Methodist. Told me once I was the answer to prayer; some answer, huh Father?"

"We are all the children of God."

"Yah, sure."

"Why are you here?"

Mike O'Connor's hands folded into fists.

Ace put his ear close to the curtain, listening to Father O'Connor breathe.

"Well, would you say a prayer for a friend?"

"I'll be happy to do that. What is your friend's name?

"Just a friend with sepsis."

"I will, and may God take care of you, as well."

"One of your powerful prayers, there, Father."

Ace stood and exited the confessional. He opened the exit door a little and said through the crack, "Better hope it works."

●●●

The mussed-haired man entered the chapel, followed by the entire committee, for Sunday morning Mass. He walked directly to Father O'Connor.

"What's going on here, Father?"

"Excuse me?"

"Her, what is she doing here?" The mussed-haired man pointed toward Moses.

"She is Sister Mary Moses from Guadeloupe, here to help me with the holy sacraments."

"You were told to always come alone."

"As I explained to the guard," Father O'Connor said, "I am not feeling well…likely a virus passed along by the school children, and I thought it best to have Sister Mary Moses handle the sacraments so as not to expose you to this malady."

The mussed-haired man fingered his cigarette lighter nervously while studying Moses, finally turning to Caswell.

"Pat her down, Caswell."

"Excuse me, Sister," Caswell said, "I must pat you down."

Moses grinned.

"Dis be da first time! Keep dem thoughts pure, mister. I be pledged to Jesus."

Caswell's snake eyes shifted to the mussed-haired man's face.

"Pat her down yourself."

The mussed-haired man wagged his finger in Father O'Connor's face, shook his head, and took his customary seat on the front pew.

Father O'Conner gripped the edges of the pulpit with his hands.

"At one point, while He hung from the cross in great agony, Jesus said, 'Forgive them, Father, for they know not what they do.'

"I doubt I would have uttered those words, especially with the knowledge that, should I ask, my Father in heaven would have sent ten thousand angels, banishing all the evil ones from the face of the earth."

The mussed-haired man looked up at Father O'Connor with dark, emotionless eyes, hardly blinking.

"There are times I grapple with why Jesus said that or why evil is permitted to exist."

Mike O'Connor paused.

"Perhaps it is to give each of us a choice, no matter our pasts, to choose good over evil, to choose the light of love over the darkness of evil. I pray each of us chooses love.

"I am honored to introduce Sister Mary Moses from Guadeloupe. I am a little under the weather, and she has kindly consented to serve the holy sacraments today."

They formed a line. Moses looked directly into each set of eyes while saying, "De body of Christ. De blood of Christ."

The line ended with the mussed-haired man.

"De body of Christ."

She extended her hand.

"Amen" he growled.

"De blood of Christ, shed for you."

"Amen."

He sipped from the silver Chalice, his eyes never leaving hers.

He turned to his right. Moses tapped his shoulder.

"Dey be much pains in your soul."

"Don't worry 'bout it, Sister."

He looked up at Father O'Connor, sitting next to the pulpit.

"I don't like this Father," the mussed-haired man said coldly. "I don't like this, one bit."

He left the chapel, walking angrily. Two men wearing identical shiny gray suits followed him. Then the entire Committee exited the chapel.

Moses turned toward Father O'Connor. He pushed a single finger against his lips and grinned his Irish smile.

The large man assigned to escort Father O'Connor, his body stretching the shiny gray Armani suit tight in the chest and biceps, opened the chapel door and waited just outside, holding the door open with his back.

"I have your ride waiting," he said.

"Thank you, Armond. I believe Sister Mary Moses and I will enjoy a walk today. I'm hoping fresh air will help shake this bug."

"It is twelve blocks, Father."

"I need the fresh air."

"Then I will instruct the driver to follow you."

"Thank you, Armond. God Bless you."

They walked through the tall building shadows with the black Mercedes following.

"Dis be creepy, dese peoples like dis," Moses said, glancing at the car.

"We need to have a conversation where there are no ears."

"Ooooh…dey be ears eben in de parish?"

"Not sure of anything anymore, about many things. For example, I'm not sure you are a nun."

"I was."

"I can tell."

"No more. Now I be married to dat blind bum we jus passed widt da dog in da drug store stoop."

Mike O'Conner flashed his Irish grin again.

"Quinn O'Malley's True Believers are here, aren't they?"

"Yes. Some of dem be watchin' us all de time."

They walked another block in silence.

"I think Chloe's boyfriend is being held in their building," Mike O'Connor said.

"I listen to dat Ace in da confessional," Moses said. "I think dat, too. Tomorrow we meet an' make de plans."

"Tonight, I write a letter to the Holy Father. Tomorrow I go with you. Tomorrow I am Mike O'Connor the bouncer, Quinn O'Malley's friend."

"Dat be gud. Keep de collar, jst in case."

CHAPTER 60
KATIE'S DREAM

*S*queak...slam.

Carla and Timothy glanced up from Poor Joe's long table.

"Got to fix that door," Timothy muttered, watching Victor Bonifacio walk toward them.

"What?" Carla asked, grasping Timothy's knee under the table.

From around the table they watched their old friend approach, Stanley, Danielle, Pete, Wayne, Rose, Richard, Katie, and Dora while fussing with the meatloaf in the kitchen.

"Machete confirms Ace is in London; had a conversation with him last evening. Moses reports that they believe Charles is being held in the skyscraper on Moorgate Street. I talked with Debra, Arturo, and Chloe half hour ago."

He pulled out the chair, sat next to Carla, and smiled at Dora walking in his direction with a mug of coffee.

"They have the intel; they are going in soon."

Carla extended both arms past her coffee cup at the same moment Danielle did from the other side. They clasped hands.

"God help them," Carla said, squeezing Danielle's hand with all her strength.

"Yes," Danielle said.

Her hands are freezing.

Katie leaned over the table and placed her hands over their clasped hands.

"I have never prayed as hard as I have this week. Last night a sudden peace filled me and I know they are going to make it," Katie said.

Victor smiled.

"I dreamed about their wedding," Katie said. "You're going to be surprised."

"Alpha Team One," Victor said.

The eyes at the long table shifted to his face.

"Arturo's team is the very best of the True Believers. Quinn and I selected and trained this group to be a special extraction unit."

He paused.

"Quinn and I were part of it, years ago; saved Fidel's life during an assassination attempt. Very special group. Start every mission chanting 'today is a good day to die...today is a good day to die.' Amazing what a person can do when they have no fear."

Victor leaned and placed his hands over the pile of clasping female fists. He covered their hands with his big hands.

"Rose and I will be honored to help with the catering and the band."

Rose whispered, "The best wedding ever."

CHAPTER 61

CHARLES' FACE

Machete fingered and then pushed the tiny black button on the end of Little Misses' leash, activating the radio transmitter under her wide collar.

Arturo listened.

Debra listened.

Chloe listened.

So too, did the folks gathered at Poor Joe's long table, five hours away.

"I have met the one called Ace," Machete said. "The presence of evil surrounds him. Little Miss trembles in his presence. I am certain he is staying on the 32nd floor, in the corner room with windows on both sides of it. I see him, every day, looking out those windows, wearing the ugly coat."

"I concur. This is Arturo. Observations from the rooftop across the plaza—corner room, 32nd floor—two men observed, one shackled—at times to a table, at night to a couch. Sending a picture."

Arturo continued, "Sniper one, what is your percentage?"

"Target is 100 percent. Glass is concerning. Initial ultrasound and light refraction analysis indicates projectile resistance."

"10-4," Arturo responded. "Next radio conference at zero-one GMT."

Machete blurted, "STOP!" pressing his transmitter button hard with his thumb.

"Go ahead," Arturo responded.

"I can remove the problem next time he passes my stoop."

"Negative. We'll discuss all options at zero-one GMT."

Victor, Timothy, Stanley, and Richard Elmore Fortin huddled, watching the tiny dots form a colored picture on the satellite transceiver. They studied the small photo for several seconds.

"Turn the lights off!" Timothy shouted to nobody in particular. Wendell did.

"Can you enlarge this?" Timothy asked, touching the image on the lower right corner.

Victor removed the flash drive and plugged it into his laptop; the enlarged photo appeared. He moved the pointer to a person's head appearing in the lower right portion of the window and clicked the mouse.

The image of Charles' face became clear.

"Carla!" Timothy said, touching the screen, rubbing it several times.

They looked at their son's image, embracing and silent, feeling their hearts thumping in unison and trembling.

"I can do it."

Everyone turned and looked at Richard Elmore Fortin.

"What?" responded everyone in unison.

Richard smiled. "I can do it."

"Arturo, we have found Charles Fife. Image enhancement shows Charles looking out the window on the 32nd floor."

In their London room, Arturo, Debra, and Chloe studied each other's eyes. Chloe stood and began walking aimlessly around the room. Debra caught her on the third revolution, wrapped both arms tightly around her and squeezed.

"We're going to get him," Debra said.

"What do you mean, Richard, you can do it? What does that mean, exactly?" Chloe said into the transceiver.

Richard spoke in a slow and deliberate manner.

"The safest way to retrieve Charles is through that window, in and out, before the scumbags have time to react. On the Ghost

Wing we have a laser guided ultrasound cannon; we can shatter that window like a frozen pickle jar. We point it at the bottom left corner, opposite Charles. Dime-sized pieces of glass will rain down to the sidewalk."

"Will Charles be hit by the glass?" Chloe asked.

"The glass will fall outward; not likely."

"What about Ace?" Debra asked.

"Two snipers on the roof across the plaza. Ace will be neutralized," Arturo replied.

"Then what? He's still trapped on the 32nd floor," Chloe said.

Arturo spoke with decisiveness, which made Victor, standing next to the long table in Big Bay, 3,565 miles away, smile.

"Both Machete and the sniper team have observed periods of time when Charles is left alone. Every afternoon from two to four, the sniper team has detected increased infrared coming from the top floor during the same time-period Charles is left alone. I believe The Committee meets from two to four every day except Sundays. Here is a plan I want everyone to think over tonight for discussion tomorrow. We plan an attack for two-thirty. The Ghost Wing takes out the 32nd floor window followed by Alpha Team One entering Charles' room from chopper one, using a sky bridge. Then, as soon as Charles is secure, Richard, I want you to circle back and take the windows out on the top floor conference room. With the windows gone, Alpha Team One can use the Gatling on XS-1 to extinguish the problem."

CHAPTER 62

THE RECKONING COMMENCES

Machete Juarez pushed the leash button and spoke, "I am here."

The satellite transceivers at Poor Joe's and Hotel Windsor crackled with the sound.

"Alpha Team here," Arturo said.

Victor pushed the transmit button on the yellow transceiver laying on the long table. "Poor Joe's here, on speaker mode."

"Hotel Windsor here, on speaker mode," Debra said. "Be advised Moses and Father O'Connor have joined us."

"I will start this conversation," Chloe said.

"Go ahead, Chloe," Arturo said.

"Debra and I have not slept since yesterday's discussion. No offense, Arturo, we think that the plan outlined yesterday is not well suited for metropolitan London. Uncle Quinn took great pride in the True Believers' ability to strike incognito, using surprise and stealth technology; to leave confusion and doubt as to who rendered the justice: hitting the Suriname Destroyer, bombing the pharmaceutical company in Nicaragua, rescuing Doctor Blue and Nora from the human trafficking mill on St. Kitts. The world wonders to this very day who was behind these actions. In and out, without a trace, leaving only confusion and speculation. I understand where you are coming from, Arturo. It is the Italian way—don't mess with our family and if you do, this is what we are capable of—in-your-face diplomacy. The True Believers are the best at what they do because we are invisible. Our threat is we will punish you without warning and disappear without a trace into nowhere, like a cobra hiding in the tall grass after a fatal strike. We cannot have our stealth helicopters attacking in broad daylight, their actions captured on the security cameras all over London to be played back on the BBC World News."

Chloe paused.

"And, we have no safe haven after the rescue, no Canada or Cuba nearby."

The transceivers went silent for nearly 20 seconds.

"I assume you and Debra have an alternative plan, Miss Mc-Millen," Arturo retorted.

Victor looked at the smile on Stanley's face and shrugged. Timothy smiled, too, at the change in Arturo's tone and his addressing Chloe as Miss McMillen.

"This is Debra; yes, we have, Arturo."

"Please share with us," Arturo said.

•••

"Ace, take a look at my wrists," Charles said, holding his cuffs as high as the shackle permitted. "I need antibiotic ointment."

Ace slammed his laptop screen down and walked to the couch.

"Looks bad, Doctor. Stinks to be you," Ace snickered.

Get him scared.

"You remember what you read on Google; sepsis is serious. Blood poisoning?"

"Yeah, I know, and if gets to your heart, you die."

"Quite a situation you have here, Ace. Look up endocarditis online...LOOK IT UP!"

Ace walked back to his table and raised the laptop screen.

"Endo-what?

"E N D O C A R D I T I S."

"Found it, says 'infection of the inner lining of the heart and heart valves caused by bacteria or fungus. Often fatal if not treated.'

You sayin' you got this?"

"I can feel the little vegetations wiggling on my tricuspid valve with every heartbeat."

Ace looked at Charles with a blank stare.

"Valve in my heart between the right atrium and right ventricle."

"I knew that."

"So, you know I need antibiotic ointment. This is critical, Ace. Or you can report in tomorrow's committee meeting that I am assuming room temperature."

Ace glanced at his watch, walked to the window, and peered down into the darkness and the *SUPERDRUG* neon light.

Street light burned out.

"I'll be right back," Ace said, attaching the handcuff to Charles' left ankle.

"Don't go nowhere."

● ● ●

"Hello there, blind bum," Ace said walking past in the darkness. "Your light is burned out," he snickered.

"Put the money back you stole."

Ace stopped.

"What?"

"My dog tells me you stole from the can."

Charles watched from his high window, leaning close to the glass despite the agony from his ankle.

"Bullshit!" Ace proclaimed, reaching his right hand into his jacket pocket. He grasped the Luger, pushing the safety off. In the dim red neon light, he pointed the gun at Machete's head.

Charles watched from the 32nd floor window. He saw the little bum spring to his feet and, with a single motion, swing a cane knife.

Whish…clank.

Ace gripped his right forearm and squeezed. With each rapid heartbeat, blood spurted from his amputated wrist, splattering against the bricks and on Little Miss. He stared down, at his curled hand at his feet and the Luger beside the tipped-over donation can.

"Where is Charles?" Machete demanded.

"Who are you?" Ace asked.

"They call me Machete."

Ace smirked and squeezed his wrist harder.

"Where is Doctor Fife?"

"Go to hell," Ace retorted.

"You first."

SWISH.

With his left hand, Ace fumbled at his neck. Blood flowed down the front of his prized Evil Knievel jacket and he wiped at it with his handless right arm. He squinted at Machete, then crumpled headfirst into the stoop.

From between the various surrounding buildings, six men appeared, dressed in black. They moved quickly and worked silently, rolling the body in a green wool blanket and placing it in a shipping box, along with the donation can. They washed away the blood with a bleach solution and placed a new donation can in the stoop next to a new folded kaki blanket.

The True Believer in charge studied the stoop, nodded at Machete, and while walking into the darkness, pointed a remote-control device at the intersection pole, activating the street light and intersection security camera.

A man dressed in Scottish tweed walked next to Earl Carter, pushing his grocery cart.

"Thank you for the use of your stoop, amigo," Machete said. "It is a very nice stoop."

Earl Carter looked in his new collection bucket, nearly filled with crisp new currency, and shook his head.

Doctor Charles Dwight Fife watched from his window.

He watched with fear and hope.

CHAPTER 63

WHO CALLED YOUSE GUYS?

Father Mike O'Connor tucked a .38 Special under his vestments and adjusted his white collar.

Moses adjusted her scapular and cowl then slipped a pistol under her tunic.

Debra and Chloe finished dressing in McNamara's Housekeeping uniforms and placed their weapons in the trouser side pockets.

Arturo and six men, wearing pressed green British Electricity Authority uniforms, entered the room, followed by Moses and Machete with Little Miss.

"You be OK?" Moses asked Machete while giving him a tight squeeze.

"So far."

Arturo inhaled a deep breath and exhaled, looking directly at Chloe.

"Well, Miss McMillen, let's do this."

"One moment," Mike O'Connor said. Raising both arms, he began to pray.

"Father in heaven, guide us and protect us today on this mission against evil.

Help us rescue Charles. Your will be done. Amen."

The room remained silent for what seemed like a very long time.

"Thank you, Father. Let's go," Arturo said, crossing himself.

"Best not to tell him I quit," Mike O'Connor chuckled to Moses on the way out.

Several times he had tried to move the couch.

"Damn!" Charles mumbled. He closed his eyes, trying to will away the pain radiating from the flesh wound around his left ankle.

He stood and immediately slipped on the floor made slippery by his urine, smashing his face on the floor. He rolled to his back and raised his arms up to study his throbbing wrists.

Haven't eaten all day.

He stared at the ceiling light.

I love you, Chloe.

"Well, shit, Charles," he muttered. He struggled to his feet and flopped over the couch. Peering out the window, he watched a gray van stop at the front door. From the van, he saw a priest and a nun exit and walk up the steps. Then a second utility van stopped behind the first van and seven uniformed men exited. He then watched a little man and a dog come out.

What the hell?

●●●

"You're here early, Father," the bulging man in the tight shiny gray suit muttered, unlocking the front door. He looked with confusion at the B. E. A. uniformed men walking up the steps.

"Who called youse guys?" the guard inquired.

"Building maintenance supervisor Peters called, quite upset, said the air conditioning and heating panel keeps shorting out… sparks and smoke. Brought the A team, won't take long, thanks," Arturo answered.

"I need authorization," the big guard replied, reaching in the direction of the wall phone behind him. He turned his face toward the phone and at the same instant, felt a sharp piercing in his right triceps.

The big man leaned against the wall with his back, sliding

down with his legs outstretched. He looked down at the growing darkness around his zipper, then up, watching the faces around him melt into bizarre shapes before the darkness.

●●●

Ace approached the white veil, pushing his face into it, feeling the cathedral sounds created by loving light on the other side. Repulsed by the joy, Ace turned and drifted away, disappearing into the complete darkness.

CHAPTER 64
DELIRIOUS

"Anyone seen or heard from Ace?" the mussed-haired man said. He looked at the empty conference room chair. "Hasn't answered his phone."

"Quite an asset, that one," Ronald from Cape Town commented.

The mussed-haired man took a long drag from his unfiltered Camel. "I don't recall you volunteering to watch the prisoner," he retorted, squinting through the smoke. "You rather have that assignment?"

"Not going to happen," Ronald snapped.

"I'll stop and check on him and the good doctor after the meeting," Kim from China said, reaching for the pretzel bowel. "I know he's been concerned about the doctor's health for some reason. I'll check."

"Thank you," the mussed-haired man said. "The first order of business is our next move. We've had no response from the last letter."

He paused.

"My phone conversation with Miss McMillen was not fruitful."

"What's that mean?" Veronica from Mexico inquired.

"Means she's not easily intimidated, Veronica. When I suggested we would be sending various body parts if she refused to cooperate, she referenced the Suriname Destroyer as a painless way to die."

"How the hell she know about that?" Tan from Singapore nearly shouted.

Matthew from St. Kitts smiled a little before saying, "Tough young lady, huh?"

The mussed-haired man snuffed out a half-spent cigarette and lit a new one then said, "We've delivered two letters now without response. Caswell's idea of luring Bonifacio out into the public for a hit isn't working. I say enough with the threats. We promised body parts in the last letter; I reiterated that during my conversation with Miss McMillen. It's time to get their attention."

The mussed-haired man rubbed his chin.

"Do we have a consensus here? Anyone with a better notion?'

The vote was unanimous.

"Tell Ace," the mussed-haired man said to Kim, "to remove the finger of his choice. We'll send it special delivery—overnight, on dry ice—tomorrow."

●●●

Doctor Charles Fife was peeing on the growing floor puddle when the door locks clicked. He watched the door open and two women dressed in housekeeper uniforms walk in, right arms extended, holding revolvers, pointing all around the room while they advanced.

I'm delirious. Get a grip, Charles. Hallucinating.

He steadied himself, leaning his left leg against the couch, watching the younger housekeeper walk toward him.

She removed her cap.

Charles' legs quivered then failed completely.

Chloe watched the man she adored collapse, his face splashing into a yellow puddle on the tile floor, his wrists cuffed together and his left ankle shackled.

Chloe ran.

She dropped to her knees and slid on the slippery floor. Gently, she lifted Charles' head, supporting it between her knees.

Quickly, a True Believer snapped the wrist and ankle cuffs with a bolt cutter.

Two True Believers lifted unconscious Charles while Chloe held his limp hand.

"The van is circling around," Debra said. "Stay with him. I've got some business upstairs."

CHAPTER 65

THE LORD'S BUSINESS

"**E**xcuse me, Father, just what are you doing here?" the first guard said while the second guard blocked the conference room door with his big body.

Mike O'Connor smiled.

"The Lord's business."

"I'm sorry, Father. Strict instructions. These meetings are never to be interrupted, even by the Lord," the guard replied. He smiled at his own humor. His eyes shifted toward the sound of the elevator doors opening again.

Then both guards reached for their guns.

The guns never cleared their holsters.

Debra and Arturo walked without hesitation directly at the two large guards, firing their silenced sidearms.

Both guards slumped back against the conference room door, crumpling to the floor.

The mussed-haired man looked down the table at the door. "What the hell was that?"

"I'll check," Caswell said. He walked to the door and turned the knob. The weight of the dead men forced the mahogany door open.

Ronald reached inside his jacket for his weapon. Arturo shot him once in the forehead.

The mussed-haired man raised both hands from the table. "Well, this is quite a surprise, Father." He said each word with cold sarcasm.

"Knew you were no nun," he said, pointing at Moses. "More likely, the Father's whore," he continued, making an emphatic obscene gesture with his middle finger.

WHOOSH.

The mussed-haired man watched the middle finger from his right-hand spin down the conference room table, around and around, leaving a tiny bizarre bloody trail. It came to a stop against Ronald's head. He turned to the left and glared at Machete holding the cane knife.

"HEY YOU!" Debra yelled from the end of the conference room table. The mussed-haired man looked at her from his chair.

"THIS ONE IS FOR QUINN."

He tried to focus on her, watching her raise the gun and pull the trigger.

The elevator door opened and three gray-suited security guards emerged, shooting while they ran. The True Believer closest to the open door returned fire before being hit.

Matt from St Kitts grasped his pistol from an ankle holster and began shooting, hitting Mike O'Connor and Moses.

SWISH.

The headless body slumped forward.

Machete walked through the erupting gun battle and knelt next to his wife.

"I be fine, honey," Moses whispered. "I be fine; de Father an' me be wearing vests."

Mike O'Connor rolled over and winked. "Like your wife said, I be fine." He wiped at the blood oozing from his left shoulder.

"I be no gud at dis," Moses whispered up at Machete. "I can't kill."

CHAPTER 66

INTO THAT DEEP MAW

From both sides of the long table in Poor Joe's, they listened to the live broadcast coming through the satellite transceiver placed in the middle.

"The Ghost Wing is airborne," Richard Elmore Fortin's voice crackled from the speaker. "ETA eleven-fifty p.m., London time."

Stanley, Danielle, Timothy, Carla, Rose, Pete, Wayne, and Victor listened to the sounds when Charles' room was entered, then the chaotic sounds when the conference room was breached, followed by the gun fight.

Danielle held Stanley tight. Together they quivered.

Timothy handed Carla a Kleenex then the old Green Beret wiped away his tears and kissed his wife.

Wayne polished the barrel of his shotgun with a bar towel.

The radio went silent, and they waited with a new agony, watching the minute hand jump 19 times.

"Charles is rescued," Chloe's voice cracked slightly. "He is safe but in need of medical attention. Three wounds. We are on our way to the airport."

She paused then pressed the transmit button again.

"The Ghost Wing may engage."

The transceiver on Poor Joe's table went quiet for several minutes.

"Dad, we'll need four beds at the hospital. Tell Timothy and Carla their son is going to be OK."

Those around the table watched Timothy and Carla clutching each other, their bodies silently shaking with sobs.

"Your daughter's plan worked," Victor said. "Quinn was right, she's a born leader."

"I hate this," Danielle said.

●●●

Flying at 60,000 feet, the stealth wing circled London for ten minutes. Richard punched numbers into the onboard computer, adjusting for wind direction and speed.

"Ready for final approach," he said to the pilot.

Richard pressed both red buttons.

At precisely midnight, London time, the skyscraper located on Moorgate Street imploded, collapsing into itself, disappearing into a deep maw filled with a great heat, consuming even the bricks.

The following day, the *London Evening Standard* headlines read:

AUTHORITIES BAFFLED BY
TREMENDOUS EXPLOSION
Community mourns loss of benefactors

CHAPTER 67
BEIJING

Kim Chan sat facing the 76-inch flat screen SHD television. Four other men around the round table turned their chairs to see the BBC satellite evening news in Beijing. They watched the BBC repeat over and over, sometimes in slow motion, the images captured by the Moorgate Street security cameras from several locations. They watched the great skyscraper, their bulletproof and bomb-resistant building, implode into a fiery pit and disappear.

"No word from London?" a man wearing horn-rimmed glasses inquired.

"Nothing," Kim Chan replied.

"It has been nearly 24 hours," the man closest to the television commented, fiddling with his reading glasses. "We should have heard something from them."

"We have not heard from anyone," Kim Chan retorted, "because dead men do not call."

"Then we should release the virus, infect the mosquitoes and release them in the States. That is the protocol established," the man said, putting the reading glasses on his face and tilting his chin down.

Kim Chan nodded, pondered, then said, "No, I think we wait. Who are we dealing with, now that Quinn O'Malley and Fidel Castro are gone? We will wait and learn."

Then Kim Chan smiled.

"After all, we are in charge now."

"Yes, Mister Chan," those around the table responded in unison.

CHAPTER 68
ANOTHER RICHARD

Katherine Kennedy McGinnis stood and beckoned everyone at the long poker table to join her. They formed a circle, locking arms tightly.

"Father in heaven," Katie prayed, "thank you for guiding and protecting our loved ones. Thank you for your blessings and your forgiveness. Mostly, thank you for your love. In Jesus' name, amen."

Victor Bonifacio raised his head and made the sign of the cross and nodded at Katie. Katie winked back.

Stanley, Danielle, Timothy, and Carla joined in a silent, squeezing circle, fused together for a long time.

• • •

Mike O'Connor and Moses refused medical attention, although Mike allowed a gauze bandage on his left shoulder.

Moses removed the bulletproof vest and rubbed at five swollen bruises and a broken rib.

"We be jst fine 'till dey fix us real gud in Big Bay."

Mike O'Connor smiled. "I take it back, Moses. You're a beautiful nun."

Several True Believers worked quietly with desperation over their wounded fellow, eventually stopping the hemorrhage from a torn right femoral artery and inserting a chest tube to reinflate his collapsed right lung.

Chloe and a True Believer worked together on Charles who thrashed about when regaining partial consciousness before lapsing comatose again. Together, they cleaned his infected wrists and left ankle. The True Believer started a large bore IV in Charles' left subclavian vein.

"Let's get him hydrated," he said, handing Chloe a bag of normal saline. He looked through the medication chest. "Hold that bag high."

"Boy, O'Malley has every contingency covered. Is Charles allergic to anything?"

"Not that I know of."

"We'll start him on Clindamycin."

"Thank you. What's your name?"

The True Believer stood.

"I am a True Believer, Miss McMillen."

Chloe smiled up at him.

"And I am your leader."

"Richard, Miss McMillen."

Chloe wiped at Charles' diaphoretic forehead with a piece of gauze.

"Then I have two Richards to thank. Where did you receive your medical training, Richard?"

The True Believer looked at Chloe's eyes for several seconds before replying, "You don't miss much. University of Minnesota."

"Golden Gophers; go Gophers! You a physician?"

"I am a True Believer."

"My dad received his Ph.D. there."

"I know. We've met."

•••

They released each other's bodies, their souls replenished. Stanley looked at the floor, holding Danielle's hand, listening to the *tic… tock…tic…tock* of the wall clock.

It's going to be a long night.

"What time will they arrive here?" he asked Victor who opened his laptop then motioned for everyone to join him.

They watched the satellite image of the S-21 Gulf Stream moving across the Atlantic.

"Flying against the jet stream—two and a half hours with the strong convection along the east coast they'll have to fly around—six thirty."

"Why haven't they radioed?" Danielle inquired, watching the screen.

"Don't know. I'll contact The Wing. Richard is escorting them home."

"True Believer base to Ghost Wing," Victor spoke into the yellow transceiver, "ETA to Big Bay."

"One hundred forty minutes, Victor. Gulfstream has lost radio communication. I have informed Big Bay Tower."

"Thank you, Richard."

"Yes, sir. It's been quite a day."

CHAPTER 69

BAMBI AND MISTER DILLON

Charles' eyes opened wide, looking straight up at the plane's ceiling.

Now what?

Chloe leaned close from her seat and touched his nose with her finger.

"Welcome back, sweetheart."

Charles grinned and attempted to sit up. Chloe pushed her face against his, forcing him down with her forehead.

Her lips rubbed his cheek. "We're on our way home, honey."

His eyes darted around the plane, looking at the men dressed in green British Electrical Authority uniforms, a priest, and Moses dressed as a nun. He whispered a croaky whisper, "Chloe, I've fallen through the looking glass."

His eyes fixed on Little Miss.

"Tell me your nickname."

"Bambi, Mister Dillon. Let's run away together."

Charles rested his head into the pillow. He closed his eyes.

"We're on Quinn's plane, Charles. We're going home."

"Nice uniform, honey. Got a day job?"

"You should see my pistol."

● ● ●

"Close it up; let's head to the airport!" Timothy shouted from behind the bar.

"Ghost Wing to base."

Victor pushed the transmit button.

"Go ahead, Richard."

"ETA sixty minutes. I have established contact with the Gulf Stream on our analog VHF intercom. We'll need two ambulances at the airport."

"I thought there are four wounded."

"Moses and Father O'Connor refuse to ride in one. Just two."

Victor shook his head.

"Mike O'Connor, should have known he'd get involved."

"You know him?" Richard chuckled.

"Know him! He picked me up and threw me out of a Dublin bar, he and Quinn. That's how we met."

Timothy grinned. "Amazing how we meet people who change our lives, isn't it Victor?"

"Chloe and Charles have been listening on the intercom. Stanley there?"

"I am." Stanley leaned close to the radio.

"Charles says he wants to marry your daughter."

●●●

"Escort plane to Big Bay Tower, do you have the Gulfstream on radar?"

"We do. You have contact, is that correct?"

"Yes, Ma'am," Richard replied.

"Tell Gulfstream to proceed to runway one-eight. Wind from the east at ten with gusts to fifteen; altimeter is twenty-nine-point-niner. All traffic is holding until they are on the ground."

"Thank you."

"By the way," the traffic control lady continued, "where are you? You're not on radar."

"Good to know," Richard replied, "Just wait until you see her on the ground."

"You are landing as well?"

"Affirmative, right behind the Gulfstream. I will activate our transponder thirty miles out."

•••

Victor Bonifacio left before the others to direct landing operations. He stood next to the air traffic controller, listening.

"You know your damn stealth helicopters are a menace to safe navigation, right Victor?" she said, watching an XS-1 helicopter lift from the tarmac.

"Bad guys can't see them either, Dawn."

"I suppose; and what the hell is Richard Fortin flying? Can't see him, either. Said I would be amazed when I see it."

Victor leaned closer to Dawn.

"What exactly did Richard say?"

"I told him we are not picking him up on radar, and he said good, just wait until I see her."

"He's landing?"

"Roger that, right behind the Gulfstream."

Victor shook his head and walked to the elevator.

•••

Richard flipped the switch, activating the Ghost Wing transponder.

"ESCORT PLANE PULL UP...PULL UP...PULL UP...You are right on top of the Gulfstream...PULL UP!"

"Fifty-two feet, to be exact, Big Bay Tower," Richard responded. "We've been flying in this formation for three thousand miles. Fifty-two feet. Gulfstream is on final approach. We will circle once and land."

The Wing pilot pulled away and accelerated skyward, watching the Gulfstream descend.

From the starboard windows, the Gulfstream passengers watched the sun arrive over their beloved peninsula and an XS-1 helicopter rising next to them. The helicopter flew close, the pilots saluting and wagging their machine several times in respect. Forty feet above the approaching runway they saw two ambulances surrounded by men dressed in black wearing red berets and a line of people looking upward.

And then they were home.

CHAPTER 70

HE'S LOST HIS EVER-LOVIN' MIND

The parents stood, arms locked in arms, watching for the Gulf-stream door to swing down. Then it came down with a hydraulic hiss, bumping on the hard tarmac.

Moses came out first, walking gingerly, smiling a big grin.

Machete followed his wife with Little Miss following him.

Mike O'Connor exited next, chin up, his Irish eyes going from face to face, saying hello.

With a True Believer on each end, a wounded comrade came next on a stretcher, IV bags above his head.

Arturo exited quickly. He walked directly to Victor and shook hands.

The remaining True Believers and both pilots came out.

"I want to walk out," Charles said, standing from his stretcher and steadying himself against Chloe's shoulder. "Mom will freak out if I'm carried."

"You ready?" Chloe asked.

Charles took a deep breath. "Yes. I've never been readier."

Chloe smiled.

The True Believer unhooked the solutions from the IV pole and handed them to Chloe.

"I love them," Chloe said, looking through the open plane door, down at their parents.

Charles' legs quivered visibly. Chloe felt his body lean harder.

"Hold me tight, honey. I'm dizzy."

They walked down the ramp to cheers. Then they were in their parents' arms, holding them. The True Believer took the IV bags from Chloe and held them high.

"I was so scared," Danielle said, squeezing Chloe with all her might. Stanley surrounded his wife and daughter with both arms and pulled them close.

"Dad, I have something for you."

Stanley watched his daughter reach into her gray housekeeper pants pocket. She withdrew a silver .38 Special handgun.

"I don't need this anymore," she said. "It'll look great with the rest of the war memorabilia cluttering your den."

Carla said not a word. She pulled away from Timothy and held her son, leaning back just far enough to look into his beautiful blue eyes with her own blue eyes. With his free hand, Charles brushed his mother's long blond hair from her face and smiled back at the first women he had ever loved.

"Made it, Mom."

Carla's lips moved without a sound.

"I love you, too," he said.

Timothy watched his son's knees fold. He grabbed his son from behind.

"Little help here, Stan!" Timothy yelled.

"I'll walk, Dad, give me a hand."

Stanley held one arm, Timothy the other, and Chloe took the IV bags from the True Believer.

Side by side, Danielle and Carla watched their husbands help their son and daughter into the ambulance and close the doors.

Katherine Kennedy McGinnis stood slightly to the side, observing. She watched each face coming from the plane and the reunions. Silently, she prayed.

Thank you, Jesus, for your miracle.

Debra O'Malley remained on the Gulfstream alone, sitting in her husband's favorite seat. She closed her eyes, seeing Quinn's smiling, whiskered face.

A hand stroked the back of her head.

Quinn.

She opened her eyes, looking up at Katie.

"Quinn rubbed my head like that," Debra said.

● ● ●

Richard Elmore Fortin instructed the Ghost Wing pilots to circle two additional times, flying very low over Big Bay and then low over the airport.

"He's lost his ever-lovin' mind," Victor said, standing next to Timothy.

"I don't think so, Victor," Timothy responded.

"What?"

"He's givin' the finger to the bad guys. He's the fighter who's taken the best the other guy has, stood up after being knocked down, and grins through bloody lips—that's it punk, take your best shot, I'm not afraid. I know exactly what Fortin is doing," the old Green Beret said, rubbing his right arm stump.

"Hope he's right, Timothy." Victor said.

***

In the early sunlight, the citizens of Big Bay stopped their morning routines to listen and look up. They watched a large gray boomerang-shaped flying machine move overhead, flying nearly silently.

"I bet O'Malley's on that thing," one old man said to his friend, standing outside Jen's Cuban Diner.

"Might be, Tom," his friend wearing a plaid shirt replied. "Could be the aliens are returning him."

"I'd bring him back, too," the first man commented, spitting a spent chew of Skoal toward the gutter.

●●●

"Ghost Wing One to Big Bay Tower," Richard radioed from the navigator's seat.

"Big Bay Tower, go ahead Ghost Wing One.

"On final approach."

"Runway one-eight. Wind east at ten with gusts to twenty. Altimeter three-zero point zero-zero. Clear to land."

Dawn, the traffic controller, watched the Ghost Wing land.

"Quite a flying machine you have there, Fortin."

"Thanks, made it myself from military surplus parts."

"I'm sure you did, Richard."

CHAPTER 71

ONE MORE PROMISE

"**S**ince when have we allowed dogs on our patients' beds?" the young night nurse asked in morning change of shift report, removing her ponytail tie and shaking her brown hair loose.

The unit manager smiled from the opposite side of the table and replied, "Have you met the man who comes in early each morning to visit her?"

"Met him two mornings ago, brought us coffee and cinnamon rolls from Poor Joe's," the young nurse replied. "He introduced himself as Stanley; said his daughter's fiancé is up in ICU. Carol in ICU told me her name is Chloe and she's staying here all the time, that she has special approval from the administration. Who's this Stanley?"

The night staff and day shift nurses in the room looked at their unit manager.

"I was a new nurse, like you, Nancy, working on the night shift," the manager said. "Stanley McMillen was the Critical Care manager. He hired me.

It was one of those crazy full moon nights with two PIA's, six victims, one DOA—she worked here in the cafeteria—and two Level Ones. I kinda' just spun around and around, feeling frantic. Old Doctor Blue put his arm around my shoulders and said, 'Call Stanley in. We need him.'

I had never experienced a calmness like that, with him here, triaging and going from one patient to the next, calm as can be, reassuring each patient they were going to be OK. We had just sent the last patient to OR, I glanced up at the clock and saw it was 3:10, when a man walked in carrying a German Shepherd. He said. 'Get me Stan, tell him Jimmy's been shot.'

Stanley and Doctor Blue worked on that dog for ninety minutes, and he made it. After the man left with all his buddies, Stanley and I were alone, cleaning and restocking room one, and I asked, 'When did we start treating dogs?' Nancy, I will never forget his answer. He looked at me from the other side of the room and said, 'We stop the bleeding. We give antibiotics to kill bacteria when they are infected, we take them to the OR and cut the bad parts out and put the pieces back together, we give powerful medications to make kidneys work and hearts beat more efficiently, open clogged arteries, and implant pacemakers. We patch...patch...patch. But, Cynthia, the only thing which truly heals is love. Did you feel the love between that man—his name is Timothy by the way—the love between Timothy and his dog? Jimmy knew Timothy would not abandon him. Love gives hope. Love heals, Cynthia.'"

The young nurse took a deep breath and averted her eyes away from her manager's gaze.

● ● ●

"I will never leave you alone, again," Machete said from his chair next to Moses' hospital bed.

"I like dat promise," Moses said, stroking Little Misses' head.

"Dey be one other thing I want."

"Yes?"

"Promise dat we go back to da lean-to an' we bury de cane knife back in de hole it came frum."

"I promise."

"In de dirt...foreber."

Machete watched Moses rub her belly.

CHAPTER 72

COME AWAY WITH ME

The nurses sitting in their cardiac station watching the heart monitor wave forms on the yellow screens, whispered back and forth among themselves.

"I hear he was being held prisoner by a drug cartel. That's how he got those wrist and ankle infections," the red-haired nurse said, fiddling with her engagement ring, nodding at ICU room 3.

"The rumor is," the older RN said, pointing through the glass at Chloe, "she rescued him."

The heavy-set nurse returned from the medication room. "That's the news at Jen's Diner. The guys at Jen's told Jake and me that she's a commando; flies all over the world doing crazy shit like that."

"Really...her?" the red-haired nurse exclaimed.

"Yup," the heavy-set nurse said, joining them behind the monitors, "the fellows down at Jen's say they heard she walked right in and shot the place up, her and that wounded lady patient on med-surg, the one they call Moses, and that Irish priest with the shoulder wound upstairs and that Commando guy in post-op. They just walked in and shot the place up and rescued him then blew the place up—that skyscraper on the news that blew up. That's what the guys are saying."

"Hard to believe, looking at her," the older nurse said, stirring Coffee-Mate powder into her coffee.

"Then the CIA flew them back in that boomerang plane out at

the airport," the heavy-set nurse concluded, reaching for the potato chip bag.

"I'd like to get to know her," the red-haired nurse said, wiping her engagement ring with an alcohol swab.

● ● ●

Charles' hospital bed angled up 45 degrees. Chloe lay next to him, holding his left hand.

"Remember the first time we touched?" Charles asked.

"In the corner booth, next to the popcorn machine. We took our shoes off and rubbed our toes against each other."

Charles smiled. "Yup."

"I was thirteen. That's the day I starting falling in love with you," Chloe said.

"All I knew is that your touch thrilled me, and I never wanted it to stop."

"That's my promise to you, Mister Dillon."

Chloe rolled a little and kissed Charles on his whiskered cheek.

"And, my promise to you, Bambi."

"Don't want a big wedding," Chloe said.

"What about our mothers?"

"Let's get married in the hospital chapel, just a few friends, OK? I'll ask Father O'Connor."

"Ok. You're in charge of getting our mothers on board."

"And when we get you out of here, let's have a long honeymoon, someplace where no one will know us."

"Where?" Charles asked.

"Richard said he will fly us to a place very special."

Charles' eyes searched Chloe's face. He watched the dimples form, and then he watched her lips move.

"Come away with me."

CHAPTER 73

PROMISES KEPT

The two old men and five younger men had nearly finished the cantina lunch special of black beans, yellow rice, and marinated pork, when the building trembled, and dust blew through the ripped screen door.

"The helicopter has returned!" the oldest man said. He stood and lit a cigar.

"Would you like to meet Machete on this visit?" the other old man inquired, in the direction of the young man with a black goatee.

"Perhaps this time I will," the young man replied, patting his pocket.

They went outside and assumed their assigned locations on the Amigo's bench just in time to see Rosa run from Fausto's back door toward the helicopter.

"I am happy you have returned," Rosa said. She hugged Moses first, then Machete.

"Are you able to drive us around today?" Machete asked.

"I am the boss. Of course, where?" Rosa shouted over the roar of the ascending helicopter.

"First to the cemetery and then to the Iztapalapa district where I was born. Can I leave this package on your desk until we return?"

Rosa took the package and returned with her car keys, extending them toward Machete.

"You like to drive my new Mercedes?"

"Moses and I will ride in the back. Is Little Miss allowed in your new car?"

"Of course, silly, it is only a car, and she is your friend. Of course."

"Very little has changed," Machete commented, watching the buildings pass by on the way to the cemetery.

Carefully, Rosa drove down a narrow dirt cemetery road. She stopped next to a marker.

"I want to be alone," Machete said.

Rosa and Moses watched Machete approach the large, carved marble marker and drop to his knees. He placed both hands on the grave and bowed his head. The ladies watched him talk for several minutes.

"It is fixed, now," Machete said, climbing into the car. "I am forgiven. Now go to the Iztapalapa district...at the intersection of Cumbres and Putia."

Rosa drove for twenty minutes. Machete looked out the window.

"There is the doctor's office. The nurse there treated me with kindness," Machete said. He pointed at a dilapidated little building with broken windows.

"Doctor Ramiz is dead," Rosa commented from the front seat. "It is rumored he crossed the cartel."

"He was not a nice man. His nurse was nice; she helped me."

"She is dead as well."

They arrived at the intersection.

"Stop here; come with me," Machete said, pulling on Moses' arm.

"There is a new shack," Machete said, looking at the lath and tar paper structure with a corrugated metal roof.

"This is the place my mother, Lilliana, and sister, Maria, died... at his very spot."

"Dey be in heaven," Moses said, "watchin' us."

"I know. Sometimes I still see them in my dreams."

"Dey still be widt you, honey."

Machete lead his wife back to the car.

"Where next?" Rosa asked.

"The lean-to," Machete answered.

The sun had hidden behind the cantina roof when they arrived behind Fausto's.

"The sun sets early this time of year," Rosa said. "Do you need a flashlight?"

"No, only a shovel."

"You know where the hardware department is," Rosa said, tossing Machete the store keys.

The ladies watched Machete emerge from the store with a new red-handled shovel and his package from Rosa's desk, wrapped in burlap. They watched him pull the canvas back and crawl into the lean-to.

Little Miss ran. She curled in the opening and watched.

"What do you think Machete is doing over there?" the young man with the goatee inquired from his end of the cantina bench.

"Too dark to see," commented the old man, unscrewing the red El Toro Tequila cap. "Perhaps you want to ask him."

"I am afraid his dog will bite."

Rosa and Moses stood side by side, watching his movement in the near darkness.

"He be digging a deep hole for Machete," Moses said.

Rosa smiled.

"De father of me baby be named Marco."

EPILOGUE

"I shall be telling this with a sigh
Somewhere ages and ages hence:
Two roads diverged in a wood, and I –
I took the one less traveled by,
And that has made all the difference."

ROBERT FROST

To be continued…

Richard Alan Hall lives in Traverse City, Michigan
with his wife, Debra Jean, and their two dogs,
Lauttie, and a red-haired hussy named Lucy.
He writes in Traverse City and Key West.